Scallywags

Cameron Stewart Miller

- Pyrate -

One of many ways to refer what is now

commonly known as a pirate.

Prologue:

The Village Of Flame

Five minutes.

That was all the time the crew of the Poisoned Rose needed. In that short span of time the entirety of Embar had become engulfed in a blanket of ash and flames. Palm trees, farms, and every home as far as the eye could see were all set ablaze.

The scent of smoke permeated throughout the village, choking out the once fresh air. Horrific screeches of the burning livestock were matched only by the equally horrific shrieks of terror that bellowed from the unfortunate villagers. Those screams only grew louder as marauders entered their homes one at a time.

A lone house sat just a stone's throw north of the village at the top of a steep hill. The flames had not yet reached the house of the small family, but it wouldn't be much longer until the wave of destruction reached the safe haven. A warm glow radiated from the house, an inviting glow that singled it out when it might have otherwise gone unnoticed.

Archibald grabbed a crude sword from the table. Much like all the others on the island, it was duller than the village idiot. He tossed it to Gerald, a beast of a man who probably could have handled more than a few brigands if it weren't for his gut sticking out like a bright red target.

"We'll move faster if I carry Finn," Archibald looked toward his wife. "Sophia, you stay right on our heels with your share of things. We'll each have our hands full," his eyes fell on Gerald as he lumbered to his feet. "So it'll fall on you to protect us. Are you going to be up for it?"

Gerald inspected the blade. "I never was the quickest lad, but I'll always protect my kin." The tears in Sophia's eyes caught his attention. "Come sister, we must leave."

Sophia kissed her young child, Finn, on the head and grabbed her share of supplies. Archibald did the same, and snatched a blade of his own, praying he wouldn't need to use it.

The toddler's sleepy groans reminded them all of what was at stake. Even worse, it reminded them of what many of their friends in the village below had likely already lost.

Gerald opened up the door and the family stepped out into the warm night. The air outside was even thicker with smoke than they had thought. Embar was filled with raging flames so bright and red that Sophia's hair could have blended in perfectly.

"We just have to hug the outskirts of the village." Archibald put a hand on Sophia's back. "The bastards' ship is on the far side of the port, see?" He pointed a finger at the hulking shape of a pyrate ship, lit only by the glow of the village's flames. "If we get down to the opposite end of the docks we can use the dark of the night to sail around the island to Mazlo. We can find aid there."

The menacing laughter grew even louder, and the shanty tune that accompanied it became even clearer. Sophia loved singing songs with the children of the village, but the dark lyrics that drifted from below were enough to swear her to a vow of silence.

"What sick bastard can sing while they do this to innocent people?" Sophia whispered to herself.

As they reached the safety of the trees, a group of ratty pyrates rushed toward the house. Sophia gasped, but Gerald clamped his hand over her mouth. He turned her head to face him and he shook his head. One sound would be the end of them all.

There were four of them, more than Gerald or Archibald could handle while protecting Sophia and Finn. They knew they should have been impossible to spot from the distance they'd created, yet that didn't ease any of them.

"Well, would yeh look at that?" one pyrate said. "Isn't this just a lovely homestead?"

"Let's get to it boys!" another pyrate said.

The men were all short, stocky, and filthy—rather unimpressive people. Their clothes were old and torn as if they'd happily worn the same outfits for years. Despite all the smoke in the air, the stench wafting from each of the brigands managed to fill the family's noses.

The pyrates looked around, and their eyes lingered on the trees where the family stood. Fear washed over the family as Sophia gripped her bag of supplies. They each held their breath until the pyrates turned their attention back to the house.

The men rushed into Sophia's home, and before anyone could breathe, a loud clattering echoed from inside. It was being ransacked. All of their belongings pillaged and destroyed. Everything Sophia and Archibald had worked so hard to build, gone.

"Quickly," Gerald huffed. "Now's our chance."

The family took off toward the village port, always remaining just inside the safe darkness of the trees. The deeper they moved into the village, the louder the sinister singing grew.

The singing of a group of madmen.

"I thought pyrates only sang while they worked on their ship," Sophia said.

"Aye, but if these are the pyrates I believe them to be," Gerald glanced back at Sophia. "This is nothing out of the ordinary."

He slowed the group down to a halt at the first sign of movement. Across from them, a group of houses burned from the inside out. A group of pyrates burst out from one of the homes and shoved three people to the ground.

"Get down," Gerald whispered.

Sophia peeked at Finn as they took cover. He'd somehow managed to fall asleep in his father's arms— the poor tired boy.

Sophia turned her attention to the horrific scene in front of her. It was Mr. Baker and his family. His wife bawled on the ground with her soot-covered child. Whatever was going on, it was clear that the family feared the worst.

"P-p-please... Take anything you want," Mr. Baker said, the tears in his eyes apparent, even from a distance. "We won't get in your way. W-w-we just—oh gods. Please, don't hurt us."

Mr. Baker had crawled his way to one of the pyrates, something that caused a twisted grin to settle over all the men. The pyrate in the front of the group looked much more clean and proper than the rest of the crew. The flames gleamed in his eyes, which caused them to take on a sinister yellow hew, almost demonic in appearance.

"That's gotta be their leader," Archibald said.

Gerald nodded. "Aye."

The pyrate adjusted his hat before striking Mr. Baker across the face. The helpless man sprawled backward as the demon stalked toward him. Even from so far away, Sophia could make out a devilish smile on the monstrous man's face.

The captain chuckled. "I have no desire teh hurt yeh, Mr..."

Mr. Baker wasn't comforted. "B-b-b-b—"

"Quit yer b-b-blubbering, and spit it out yeh damned fool," the captain snapped.

"Baker."

"Ahhh... Mr. Baker," the captain's voice calmed as he rested a hand on his flintlock pistol. "I have no desire teh hurt yeh, Mr. Baker. Me and me fine crew are simply here in yer fair village teh ascertain a very specific plunder, yeh see?"

Sophia was taken aback by how educated the pyrate seemed. While he spoke like the other brutes, something about him seemed dangerously different. Most pyrates probably had no idea what a word like *ascertain* even meant.

"W-what is it?" Mr. Baker perked up. "Maybe I could help— "

The captain let out a hearty laugh. "Well, yeh see—I doubt very much that yeh'd be interested in helping me with teh plunder that I require."

His fiery eyes fell onto Mrs. Baker. He nodded, and his men grabbed her, separating the woman from her child. She let out an ear-piercing scream—the kind of scream a person hears in their nightmares years after the horrific experience is but a distant memory.

"N-no. Anything else, but just please, not them. I've

got a few pieces of silver. I'll give you those!" Mr. Baker said, putting himself between the pyrates and his family, "Please! Take me instead!"

"Come now, Mr. Baker." A smug smile crawled across the pyrate's face. "Begging isn't becoming of any man."

The pyrate started to walk away, likely leaving whatever was supposed to happen next to the rest of his men. Mr. Baker's breathing had become laboured and angry. He stood and charged toward the pyrate with a desperate shout, but the monster twirled around and pulled a pistol.

- BANG! -

Finn began to stir, but Archibald covered his eyes. The child didn't need to see the horrors of the night. The chances were, that was just one of the many terrible scenes he'd need to be shielded from.

Mr. Baker brought a hand to his chest as blood poured from the fresh wound. The bright-red blood that oozed from his body was lit up by the flames, making it plain to see that he'd been shot in the heart.

Sophia brought a hand to her mouth as her old friend, Mr. Baker dropped to his knees. She'd known him since she was a young girl. The two of them attended academy together deeper in the island before the great fire, but that was all gone. No one could survive a wound like that.

The Captain looked at Mr. Baker's child and clicked his tongue. "Tis always a shame when a young lad grows without a family." He pulled out another pistol and pointed it at Mrs. Baker. "If only yeh were a touch thinner—prettier ."

Sophia turned away as Mrs. Baker's cries grew louder.

- BANG! -

Sophia turned to see a body on the ground, and the lone Baker child just a few feet away.

"Mama?" the child cooed. "Papa?"

"ROUND UP TEH REST OF TEH WOMEN, BOYS!" the captain shouted.

Finn turned his head and saw the sinister pyrate as he smiled, his grimy teeth clear against the flames behind him. It was a terrifying sight for anyone, so someone so young had to be ready to burst into tears. Still in a sleepy haze, he buried his face in his father's shoulder.

"Lord—" Archibald said to himself as he ran his hand through Finn's hair.

"We have to go get the Baker boy," Sophia choked out through silent sobs.

Gerald shook his head. "If we step out of the trees we're as good as dead. We're risking everything just by leaving the brush to get to the boat. If we step out for that boy, we're done for."

"That's not fair."

"If you want Finn to grow up without a mother, then be my guest," Gerald said before he continued toward the port, "I wouldn't recommend it, though, Soph."

Archibald looked at Sophia then back to the body of the Bakers, and the orphaned Baker boy.

There was no winning.

He shook his head and followed Gerald.

If it were any other day, any other situation, Archibald would have been the first man to step in. He was kind-hearted, and he knew wrong from right. Seeing how much people could change in dire situations left

Sophia unsure of how to feel. With nothing left to do, she swallowed her sadness and followed along.

The family crept through the bushes, taking care to avoid any fallen sticks. As they went, they watched more scenes similar to what they had witnessed with the Bakers, each as horrible as the last.

Sophia's hands were as clammy as her face and her knees felt as if they were ready to buckle. It was as if she'd gone on a trek across the island, but she hadn't even gone a tenth of the length yet. The mixture of fear, adrenaline, and the need to protect her child was all that drove her forward.

Gerald stopped them. "Wait, wait, wait—"

They came to the edge of the trees once more. A large open road was all that separated them from the port. A few open paces stood between them and safety on the sea.

They paused and listened.

The horror seemed so far away.

Gerald looked at his family with fear in his eyes. "It's now or never."

The night had found an eerie calm. The screams had all stopped, and the only other noises left were the crackling of fire and the waves of the sea.

"Hey! I found some more!" a voice rang out.

All of their hearts stopped. They'd come so far, and now, it was all for nothing.

A lone pyrate stepped onto the road. "C'mon boys!"

The pyrate charged toward them, and after a few moments, the lone pyrate had become a band of more than fifteen.

"Quickly!" Archibald said.

The horrendous singing started again, growing louder as they ran. They were moving faster than they thought their feet could carry them, but it didn't matter. Before they reached the stairs to the docks, a wall of a man trudged up toward them with a sad expression.

Sophia examined his face, he was far younger than he looked at a glance. Only a few years younger than her. He had to have been a boy, but if he was, he was a brute of a boy.

"You need to move. I won't hesitate to kill you," Gerald said.

The pyrate shook his head and reached behind him. He pulled out an enormous hammer, but it didn't look like he wanted to use it. While the other pyrates weapons were all smeared with blood, this one's weapon was pristine.

Gerald lunged at him, but with incredible speed, the pyrate whacked him with an arching strike. The sound of cold steel smashing against flesh sent Sophia into an entirely new panic. Gerald flew backward into the road, sword still in hand.

A slight groan put Sophia at ease.

He was still alive—for the time being.

Sophia and Archibald backed into the road and were surrounded by the rowdy band of pyrates. Destruction lay all around them. A sheet of ash, crumbled walls, and fallen doors littered the ground. Their beautiful home had been turned to ash and ruin.

The pyrates fell silent and they made a path for their captain. He stepped in between his crew and sauntered toward Sophia. Just a few paces away, a sinister smile crawled across the captain's face once again.

"BASTARDS!" Gerald stood up and held his sword up once more. "YOU WILL NOT TOUCH HER!"

Quicker than Sophia could comprehend, the Captain pulled one of his flintlock pistols once again.

- BANG! -

Gerald crumpled to the ground—dead.

"No one gives me orders," the captain said.

Sophia stared down at the lifeless body of her older brother. "GERALD!"

Her hands moved as if they had minds of their own. She pulled Archibald's sword from his belt, ready to take on any man dumb enough to step forward. Supplies didn't matter anymore, but survival did. She held the blade toward the pyrates, sending them all backward.

Sophia's adrenaline betrayed her.

She stepped too far from Archibald, and the pyrates capitalized. In a horrific sight, they pounced on her husband and son.

"No!" Sophia stepped forward, but stopped when she heard the captain's laugh.

"Ha-ha-ha! I like this one!" The captain stared at her with admiration. "She's a fighter."

"Mommy!" Finn cried.

"No! No! I give up. You can take me. Do whatever you want," Sophia said. "Just don't hurt Finn."

Archibald wiggled and shook free from the pyrates. He punched one across the face and pulled a pistol from the belt of another. With another violent punch, he reclaimed his son and pointed the flintlock pistol toward the band of brutes.

Sophia started toward Archibald, but the Captain raised his other pistol and pointed it at her.

"I like teh whole family." the captain said with a whistle. "A whole bunch of fighters, I can see why teh two of yeh came together. Unfortunately for yer husband and yer lad, me crew is full up at teh moment, so—"

The captain snapped his fingers, and from the crowd, a hiss trickled into the ears of the frightened family. A small bomb was flung out from the crowd and it landed right at Archibald's feet.

Hissssssssssssssssssssssssssssss—

He looked down at the bomb, and then lower at the door he was standing on. Archibald jumped backward, tossed Finn to the ground, dug his nails into the ground, and lifted with all his might.

Hissssssssssssssssssssssssssssss~

It wasn't going to shield the entire blast, but it was better than nothing. In one motion, he pulled the door up, put his back against it, and grabbed Finn. He pulled him close to his chest as he closed his eyes—

BOOM!

The shredded door went flying down the road, landing alongside whatever remained of Archibald and Finn. Sophia watched as the love of her life and her pride and joy hit the ground, motionless.

Her entire life had been stripped away.

She couldn't get a single sound out.

She couldn't move a muscle.

***

"Mommy?" Finn mumbled.

He began to stir just in time to see the pyrates carry his mother onto their boat across the dock. There was no telling whether or not the screams he could hear were hers or one of the other women they'd snatched.

His head was in the worst pain he'd felt in his short life. Finn closed his eyes for what felt like a moment, but when he opened them again the boat was no longer in the docks.

"Mommy?"

He stumbled to his feet and rubbed his eyes. Blood dripped down his face, but even as a child, he knew he shouldn't check it. Instead, he looked out to the sea and watched a lone ship as it sailed away. Across the back of the ship were a few blurry words.

Poisoned Rose.

Finn looked back towards his father, who began to stir on the ground, blood pouring from his shoulder. He clued into what had happened to his father as he took one last look back to the ship.

He spotted it just in time to watch a dull orange glow flash across the hull. After a few moments, the entire ship began to glide down into the water until it was fully submerged in the ocean.

"Mom?"

Chapter 1:

The Boy From The Burnt Village

"Finn?" a familiar voice rang out in the distance. "You better not be sleeping up there again!"

Finn drifted out of his usual midday nap with an annoyed groan.

He leaned up and rubbed an eye as he looked down at his snoring companion. Bug must have decided that his stomach would be a much more comfortable place to nap than the hot tiles that dotted the roof.

"Fiiiiiiinn?" the voice called again, this time closer.

He ran his fingers through Bug's fur. "Almost time to get moving, boy."

Finn pushed his long curly hair back and looked out to the town below. The look of Embar had barely changed since the day he was born, and Finn figured it wouldn't be changing anytime soon. Even despite the destructive attack in his youth, the village had recovered well.

Off in the distance, ships were coming and going with the flow of the waves. The way the blue-green ocean crashed into the sleepy town below looked more magnificent than any famed artist could have attempted to capture.

"Finn?" the voice called from below. "Finn, are you up there?"

Bug's eyes snapped open, finally realizing just who the distant voice belonged to. The furry little pup let out a yawn, but it looked more like the creature's tongue was attempting to escape its mouth. As he stretched out across Finn's body, Bug's fat rolls bunched up, reminding Finn that the pair needed to go on more walks.

"C'mon," Finn put a hand on Bug's head. "Nap time's over." He set the dog next to him and leaned over the edge of the building. "Yeah, Diego. I'm up here."

Diego looked as irritated as ever.

That was never a good sign.

"How many times are you going to do this?" Diego's wide eyes could have rivalled the bulging of Bug's, which is exactly how Finn knew he was in for some trouble. "Goofing off, taking naps, going to visit that crazy old lady—keep it up and the town's going to label you a pyrate and be done with you."

Pyrate had become the dirtiest word one could use on Embar. Those brave enough to use it were doing so at their own risk. The survivors of the attack from years ago were always willing to thump almost anyone who used the word. Vi was pretty much the only one who could get away with it.

Finn rolled his eyes. "Then send me off to sea."

"You'd probably like that, wouldn't you?" Diego said with a sigh.

Finn pulled a length of rope, complete with a hook from his belt. He latched it on a nearby pipe and tapped Bug. "Ready for a quick ride, boy?"

After a small tug to test the stability, he grabbed Bug and hopped over the side of the building. The whoosh of the air was exactly what he needed to wake up. He swung to the ground and jostled the rope until the hook dropped down.

He looked back at the old building for a final time. Archibald had told the boys that it used to be his home, but Finn had no memories in it. Now, the home sat at the top of the hill overlooking Embar, a memorial to the horrific night the villagers experienced all those years ago.

When he looked back toward Diego, Bug had already run over to hide behind him. They both looked equally horrified by Finn's unique route off the roof. Neither of his best friends were all that adventurous.

Finn raised an eyebrow. "What?"

"You're the only person I know reckless enough to jump off a building," Diego pulled a small piece of crispy bread from his pocket and fed it to Bug. "Trusting that a thin piece of rope will keep you safe."

"What's reckless about it? I know the distance." Finn attached the rope to his belt. "It's just like when I'm cleaning windows, someone's gotta be dangled in the air to do it properly," he said with a shrug. "Just because you don't like to do any heavy lifting around here…"

"It's not that I don't like heavy lifting," Diego's voice wavered. "It's just—"

The way Diego's gaze shifted told Finn he'd hit a nerve. "I know. Everyone's built different right?"

"Something like that."

Finn knew that Diego had a bit of a complex. For whatever reason, Diego always viewed him as someone who stole the spotlight. It was never Finn's intention to come off like that. In fact, he would be more than happy to leave the island and get out of everyone's way.

"So, what're you after?" Finn said. "Someone's going to think a lady's in trouble up here with all that hollering you were doing."

"Funny." Diego tossed a piece of bread at Finn. "Well, you did promise pop that you'd help out in the shop today."

The realization of his screw-up hit way harder than that piece of bread. "Aw, crap."

"You forgot."

"I didn't forget. I just wanted to be in the right headspace."

"So what you're saying is—you forgot."

Diego could be a bit of an annoying brat at times, but Finn did his best to keep his irritation in check. There were only a few ways he could one-up Finn, and as much as people picked on him, no one was going to bet against Diego's steel trap of a brain.

"Being properly rested is just as important as working all day" Finn headed toward the town. "C'mon, Bug."

"The shop's been busy the last little while," Diego said as he caught up to Finn. "Pop is gonna be mad."

As they headed down the hill, Finn spotted an unusually large crowd gathering by the docks. They crowded around a ship he'd never seen before. Whatever it was, it was probably the most excitement the village would see for months.

Finn pointed a finger—"What do you make of that?"

"Probably just another slimy merchant who brought along another group of pretty girls." Diego leaned forward and squinted. "Well, that or the town got a new ale merchant."

"We should check it out."

Diego frowned. "How many times do you need to be disappointed by the old witches' stories?"

"Relaaaax." Finn's eyes remained trained on the distant commotion.

There really were only a few things that the commotion could have been. Embar wasn't one of the best and brightest villages across the seas. It was always possible another band of pyrates could stop by, but if

Finn's hazy memories served him well, that would mean he'd already hear screams. Still, it was possible it was the very thing Finn had always hoped for.

"You do this every time there's a new ship in port," Diego said. "You get all excited thinking that just maybe this time it'll be Fortune whatever—"

"Fortune Palmer," Finn corrected. "The greatest pyrate—"

"The greatest pyrate this side of the seas." Diego knew the routine well. "I know, I know, but then every time it's just someone peddling some more exotic animal butter. If you'd stop letting that woman feed into your delusions, maybe you could finally settle into a job and find yourself a nice girl."

It didn't take long for Finn to grow tired of pyrate hatred. That kind of hatred was pervasive amongst most people on the island, with Finn remaining the odd one out. He couldn't blame anyone for feeling the way they did, but it was always best to simply change the conversation whenever it came up. It was just his luck that Diego had given him the perfect way to flip the conversation.

"Speaking of finding a nice girl," Finn gave Diego a cheeky grin. "How're things with Minerva?"

"Minnie?"

"Cute."

"Shut it. Things are good." Even with his sun-tanned skin, Finn could see a deep blush on Diego's face. "I don't know why you'd bring her up, though."

"You don't, huh? Gee, I'll have to let her know what her *hero* thinks of her."

"Oh, come on, Finn. Don't do that. Please?"

He may have been embarrassed by it, but Diego's biggest weakness was Minerva, for better or worse.

"I'm just kidding." They reached the bottom of the hill, trading the feel of dirt and grass for the feel of hot cobblestone. "You can just admit you like her, I don't care that she's—got lots to love."

"I know you don't care, but I'm not so sure about the others."

Finn waved to a group of girls by the tailor's shop. "Who cares what they think?" They all giggled and waved back at him. A few villagers passed by the boys, each saying hello to Finn and ignoring Diego.

"Easy for you to say when everyone here loves you."

"People don't love me." Finn rolled his eyes at Diego's melodrama. "I just meet a lot of people. I don't think I've seen you talk to anyone other than pop or Minerva since we were kids."

There was a chance he'd been mistaken, but as far as Finn knew, that was the truth. Diego never went out of his way to learn about the other villagers of Embar. Even when he'd run errands for Archibald, Diego would keep his eyes on the ground and only speak when he had to. One day, he'd have to learn to be his own man, and that worried Finn.

"DIEGO!" a shrill screech echoed from the edge of the street.

Finn cringed. "And you were saying everybody loves me."

The boys turned to see the largest girl in the village, Minerva, running down the street. Bug decided it would be best to hide from any potential squishing, so he hid behind Finn's leg. It was probably the right call.

Finn always found Minerva unbearable, but the way Diego lit up every time he saw her gave him the strength he needed to put up with her. Even if he could get a bit embarrassed at times, Diego truly cared for her.

She wrapped Diego in a bear hug, but both the boys noticed there were tears in her eyes. Something like that was pretty common for Minerva, but Finn had a feeling his boring day was about to get a lot more interesting.

"Everything—okay, Minnie?" Diego choked out as she squeezed the air out of him.

"Gord was being an absolute monster again." she let go and wiped her eyes. "I told him you'd teach him a lesson."

"You can't say things like that." Diego's eyes looked like they were ready to jump out of his skull. "What's a guy like me gonna do against a guy like him?"

"Beat him up."

The boys locked eyes. "I appreciate how much you believe in me, Minnie, but—" Diego's panicked face just about made Finn crack up. "I—uh—I think you have *seriously* underestimated my size."

Minerva ran a hand along Diego's thin arm. "Just because you're smaller doesn't mean you can't do great things."

She could be an annoying handful, but it was clear that she cared for Diego as much as he cared for her. Probably more.

"Not that he can't do great things," Finn gave Diego a playful shot in the shoulder as he continued. "But Gord is probably the biggest guy in the history of Embar. He could be out on the seas travelling with a band of freaks to entertain people."

"See?" Diego gestured to Finn. "My own brother isn't even sure about this. He'd know better than anyone."

Minerva wasn't having any protests. "That's just because he's used to everyone either being afraid of him or sucking up to him, and that's just because he's—"

"Wait," Finn cocked his head. "There are people that are afraid of me?"

"Well, you have beaten up half the village," Minerva said with a shrug.

It was true that Finn had been in his fair share of fights, but never without good reason. Diego made himself an easy target, so he'd often step in to help him. Outside of that, Finn got along with most people because he didn't care enough to get roped into a brawl. He was more interested in a clash of blades than he was in throwing a few hands.

"I beat up half the village for picking on Diego," Finn corrected.

"And I appreciate you for that." Diego nodded at Finn before turning back to Minerva. "How far behind was he?"

Finn spotted Gord down the street with his two little goons in tow. Even at a distance, he looked imposing when compared to Diego's meek frame. Finn wasn't exactly a specimen, and even though he was almost a head taller than Diego, Gord still managed to tower over the both of them.

"Looks like—not all that far. Need me to handle this?" Finn asked.

"If you don't mind."

"You need to help him at least!" Minerva said. "Defend my honour!"

"Any ideas?" Diego asked.

Finn looked around for anything that might help him in the fight that was on the way. There was a rickety shop sign above them, and a cart full of what could have been dirt, but smelled more like manure nearby. Not exactly great equalizers in a fight against a giant.

"Not one," Finn said.

chapter 2:

What Goes On At The Docks

Whether Gord meant to or not, he looked as if he were ready to kill a man. Some people liked to take their time entering a conflict, but he was storming right toward Finn and Diego. Hearing that Diego would beat him up wasn't the kind of thing someone like him let slide. His bruised ego needed to prove to everyone that he was the strongest around.

"Bug, stay behind Diego," Finn said.

Bug barked and obeyed. Finn never needed to tell him anything twice.

"Look, it's the portly-lady-lover," Gord said to a chorus of laughter from his buddies.

Finn ran a hand through his long hair. "Those are some harsh words coming from the only guy in town losing his hair before twenty."

There wasn't a lot to use as ammo to poke fun at Gord. He was tall, athletic, and probably would have had just as many women pining after him if he wasn't so insufferable. The only issue he had was his slowly and clearly balding head, something Gord was a bit sensitive about.

Gord's nose crinkled. "You're going to want to

apologize for that before I use your face to dig your grave."

"It'd save me from having to look at your mug—" Finn shuddered. "Yikes. I'd hate to see the unfortunate souls that spawned you."

The comment fell out of Finn's mouth before he had a chance to think it through. Gord's parents were among those killed the night of the attack. Finn felt bad for a moment before he remembered that the comment was going to make a difference. A fight was coming no matter what he said.

Gord's already angry expression got even scarier. "I'm going to beat the piss out of you just so the orphan can watch what'll be coming for him next," he finished with his gaze on Diego.

"I'll be sure to mark you down as the ugliest person to try," Finn fired right back. "Right next to your two little buddies there."

Gord lashed out with a few punches, but Finn managed to dodge them all. He ducked another punch, and as Gord reached down to grab him, Finn latched onto each of his arms. With a quick roll backward, he tossed his foe clean across the road.

"Can't even hit me," Finn laughed. "You talked a hefty game, big guy. What's going on?"

One of Gord's cronies rushed toward Finn. Hearing the scraping of boots on the stones beneath their feet, he pulled his grappling hook from his belt. He whirled it and tossed it toward the rickety sign he spotted earlier. As the boy passed underneath Finn tugged it—

-CRASH!-

He winced at the unconscious bully. The headache Finn was going to have from Minerva's grating voice had nothing on the headache that kid was going to have.

"AHH!"

Finn whirled around in surprise from Diego's shout. The other boy had taken the opportunity to rush toward him. Finn grinned. As the boy approached Diego, he'd have to get right in line with the manure-filled cart.

He eyeballed the toss and as the boy passed by the cart, he threw his grappling hook. The boy tripped face-first to the ground, giving Finn the chance to close in. As the boy got up, Finn hit him with the biggest shoulder tackle he could, sending him flying into the cart of manure.

Finn felt a hand on his shoulder that he thought was Diego. "Watch out!" Hearing Diego's cry, Finn got the feeling that it wasn't his brother's hand.

He turned around into a wicked left hand, courtesy of Gord. Finn was pretty good at taking a punch, but that was when he was ready for one. The surprise shot dropped him to the ground, and he could feel blood trickling from his nose. A solid kick to the gut sent all the air shooting out of his body.

The coppery taste of blood hit his tongue as he looked over at his defenceless brother. Gord stalked toward him, but Finn had no qualms with returning a sucker punch.

Gord spat at Diego. "I'm gonna mess your face up so bad, little miss portly over there isn't even going to—"

To Finn's shock, Diego threw a punch at Gord, but it didn't look like it hurt all that much. Minerva got in on the action and launched a few slaps of her own at the bully. Even Bug jumped into the chaos with a vicious chomp to Gord's leg.

As Gord jumped back, Finn whirled his grappling hook one last time. He let the rope go and the flat end of the hook slammed into the side of Gord's head, sending him spiralling to the floor.

Diego took a deep breath. "I saw my whole life flash before my eyes."

"The worst he woulda done is give you a black eye —" Finn said. "I think—probably—"

"He punched you once and your nose is bleeding!" Diego scoffed. "Think of what he would have done to me."

Finn wiped the blood from his nose. "No big deal, see?" He turned his attention back to Gord. "Why don't you pick up those two morons you call friends and leave Diego and Minerva the hell alone?"

"Forget these idiots." Gord looked up at Finn with hatred in his eyes. "You just made an enemy out of me. I'm going to make sure you pay for this."

Finn wiggled his fingers. "Oh, I'm so scared. If I ever need an opinion on how a hook to the head feels, or how it feels to bathe in animal crap—I'll be sure to come find you guys."

Gord stared a hole into Finn, but eventually, he let up and headed to help his embarrassed friends. That was probably just going to cause even more problems in the long run, but there was something freeing about a good fight. It was that feeling that told Finn he belonged out on the seas, facing adversity at every turn.

Minerva hugged Diego. "That was so amazing."

"What are you talking about?" Diego let his head hang. "That was all Finn, as usual."

"Sure, Finn beat them up good," Minerva shrugged. "But you didn't back down when he came storming toward you. You stood up to him, for me."

Diego narrowed his eyes. "That's not exactly—" Finn raised an eyebrow and gestured toward Minerva. Luckily, Diego clued in. "Yeah, I did, didn't I?"

"I promised mother I'd be home by now, but I'll come by your pop's shop tomorrow? I'll even bring a homemade pie and then maybe a little—" Minerva puckered her lips at Diego. He nodded and she kissed him on the cheek.

"*Oh, look at me, I lead such a poor life,*" Finn snickered. "*No one loves me at all. Boo-hoo.*"

"Shut up." Diego gave him a light push as Minerva disappeared down the street.

A few people had been watching all the commotion from their windows. Finn gave them a wave and they all waved back. He really could get away with just about anything in Embar.

An elderly woman's laugh pulled their attention. "You children today—so violent."

"We aren't children anymore, Vi," Finn said.

"Well, that doesn't mean you don't have time to hear my stories anymore does it?" Vi asked.

"You know I always have time for your stories."

Hearing Vi's tales were a daily ritual for Finn. She was the only person in the village who wasn't born and raised there. She simply showed up one day, and the rest was history. Some say her stories are utter lies, but Finn always felt that Vi's vivid stories came from firsthand experience.

"He really shouldn't," Diego cut in. "You keep filling his brain with lies and stories about people that probably don't even exist."

"Hush, child," Vi said.

"I'm older than Finn."

"Yet you act like you're five years his junior."

Finn slapped Diego's back. "She's got you there."

"Oh, shut up."

"Watch your mouth, boy. Finn is going to be the talk of the village one day. You'll wish you spoke more kindly to him soon." Vi set her broom down and sat in her rocking chair. "I can feel that in my bones, I can. More than any other truth, I say."

Vi was the oldest person in the village, although that wasn't much of a feat. Many of the adults of Embar had died years ago when the pyrates attacked, leaving just a handful to raise the next generation that had already been born. She was shunned when she had first arrived, but she proved quite useful to the village in the aftermath.

"Finn already is the talk of the town. Not to mention he just beat up the biggest and scariest guy around." Diego looked in the direction of Archibald's store. "I'll be surprised if ten different girls don't show up to the shop tonight asking for him."

Finn rolled his eyes. "Jeez, Diego—you sure *you* don't want to court me?"

"Mmm. I can feel that," Vi said as she rocked in her chair. "The people of this village do fancy you quite a bit, child."

"Can you feel it in your bones?" Diego scoffed. "You probably just heard a group of girls gossiping about how cute he was or something like that."

Vi snatched her walking stick and swiped it toward Diego. "Quiet you."

"I've been meaning to ask you, Vi, I had a dream a few nights ago—about the night of the attack," Finn said. "I could see the ship that took my mum one second, and then the next it vanished. There isn't a ship fast enough to do that, is there? It would take way longer than just a single moment to reach the horizon, right?"

"The Poisoned Rose," Vi said as if she were recalling the death of a loved one. "Fast enough to disappear? Certainly, but not while sailing above the water."

"Above the water?" he asked.

Finn had been under the impression that he had hallucinated the ship disappearing. Only a crazy person would think a ship could sail beneath the ocean. Those pyrates weren't just any ordinary brigands.

Diego scoffed. "Next thing the witch is going to tell us is that pyrate ships have legs and feelings."

"Quiet, boy!" Vi snapped, "Legs, no. Feelings, no. Life, aye."

"You're saying ships are alive?"

"Not all ships, no." She shook her head. "Some ships —very special ships, have a heart."

"You can't actually believe any of these lies." Diego tugged Finn's arm. "Let's get out of here. We can go check if the shop suddenly has a brain."

Vi glared at Diego. "I speak no lies. Never have. Where is it you boys are headed? Best be to the docks."

"The docks?" Diego asked. "Why the docks?"

The old woman struggled to point a finger at Finn. "Because he'll find what he has always yearned for at the docks. I can feel it."

Diego sighed, "So, someone walked by talking about what's going on at the docks."

He could make all the sarcastic remarks he wanted, Finn knew exactly what Vi meant. There was only one thing she could mean, only one person she could be referring to.

Finn stared at Vi. "Fortune Palmer."

"Aye."

Finn sprinted toward the docks with Bug right on his heels. One way or another, Finn was about to join the crew of the legendary pyrate, Fortune Palmer. He kept his focus on the docks ahead, so he hadn't noticed as Diego struggled to keep up with him.

"Hey! What—are you—expecting to—find there?" Diego asked through huffs.

"You heard Vi," Finn looked down at Bug and almost laughed as his tongue flapped in the wind "Captain Palmer is down there."

"How—could she—know—who's at the docks?"

"I don't care. It's worth at least checking it out."

When they reached the docks they came to the edge of a crowd of people. After a moment to catch their breath, Finn and Diego pushed their way to the front of all the villagers.

It was true.

All the commotion wasn't over some new merchant. It wasn't over a group of busty women. The commotion was over a group of pyrates that had docked. If the old lady was right, it was Fortune Palmer and his crew.

A brutish man in long black leather stood across from a beautiful raven-haired woman in an intricate purple coat. The scene reminded Finn of his earlier stand-off with Gord and his cronies, except the woman was clearly outmatched.

Whatever was going on, it looked like that woman had really managed to piss off Captain Palmer.

Before Finn had a chance to speak to him, Captain Palmer drew his sword and charged at the woman. In a matter of seconds, that poor beautiful woman was going to be stuck on the wrong end of a very pointy blade.

The issue was, that's not what the Fortune Palmer from Vi's stories would do.

chapter 3:

At Absolutely No One's Service

The crowd shrieked as Captain Palmer rushed toward the smaller woman, but she remained a defiant statue. It was like watching a hippo charge a dove, and despite wanting to look away, everyone wanted to see what would happen next.

Every muscle in Captain Palmer's body tensed with his approach. He swung his sword, but the woman moved out of the way so fast, and at the absolute last second, nearly sending the captain to the ground from the force of his own strike.

Diego nudged Finn. "That woman must be from the other side of the world. I hear they're ungodly fast."

"Who told you that?" Finn narrowed his eyes. "Vi? All the sudden you want to listen to her stories?"

The woman spun around and as her coat fluttered up, an ornate sword and pistol came into view. She laughed as she drew her blade, but rather than taking a ready stance, she pointed it toward the ground. As Captain Palmer rushed at her again, she simply smiled and adjusted her hat.

"Is that guy Captain Palmer?" Diego asked.

"I don't know."

"What do you mean you don't know?"

"Well, obviously I've never seen him before," Finn squinted at the brutish man. "And Vi never really described him to me. With what she said, that's gotta be him, right? A guy like that could have done everything from Vi's stories."

Captain Palmer reached the woman and their swords clashed. Thanks to the size difference, the woman was having a difficult time pushing back against the captain, but she didn't look concerned at all. She backed off and as he came in with more strikes, the woman parried each one with a grin on her face.

"That lady is really good with a sword. You know her?" Diego asked.

"No, and I'm pretty sure someone would have said something by now if she lived on the island. I've never seen her before."

Their swords clashed a few more times and with a quick rotation, the woman flicked Captain Palmer's sword out of his hand. It flew threw the air, and the woman stepped back, she caught the sword and bowed.

The crowd let out a collective breath since the odds of the woman being hacked into pieces were done with. That was until the woman flipped the sword and handed it back to Captain Palmer.

Diego's face scrunched. "What's she doing?"

Finn's mind was racing after watching his childhood hero lose to a woman. "I—I think she's going to give him another chance."

"Why?"

"I have no idea."

Captain Palmer snatched the blade with a growl and lashed out with a few more swings, all of which the woman dodged. The way she moved, it was as if she was reading Captain Palmer's mind. The whole fight looked easy to her.

The two pushed their blades against one another again, but Captain Palmer launched a quick fist into the woman's face. A man of that size should have knocked a woman of her size to the ground in a single blow, but instead, she staggered back and checked for blood.

The woman almost looked impressed that someone would dare to strike her like that. She wasn't bleeding, but Finn had a feeling that she would have gotten a serious kick out of it if she was.

"Looks like Palmer isn't below fighting dirty," Diego said.

"What do you expect?" Finn asked, his eyes still glued to the action. "He is a pyrate."

"I thought he was supposed to be one of the good ones."

"Well, what really is *good* for a pyrate?"

After the surprise punch, the mood of the fight flipped. The woman stormed forward and lashed out with a few swings of her own. The speed at which she was capable of striking put the captain on the back foot, and they once again clashed blades.

The woman wound up a nasty kick and placed it square between Captain Palmer's legs. She got him so good that his whole body lurched upward as she connected. He dropped to his knees, then the ground, and then writhed in agony.

"I hope he didn't want to have kids someday." Diego joked, earning himself a nudge from Finn.

The woman snatched the captain's sword and snarled, "That'll teach you to strike a lady."

Finn couldn't believe his eyes. A woman had just beaten the greatest pyrate to ever sail across the seas— twice—and she made it look easy.

"There's no way that's him, right?" Diego asked.

Even in his current state of disbelief, Finn could tell

the look of worry plastered on Diego's face was for Finn, and not for the events in front of them.

"I don't know." Finn's eyes darted around, looking for any explanation. "He's supposed to have taken on an entire crew single-handedly and only came out with—a single scar."

Finn focused on the woman as she turned to the crowd and bowed once again. When she stood upright two things became clear. First, she had a beaming grin that could have lit up the darkest night, and second, she had a thin scar running from the edge of her left eyebrow down to her cheekbone. It appeared as if a perpetual tear was streaking down her face.

Captain Palmer wasn't a he.

Captain Palmer was a she.

"Captain!" A bandana-clad man waved down from the nearby ship. "Are yeh done playing 'round with the locals?"

"Not much fun around here," the real Captain Palmer said as she spun to greet the pyrate. "If this is the best they have to offer, we really were better off heading to Bridger straight away."

"Supplies, Captain. Supplies."

"So we lose a few men," she shrugged. "We're in the business of replacing the lot anyway."

Finn could feel an involuntary smile shoot across his face. That was exactly what he'd always hoped to hear. Not only was Fortune Palmer standing right in front of him, but she was also looking to find some new crew members.

Captain Palmer tossed her opponent's sword into the sea. "How much longer do you lazy lot need?"

The man on the ship disappeared for a moment before leaning back over the railing. "Won't be ready 'till nightfall, so t'would be best if we spent the night. Let's try not to beat the piss out of the entire town, aye?"

"I don't think this now perpetually childless fellow belongs here." She looked at the frightened crowd. "Doesn't exactly appear local."

Something in the corner of Finn's eye caught his attention. Another stranger he'd never seen before. A man lingering just beyond the edge of the crowd shrouded in dark robes. It was a strange sight, but Embar did get its fair share of strange visitors from time to time. Pyrates always tend to attract strange company.

"Regardless," she continued, "Those plans won't do. We leave at nightfall. The less time the Blues have to catch up, the better. I'm going to figure out what they drink here—and drink it all, savvy? See you at nightfall."

"Aye, Captain," the man said before disappearing back onto the ship.

The excitement had died down and so too did the rowdy crowd. Some might have left out of fear, and others out of a lack of interest, but almost everyone lingering in the dock was giving Captain Palmer a dirty look.

She took note of the stares as she sheathed her sword. "Happy lot here, huh?"

Diego shook Finn's shoulder. "That was pretty awesome—" Finn rushed toward Captain Palmer. "Finn, wait!"

"Excuse me," Finn said as he approached her.

"Oh, how nice," Captain Palmer said without so much as a glance in his direction. "Someone in this village actually has some manners."

"That's funny coming from a pyrate," Diego said from behind Finn.

Finn shot him a glare. "Sorry." He turned back to Captain Palmer. "Are you—are you really—"

She bowed. "The Devil's Charm, Captain Fortune Palmer, at absolutely no one's service."

Those were the words he'd always dreamed of

hearing in person. It wasn't the exact way he imagined it, but it was still incredible. Finn started shaking her hand, but no words were coming out. He knew he had to look like a complete lunatic.

She looked toward Diego. "Is your—excited friend here alright?"

"I'm sorry," Finn let go. "I just thought that—that you'd be—"

"A man? Get that a lot. Not quite sure why. Pretty sure I've got all the lady parts required." Captain Palmer looked herself over and shrugged. "Is it really that hard to believe that a woman could be as capable in a fight as a man?" Her sights set on Finn. "What is it I can do you for, lad?"

There was no way Finn could have prepared himself for his meeting with Captain Palmer, but she was nothing like what he thought she'd be. He pictured a hulking brute with a big bushy beard, and on the odd occasion, gold teeth. Not a thin, beautiful woman only somewhat taller than himself.

"C'mon, c'mon, I haven't got all day." She clapped her hands in front of his face. "Places to be, things to drink."

"I want to join your crew." Finn blurted out, with Bug following up with a supportive bark. "I should say, we want to. Me and Bug."

She looked at the strange duo for a moment. It could have been just a few seconds, but it was a moment that felt like a lifetime.

She opened her mouth to speak, but she stopped herself and rose a finger. She finally burst into laughter and headed toward the town. "Thanks for the laugh, lad."

Finn turned back to Diego for any sign of support. Diego just cocked his head and narrowed his eyes. At least Finn wasn't the only one confused by the situation.

He stayed right on his idols' heels. "Hey—"

"Oh, I'm sorry." Captain Palmer composed herself. "You're serious? You don't just ask to be a pyrate and become one. It's a lifestyle. You're born into it, whether you know it when you're born or not. You—you don't look like a pyrate at all. It's not in you."

The biggest Captain Palmer fanboy on the planet had his entire life crumble in an instant. "Please, I just want to learn." He didn't even have the will to move forward. "My whole life I've heard so many stories—"

"About how I'm the greatest hero to ever sail the seas?" Captain Palmer asked. "About how I've battled entire dastardly crews single-handed? About how I've uncovered many fabled treasures? I've heard it all, lad." She cocked her head with a cheeky grin. "In fact, I lived it all. You think you're the first one to ask to join my crew?"

Finn had no idea what to say. He'd never heard a woman speak with so much conviction. It was disarming, but he couldn't tell if it was a good thing or a bad thing.

"It's going to be a hard no from me." Captain Palmer started down the road and waved a hand. "So long!"

chapter 4:

Flynn Tonrend Saves The Day

Finn stared at Captain Palmer as she walked further and further into the village. Everything he'd ever wanted was walking away from him. If people couldn't just ask to join the crew then Finn was going to show her exactly why he belonged by her side.

"C'mon." Diego grabbed Finn's arm. "Let's just go back to the shop and forget this all ever happened. You got your—"

"I'll see you back at the shop," Finn said.

Diego had overstayed his welcome. He might have had good intentions, but all of his protests made it feel like his own brother didn't want him to live out his dreams. There was pain in Finn's heart, and part of that pain was because of Diego.

"Finn—"

"If all you plan on doing here is telling me to forget it, then you can leave." His eyes fell back on Captain Palmer. "I need to talk to her, so you can just head back to the shop, okay?"

"I just don't want you to—"

"I don't care." Finn snapped, "This isn't about you."

"No. It's not. It's about you—like always." Diego scoffed. "Go on, do whatever you want. I'll go tell pops exactly why you didn't show up—again. Mid-day naps, fights, and pyrates."

"That's the last time I save your ass, Diego."

Finn shook his head and turned his attention back to Captain Palmer.

He had to join her crew.

No matter what.

He caught back up to the captain and grabbed her hand. "I'm not done talking to you."

She stared at her hand in his. Happy would have been the last word Finn would have used to describe the look on her face. He imagined it was the same look she'd have if someone caused her to spill some precious liquor.

She snapped her hand free and looked down her nose at him. "You'll do well to only touch a lady once you've gotten permission, boy."

Finn rushed around her as she continued on her way. "Don't call me boy."

"Fine—girl. You really are getting on every single one of my nerves, you know that, girl?" She glanced at Bug. "Quite an ugly dog you've got there by the way."

"You haven't even given me a chance to show you what I can do." Bug started to bark, but Finn wasn't about to get distracted. "Your crew could use me."

"I decide who the crew could use." She waved a hand around his body. "This whole young, bright-eyed, enthusiasm thing is grating. Cut it."

"Not until you—" The glint of sunlight hitting steel shone from a darkened alley. Finn was so caught up in begging Captain Palmer that he hadn't realized what Bug was trying to tell him, that robed man from the docks had followed them. "Get down!" Finn tackled Captain Palmer to the ground.

The whirling of steel whooshed just past his neck

where the mouthy pyrate had been standing. An earful was going to be coming his way, but he knew that his hero now owed him her life.

"You're going to pay to have my coat—" Captain Palmer stopped when she spotted the small blade stuck into the side of the building opposite the alley. "That knife... Hello, Shad."

Captain Palmer and Finn got to their feet as the robed man stepped out from the alley. "The boy's a little young for you, Devil's Charm."

"Every pyrate has their followers, Shad." She held out her arms. "Turns out that none have quite as many as I."

Captain Palmer's energy had changed entirely. She seemed crude, dismissive, and annoyed while dealing with Finn, but now she was calm, confident, and ready for a fight. Something about her demeanour was awe-inspiring. All the stories Finn had heard had to be true.

Shad clicked his tongue. "The more fame you garner, the more detractors you garner as well."

"When is there not a bounty on me?" she asked. "What's this? Your fifth attempt at capturing me? Pretty sure I left you locked in a barrel last time. How do you think this is going to end?"

"The difference this time is that I don't have to bring you back alive."

"Lovely."

When he woke up from his midday nap, Finn was expecting an ordinary day. Things had gone so supremely out to sea that he was stuck in the midst of some kind of fated duel. Something like that might have scared most people, but Finn wasn't most people.

He stared at the two rivals. "What in the world is going on?"

"He's a pyrate hunter," Captain Palmer said as if the situation was nothing new. "I believe Shad here is actually ex-Royal Navy, correct?"

Shad nodded and fixed his eyes on Finn. "This village really is tucked away at the edge of the world, isn't it?"

"I'm not entirely convinced this lad isn't just incredibly sheltered from life, though you could be correct. There doesn't seem to be *any* advancements here."

Finn stared at Shad. "But why would you want to kill her?"

Both Captain Palmer and Shad raised an eyebrow at Finn. "Money."

Shad rushed toward the captain and she shoved Finn as hard as she could. Shad threw his robe to obscure her vision, but something about Captain Palmer's confident grin said she knew it was coming. Regardless, he used the obstruction to get in close with knives in each hand.

Rather than simply dodging, Captain Palmer launched into a back handspring and hit Shad hard in the jaw as her boot came up. It was unfortunate for Shad that the obstruction worked both ways.

"That was so cool." Finn figured his eyes must have been sparkling. "It's like that story where you went after the cursed gold in that old Rohiri temple. You used that move to launch a pyrate into the waters below, right?"

She gave Finn a puzzled look. "There's groupies and then there's you. How do you even know that?"

Shad recovered and struck out with a series of slashes. Captain Palmer danced around the wild slashes and landed a few quick strikes on the pyrate hunter. Finn only clued in when he saw the flashes of her fists, she hadn't even bothered pulling out her sword.

The two separated, and when an unexpected knife throw gave her a split second to dodge, it was time for her to get serious. The close call could have shaken her, but it didn't show on her face at all. She unsheathed her sword, and Shad did the same, ready for another round.

Finn wondered how someone could learn to fight with a long sword and short blade at the same time. It was a concept that seemed confusing to even attempt. With how comfortable Shad looked, it wasn't the first time he took a stance like that.

"How many knives do you have this time?" Captain Palmer blew a streak of hair from her face. "Four? Nine? One of these days you'll need to surprise me with none."

"I like to keep you guessing. Would it make you feel better if I told you I had a hundred?"

"Well, that's just not realistic."

Something was off.

Shad had been pushing the attack beforehand, but he stopped as soon as the captain had pulled her sword. If he were there to kill her, he would be prepared for her to pull out her go-to weapon. Why would he slow the pace back down when he already almost hit her with a knife?

Whatever the reason, Finn got his grappling hook ready in hand.

Captain Palmer glimpsed Finn readying his weapon. "Don't you dare interfere, girl."

Shad's face scrunched up. "That's a—"

Captain Palmer darted forward and the two clashed blades with a speed Finn had never seen from anyone. Even Vi's stories couldn't do Palmer's skill and speed justice.

Finn had practiced with a sword on his own and knew he'd likely be able to match the skill of some navy veterans. They'd make land in town for a few days every now and then. He'd watch them practice their meagre skills, so Finn felt confident, but these two were on another level.

In a desperate attempt, Shad tossed his knife upward, but Captain Palmer slashed it in midair. Using the knife as misdirection, Shad approached and threw a high knee. He missed, but this time a knife flew out of his boot.

He snatched it out of the air and started swinging it toward the captain's face.

"Watch out!" Finn called as he swung his grappling hook toward Shad.

There was no way she could dodge it in time, but Finn wasn't about to watch his hero die.

The hook wrapped around Shad's wrist right before he could connect. Finn was too far to be sure how close the save was, but he wondered just how close the knife came to ending the legacy of Captain Fortune Palmer. He tightened his grip on the rope and gave it a hard tug.

Shad looked toward Finn with his teeth bared. "I had her, you little piece of—"

Shad dropped the sword in his free hand and tapped his arm against his body. A knife fell from his sleeve to his hand, and Finn knew he was in trouble. He whipped it toward Finn, and despite trying to dodge, it caught him across his arm.

"Note to self, knives really hurt," Finn said.

Captain Palmer brought the hilt of her sword down onto the top of Shad's head and he hit the ground hard. When he didn't spring back up, Finn knew the fight was over.

She looked through a few barrels outside of the surrounding buildings and found some rope. After tying up Shad, she rolled him into a nearby alley with her foot. It wasn't much, but he probably wasn't going to be found anytime soon.

"I've about had it with today's excitement." Captain Palmer sheathed her sword and wiped her hands. "Is it so much to ask that I pull into port one time and I'm not stuck fighting the whole day?" She turned her attention back to Finn and his wound. "You'll need to go seek medical attention for that."

"It's not as bad as it looks," he winced "What about him?"

She shrugged. "He'll wake up at some point, someone will untie him, then we'll do this all again another time on another island."

The two of them stood there a moment and stared at one another. Finn gave her a look like he was waiting for her to say something. Captain Palmer returned a look of confusion.

"Well?" Finn asked.

"Well, what?"

"I saved your life back there." He tried to contain his excitement. "Isn't there some weird pyrate code thing where I save your life, and you owe me a favour?"

"You've listened to one too many stories, lad."

"That's better than girl." He took a breath and readied himself. "Can I please join your crew?"

She examined Finn and brought a hand to her chin. "What's your name?"

"Finn. Finn Townsend."

"Well, Flynn Tonrend, it's your lucky day." Finn could feel his heartbeat in his hands as she continued. "Because all the vacancies on the crew of the world-famous Curse of the Albatross will be filled in Bridger. You may remain here and live out the rest of your mundane life—filling barrels with goods, or whatever it is you people do here. The answer is no."

The craziness of the day was finally getting to Finn. His disappointment was only adding to how exhausted he felt. He figured he must have looked absolutely pitiful because the captain hadn't walked away from him yet.

She sighed, "Tell you what, lad—"

"Finn."

"Flynn"

"It's *Finn*."

"Alright, kid. Don't push it."

"I'm sixteen. Today's my birth—"

"Sixteen and awfully annoying still makes you a kid." Captain Palmer tapped a finger against the brim of her hat. "Look, if you can point me in the direction of the nearest tavern, I'll at the very least think about maybe allowing you to potentially come aboard my ship at some point in the distant future, savvy?"

Finn knew she was just telling him what he wanted to hear. He lifted a finger in the direction of the only tavern in town, and without another word, Captain Fortune Palmer disappeared into the town.

Chapter 5:

Dear Old Dad

Finn swung the creaky shop door open to a familiar musty scent. The store had been doing quite well as of late, and as such, many of the shelves were barren and dust-covered. Fresh supplies for the shop wouldn't be arriving for a few days, but that wasn't necessarily a bad problem to have for a boy named Finn.

He didn't even make it through the threshold before Archibald was on top of him. "You broke your promise."

"I'm sorry," Finn said, trying to hide his annoyance.

"No, you're not sorry," his father said. "If your promises meant anything to you—you'd keep them, yet here we are time after time. A man who can't keep a promise is no better than a pyrate."

Finn couldn't get the events of the day out of his head, and that morning he might have thought of that as a compliment. Now, being called a pyrate didn't feel quite as good as it might have used to.

"Is Diego—"

"You're bleeding." Archibald grabbed Finn's arm. "Was it the damned pyrate Diego mentioned? I'll kill him."

"Her. That pyrate was a her—and no." He pulled

his arm free. "It's from something else. It's been a long day, pop."

"Sit down." Archibald could tell something was wrong with his son, but he wasn't quite sure what it was.

He led Finn to the counter before heading upstairs to find some of the additional supplies they kept for emergencies. The muffled voices of Diego and his father oozed down the staircase, but their hushed tones made it too difficult to make out any words.

Finn looked for his pup, but Bug had already wandered off into the store, no doubt looking for his small wool bed in order to take another nap. If that dog had his way, he'd be nestled in a soft bed all day, each and every day.

Diego tip-toed down and leaned beside him on the counter. "I take it things didn't go so well?".

"Some crazy pyrate hunter tried to assassinate Captain Palmer and then they fought for a while. I actually helped her beat him."

"Helped her beat him," Diego looked down at the gash on Finn's arm. "Or got hurt, and she saved you?"

He glared at Diego. "I helped."

"So, what? Does that mean you've got an open invitation to become a mighty pyrate?"

"She told me she might think about it."

"Is that a good thing?"

There was a tiny spark of hope in Finn's heart. Hope that Captain Palmer might send out word to recruit the boy who had helped her in combat. Hope that he could join her crew. Thoughts like that were nothing but a dream, and he knew that.

"I don't think so," Finn said, all the air leaving his chest.

"Well, at least now we know that we can move past all this pyrate stuff right?" Diego sighed and leaned back, his tone becoming cheery. "We'll find you a lovely girl, we can take over the shop from pop, and we'll—"

"Why do you want that so badly?"

"We have our whole lives set for us here." Diego stared at Finn. "Every single thing we could ever need. Why don't you want all this?"

Diego looked around the dingy shop like it was the first time he was seeing it. He was always in awe of everything Archibald had accomplished after the attack, but it felt hollow to Finn. Pride in accomplishments was important, and while he was proud of all the work his father had done, the life of a shopkeeper wasn't for Finn.

"Are you kidding? Condemning myself to the same pointless tasks every day?" Finn brought a hand to his head. "Wake up, open the shop, deal with a bunch of people I'll never care about, and repeat. Why would I want that when I could go explore the world? When I could go look for my mom—for the man that killed your parents. Don't you care about that?"

"No, because I don't let that crazy old woman fill my head with pointless hope." Diego grabbed a small pitcher of water and filled a bowl, setting it on the ground for Bug. "You think the band of murderers that took your mom kept her alive all these years? Do you think they escaped? Why wouldn't they have just come home?"

"You may have given up, but I won't." Finn glared at him. "Not until I know what happened to her."

It was rare for the boys to discuss their parents at all. Finn's mother was a sore spot for Archibald, and a conversation like that would often just lead to a shouting match. Diego simply giving up and resigning himself to never knowing who killed his parents was something that always bothered Finn.

"The only way you'll do that is by stowing away on their ship." Diego regretted having said that when he watched Finn's expression change. "That was *not* me giving you an idea."

"Yes. yes, it was." Finn's heart started pounding. "They said they wouldn't be ready to go until nightfall, so that must mean they're bringing supplies aboard, right? I could stow away, and then when we're already far enough from Embar, they'll just have to let me join."

"Or they'll toss you overboard and laugh while they watch you get pulled under," Archibald said from the top of the stairs.

Finn had been scolded by his father before, but his tone wasn't anything close to the usual. He wasn't angry. He was filled with hate. Hatred for the kinds of people that took the love of his life.

"You have no idea what you're trying to get mixed up in." Archibald continued as he made his way down with an arm full of supplies. "Pull up your sleeve."

"I have to try, pop." Finn started rolling up his sleeve. "I have to find her."

"Finn—"

"Forget what Diego said, she's alive. She's out there somewhere and *you* never looked for her." Finn could tell his words were like poison. "If you won't do it then I will."

"Pop needs our help to run the shop," Diego said. "Life isn't exactly easy with one arm."

Finn looked at where his father's arm used to be. It could be hard for him to recall that dreadful night, but the loss of Archibald's arm made it a lot easier. That loud explosion and sudden rush through the air was something Finn would never forget.

"Then just take on a little more responsibility," Finn said through gritted teeth. "You're better with the shop than I am anyway, plus you bake. Probably best if someone who actually enjoys the work is the one running the place."

"That's enough out of the both of you," Archibald said. "Finn, your mother is dead. Those bastards took her and—I'm tired of you doing this and upsetting everyone in the process. Do you even know what those monsters are capable of?" He wrapped a bandage around Finn's arm. "She was likely dead the night they took her—after—those bastards did what bastards do."

Finn looked at the bandage and rolled his sleeve back down. "You never tried to find her."

"SHE'S DEAD!" Archibald's voice could have shaken all the windows.

It was never pleasant hearing his pop scream. If he was facing the door, he would have expected to see all the neighbours poking their noses through the door. Yelling wasn't out of the ordinary, but angry screams were.

"What do you want from me, son?" Archibald continued. "Was I to patch myself up? Pick up my bloody severed arm, swim to their ship, and beat them to death with it to save her? I never went after her because those pyrates don't take prisoners, and if I tried, it would have been two children without a family."

It was a tough spot to be in. Finn knew he would have hopped on the first boat he found in order to hunt for his mother, but it wasn't that simple. If Archibald had done that, both Finn and little Diego Baker would have likely met a cruel, sad end. Still, Finn couldn't understand.

He stared into his father's eyes. "A real man would have done anything he could for the one he loved."

"I did exactly that," Archibald stared right back. "And maybe one day you'll understand that. Right now, you're just a weak boy with no idea of how the world really works. At least I'm a man that can keep his promises."

"A promise means nothing if the one you promised everything to isn't even alive anymore." Finn hoped his father could feel his anger. "You let her die."

"You aren't being fair to pop," Diego said

"He's not even your real father," Finn snapped.

He didn't mean for his anger to hit Diego like a knife in the back, but his reaction told him that it had. More than a few people around the village referred to Diego as either the orphan boy or the Baker orphan. The tragedy of his family was one that never escaped him.

Archibald grabbed Finn by the scruff of his shirt. "And who's responsible for that? Bloody pyrates."

"So that's it?" Finn pushed Archibald's hand away. "Everyone just lets pyrates do whatever they want? Kill and take whoever they want?"

He was at a loss for words, and it seemed like the others were too. It was an argument they'd had a thousand times, but one that never had a firm ending. With nothing left to say, Finn stormed up the staircase with Bug thumping up the steps behind him.

Soon, the sun started falling across the sky.

Finn had slid a window open, but he was in such a state that he couldn't remember when he had opened it. The cool breeze from outside beckoned him out of the house.

It would have been so easy to slip out.

He could show them all just what he was capable of. Become the most capable pyrate ever known, and return with not only tales of perilous adventures, but knowledge of those that devastated his village.

The door creaked open, catching him off guard. After a fight like that, he assumed they'd leave him alone for the rest of the night.

Archibald stepped in with two different cloths, one small and fat, and the other long and thin. Finn looked at his father, unsure of whether or not he'd receive another tongue lashing. It wasn't out of the realm of possibility for the items under the cloths the be part of some kind of punishment.

"What do you want?" Finn asked.

"I haven't forgotten it's your birthday." Archibald held out a long piece of cloth. "Here, it belonged to your mother."

Finn unwrapped the cloth and was met with an intricate sheathe. It was made of vibrant materials that were rare to come across on Embar. He drew the glittering blade from it and gawked at it. It was sleek, silver, and finished with an ornate hilt. To Finn, It matched Captain Palmer's sword in terms of beauty and craftsmanship.

"It's incredible."

"You best take good care of that. I know you haven't had a lot of practice with a blade, but I've seen you practicing when you think I'm not watching," Archibald sighed. "I have a feeling you'll be needing that."

For a moment, it looked like Archibald's eyes fell on the open window before he looked at Finn.

"This was really mom's? Why did she have a sword?"

Archibald nodded. "Sophia was always receiving gifts from the men who were pining for her. She wasn't the greatest with it, but she felt better having some way to defend herself. This is one of the few things I have left to remind me of her." He set the other cloth down on Finn's bed. "In a way, I'm glad she didn't bring it with her that night."

Finn untied the second cloth, and some rations of food complete with a small canteen fell out. Finn could tell that the warm chunk of bread was made by Diego. It wasn't much, but it was enough to get Finn by for a couple of days.

"What is this for?" Finn studied his father's face as he sheathed the blade. "So, that means you'll—"

"Supper's in an hour." Archibald brought a hand to Finn's face. "I'll see you then."

His father was never big on goodbyes, and Finn could tell that was what was happening. It was his blessing for Finn to follow his dreams and find his answers.

Finn hugged him. "I'll see you in an hour, pop."

They let go of each other, and Archibald crouched to pet Bug. "Protect each other. Don't mention anything to Diego either." Archibald started to leave, but lingered in the doorway. "You know how he gets—about supper."

After his father shut the door, Finn pulled out an old book and reached for an inkwell he kept on his desk. Most people from Embar didn't care for reading or writing, but Archibald had taught both him and Diego of the importance of language—

Diego,

I know you'll have a lot of questions. Why did I leave? Was it because I was angry at you and pop? Was it something else entirely? It's like I told you, I need to find out what happened to my mom—and that means finding the man that killed your folks. This is goodbye, but it's only goodbye for now. I promise you, one day I'll return to tell you and pop all about the *crazy adventures I got up to on the seas with Captain Palmer. You take good care of pop until I get back, and make sure you don't ignore Minerva. You're going to have to stand up for yourself for a little while, but I know you'll do just fine. You always do.*

Forever your brother, even if not by blood,

- Finn

He looked down at Bug and laughed at the goofy, tired look on his furry companion's face. The poor little guy had no idea what sort of adventure they were about to head off on. Finn turned around to face the window as the sun started to dip below the horizon.

"Time to go, Bug."

chapter 6:

Stitches, Captains, And Contracts

Finn's plan had gone surprisingly well.

As it turns out, a sixteen-year-old stowaway and his chubby dog weigh similar to whatever supplies the crew of the Albatross was bringing aboard. The real issue was knowing how long it had been since he had made his way onto the ship.

He figured the best course of action would be to wait until he woke up—if he ever managed to fall asleep.

That part of the plan stopped mattering when he was jostled awake by the barrel he had hidden in being tipped over. He spilled out with Bug and looked up at a mousey girl who gave him an intense stare. She didn't look angry, more amused with a hint of annoyance.

"Oh, good. Who needs medical supplies when you can have some kid and his weird dog?" She grinned. "I guess you two will make good practice dummies."

"This definitely isn't my bed," Finn groaned. "How'd I end up here?"

"You don't have to play dumb, stowaway." Without looking at Finn, she looked inside a few other barrels. "I don't really care why you're here. What's your name?"

"Okay," Finn stood up and held out a hand. "Finn, and this here is Bug."

The woman let out a bit of a silent chuckle as he introduced himself, though Finn had no idea why. She exuded a strange energy, and he figured that any woman willing to spend time on a pyrate ship had to be a bit *different*.

"Finn. That's a fun name for being out at sea," The woman looked down at his hand but didn't take it. "But that's definitely a dog, not a bug."

Finn rolled his eyes. "What's your—"

"The name's Cecily! But most people around here call me Stitch, for obvious reasons."

"Ship doctor?"

"You got it." She adjusted her glasses. "Well, I used to be a tailor, buuuut you get what you get when you're on a pyrate ship."

There couldn't be much overlap in the skills of a doctor and a tailor. Even believing a tailor could competently pull off basic stitches on a human was a bit of a stretch. With how young Stitch looked, she probably hadn't been the ship doctor for all that long.

Finn wiped some dust from his clothes. "Remind me to avoid ever needing any stitches."

"Those are my speciality."

"I got that." Looking around at his dark surroundings, he noticed he was surrounded by worn-out barrels. "This isn't exactly what I expected from the ship."

"I would hope not. Who in their right mind imagines the storeroom of a pyrate ship?"

"Are you for real?"

"I try to be. Why? Am I see-through or something? Am I becoming a spirit?" Stitch patted herself. "Nope. All good."

A woman so strange had never landed in Embar. Women from other islands had visited on the rare occasion, but most of them were quiet and meek—or simply there to entertain the men. Stitch oozed the same kind of confidence that Captain Palmer had despite being ten times stranger.

"Right." Finn looked to Bug, but even he looked confused. "What time is it?"

"Morning," she said plainly.

"And what do we do now?"

"I guess I have to take you to see the cap."

"Cap? Captain Fortune Palmer? This is the Curse of the Albatross right?" Finn asked in mild panic.

It would have been his luck to attempt to infiltrate the Albatross, only to wind up on a ship headed in the opposite direction.

"Huh. Is that what this ship is named?" Stich asked. "That is so cool."

Finn looked down at Bug again. "What have we done?"

"Come along, I'll take you to Captain Palmer." Stitch headed toward the door. "Most people don't call her by her full name, I assume you're a friend? You look a little young—a nephew?"

Finn was going to take whatever he could get. "Yeah, something like that."

"Oh, goodie. Well, it's always nice to have someone to talk to on the ship. Most people here just grunt and make scary faces." She pulled the corners of her mouth down to make a scary face of her own. "You have a nice face, not exactly my cup of tea, but I hope you stick around."

They headed through the door and into a long wooden hallway filled with doors. When Finn had seen the ship in the port it looked a bit beat up, but the interior was beautiful. All the wood looked specially hand-crafted. There wasn't any finer craftsmanship anywhere on Embar.

"Hope I stick around?" he asked. "People tend to leave?"

"No."

"Then what do you—"

"People tend to die," Stitch said with a kind of glee that told Finn she didn't have much regard for the average life.

"Why did I not see that coming?"

Stitch looked around. "See what coming?"

Finn brought a hand to his face. "Never mind."

They turned a corner and up ahead Finn could see a hatch with daylight flooding through the cracks. In just a few moments he'd be on the deck of the ship he always dreamed of sailing on. The only issue was that Stitch was kind of ruining the moment.

"You're weird," Stitch said with a grin. "I like it."

"Thanks, Stitch. I like you too."

"Yay! A new friend," she beamed. "Tobi'll be so proud of me."

The top deck was bustling with various crew members doing whatever it was that a pyrate crew does. They were all busy, but Finn couldn't identify what anyone had been assigned to do. A few unfortunate souls looked miserable as they swabbed the deck, and Finn prayed he wouldn't end up like one of them.

"So—where is—" Finn began to ask.

"She's the one steering this thing right now," she said as she mimed steering a ship. "Well, I hope so at least."

The dark brown wood of the ship looked like it was ready to fall apart, but there wasn't a single creaky board under Finn's feet. He wondered if it was a kind of trick —make the outside of the boat look as if it were in poor shape when the entire thing was actually sturdy as a brand new vessel.

They headed up a set of stairs, and with each step, more of the ship's wheel came into view, along with Captain Palmer. Stitch and Finn were right in front of her as they came up the stairs, but the captain was in her own world.

"Excuse me, Captain," Stitch said as she waved a hand. "Yoo-hoo."

Captain Palmer snapped back to reality from wherever her mind was, and her sight fell on Finn. "What are *you* doing here, girl?" Bug barked at her, causing Captain Palmer to curl her lip. "And of course with that ugly little thing."

"That's what I came to talk to you about." Stitch sat on the nearby railing. "I found your nephew—niece? Or your friend—he wasn't really clear on the relation. Point is, I found him napping in a barrel that should have been full of my medical supplies."

Captain Palmer scowled at Finn, but the scowl morphed into a smile—and then into boisterous laughter. He wondered when anything on the ship would start making sense. Stitch joined in on the laughter, but the captain shot her an annoyed look as if she was the only one allowed a bit of fun.

"What a series of days—" Captain Palmer turned her attention back to Finn and cleared her throat. "Well, at least now I know I can't call you girl, kid. You've got balls."

"I told you I wasn't going to give up," Finn said.

"Trust me, it was so annoying—I wasn't going to forget *that* anytime soon. I'm honestly just deciding if I want to keep you aboard, or if we should toss you and have a nice laugh."

Finn groaned at the accuracy of his father during their argument, "If it helps at all, I'd prefer the first option."

"Quiet, you. You don't get any say in your fate. This

is official pyrate business." Captain Palmer walked around the wheel and leaned over the rail to the lower deck. "Walker! We have a bright-eyed young stowaway wanting to join the crew. Keep him, or toss him?"

Finn leaned over as well and was met with the man he had seen talking to the captain in Embar.

"He any good in a fight?" Walker asked.

Captain Palmer flicked her eyes from Finn to her first mate. "Unfortunately, it seems he might be."

However backhanded the compliment was, Finn was thrilled. He knew he could grow on her with enough time to do so. If he was already deemed as valuable, his chances looked even better. Something told Finn that Walker's opinion meant far more than the average pyrate thanks to his rank on board.

"Keep 'em." Walker shrugged. "We need more fighters. 'specially with the Blues on our tail."

She groaned and returned to the wheel, "I guess at the very least the kid'll make a good meat shield."

Finn waved. "Still right here."

"I'm well aware of that."

Stitch shot a hand up. "I'd prefer if we kept Finn aboard."

As soon as that sentence left her lips, Finn was worried about his odds of staying all over again.

"Really?" Captain Palmer raised an eyebrow at her. "You want to keep the lad? But will he make a good pyrate?"

"I think so." Stitch looked from Finn to her captain. "From the second I tipped him out of that dusty barrel, I had a feeling he'd fit right in. Then we became such fast friends—we even talked about spirits! We gotta keep him!"

Stitch was a strange woman, but she spoke in such an earnest way that it was hard not to like her. Even though she was likely a few years Finn's senior, she already felt like a little sister.

"Very well," Captain Palmer said. "Welcome to the Albatross."

Finn had no words. Things could have gone bad enough that he'd already be under the sea, but now, he was going to become a pyrate. Not just any pyrate, but one of Fortune's pyrates.

Captain Palmer hadn't noticed Finn's cheesy grin as she continued. "Stitch, I trust you're quite busy? I'll deal with our stowaway personally."

"Yes ma'am." Stitch hopped off the railing and headed toward the stairs. "Welcome aboard, Finn."

Before he could say anything, Stitch disappeared back into the ship. "She's so strange."

"She may be strange, but she's never been wrong about a person's character. The oddballs are always the best judge of character." She let out a sharp whistle. "Walker, come take the wheel."

"Aye!" Walker called from below.

Finn looked to where Stitch had left. "Not that I want to ruin things, but I only met Stitch a few minutes ago. I don't know how much she really knows about me."

"Doesn't matter." She handed the wheel to Walker. "Once you've spent enough time here, you'll learn that a gut feeling is more important than anything you could think your way through. Stitch knows people's hearts, that's even more valuable than her medical abilities."

"Alright, so what happens now? The crew—"

"There's time for that later," Captain Palmer said as she stuck a hand in his face. "I'll show you around the ship. I assume you've never been on one before. Then, we'll have you sign your contract. After that, it's all up to how long you manage to survive."

Of all the tales that Vi had told him, she'd never once mentioned contracts. Using something as official as a contract was strange considering most pyrates probably didn't know what a contract was, and even more of them couldn't read.

"A contract?"

"Aye. You want to be a pyrate? It's a life-long commitment. Break it, and you won't like where your soul ends up," Captain Palmer said.

"The Locker?" Finn asked, filled with horror and wonder.

"Captain," Walker cut in. "The Blues are gaining on us—far quicker than I'd like."

Walker pointed backward at a ship looming in the distance. Even while it was leagues across the sea, Finn could tell that the ship was as finely built as they come. The ominous sight reminded him of a cyclone at sea, ready to wreak havoc on a port at any moment. He didn't know what Blues were or how bad it would be if they caught up, but Captain Palmer didn't look worried.

"They are?" She rushed to the nearby railing. "I thought we'd have no trouble leaving them behind. That must mean—"

"Shall we head under?" Walker clutched the wheel. "I don't think they can match our speed then."

"No. I'm up for a little battle." She glanced at Finn. "It gives us a chance to see what our little stowaway can do. We'll take them by surprise and make quick work of them all. Penny won't expect something like that."

Finn wasn't sure what Walker and Captain Palmer were talking about, but their mischievous grins told him it wasn't going to be good.

chapter 7:

Penny Of The Blues

"Well, stowaway, are you ready for a fight?" Captain Palmer asked as she adjusted her belt.

"Stowaway?" Finn asked. "I thought I'm supposed to be part of the crew now—"

"Not until you sign that contract," her dismissive tone made it clear that the time for that discussion was long gone. "You said you'd heard stories about the likes of me and my crew for years, yes?" Finn replied with a simple nod. "Then tell me the first rule of my ship."

Finn beamed at the thought of reciting the rules of the ship. It had been a while since he'd heard them from Vi, but he'd asked to hear them at least once a week when he as a boy. The thought of pyrates that don't kill was just one of the many reasons he always looked up to Captain Palmer.

"The crew of the Albatross sheds no blood if they can help it." Finn recited. "Their enemies live on to share the tale of the utter defeat at the hands of the greatest pyrate this side of the seas."

Walker nudged his captain. "The kid's clearly heard one too many stories."

"Yes, a little dramatic," she said with a chuckle. "But

he'll be right at home. He was close enough—you are not to kill anyone so long as you remain a member of this crew, savvy?"

Finn smiled. "Aye."

Walker clicked his tongue. "Kid catches on quick."

Captain Palmer stepped to the front railing overlooking the deck. "READY FOR BATTLE! THE LOT OF YOU! NOW!"

Men rushed every which way, tying lines down, and grabbing weapons. The ship in the distance was closing in fast, and Finn worried the crew wouldn't be ready in time. The dark blue sails of the ship struck Finn. Unlike most ships he'd ever seen, the vessel felt regal.

"You've got a blade and a grappling hook on your belt. I know you can use one, how are you with a blade?" Captain Palmer asked as she held up two fingers to a nearby crew member.

Finn pulled out his sword and gave it a few quick swings. "I've practiced."

"That's—reassuring."

"Who are the Blues?" Finn asked. "Navy or something?"

"Spot on actually," Captain Palmer said as she looked over her weapons. "Unfortunately, if this ship is fast enough to surpass us in speed, it's a specific individual."

"Specific individual?"

If it was anything like the individuals on Embar, Captain Palmer might have been a bit too relaxed. If a ship was filled with men as skilled as Shad, there was no way she could fend them off. Perhaps the rest of the crew was more skilled than they looked, but Finn couldn't be sure about that. Walker was the only other crew member Vi had ever even mentioned by name.

"Walker, please see to it that Trigger is prepared for battle below deck," Captain Palmer said. Tell him, cannons high, and inform Tobi that if things go wrong, he may be in for quite a bit of work when we reach Bridger."

"Aye," Walker said before rushing below deck.

The crew member the captain had gestured toward rushed over with two ropes attached to the mast high above. How the pyrate managed to get lines tied above Finn without him noticing was just one of the many questions he had, but he figured that was just how skilled the crew of Captain Palmer's ship really was.

"Hand those to the kid," Captain Palmer said.

"I get to hold rope?" Finn asked as he took them.

She leaned forward as if she were talking to a child. "It's your first official pyrate job—keep a tight grip on those ropes."

It wasn't exactly what Finn had imagined as his first job on a pyrate ship. He figured he'd get to climb the crow's nest and spy for land. Holding a couple pieces of rope wasn't anywhere on his list of jobs he'd love to do.

"Yes ma'am." Finn grumbled.

Captain Palmer glared at him.

He straightened up. "Aye."

Her glare turned into a pointed smirk as she glanced at the approaching ship. "You can't forget that even though you are forbidden from killing, the enemy will likely always be trying to kill you. Savvy?"

That was a scary thought.

Finn paused for a moment before he spoke again. "Aye."

The ship was moments away from a skirmish when Walker returned to take the wheel. He may have looked a bit nervous about the coming conflict, but Captain Palmer looked giddy. She walked over to Finn and took one of the ropes.

"What's the plan, Captain?" Walker asked.

"Be prepared to weigh anchor," Captain Palmer said

as she tightened her belt. "The kid and I are going to swing onto the front of their ship when it gets into range and we're going to end the battle before it begins."

"We're what?" Finn asked.

"Problem?" she asked with a wry smile.

"You don't want to come up with a real, well-thought-out plan?"

"I thought up a plan. In fact, I just told it to you."

"Yeah, but—"

"Everything I do, I do well."

"Sure, but—"

"Ready?" Her eyes gleamed as she turned her attention to the approaching ship.

The black and blue ship was just behind the Albatross. A small group of men in dark blue uniforms lined the deck of the ship, though none of them looked as ready for combat as Captain Palmer.

Finn heard Bug whining behind him. "You stay here, boy. Walker will keep you safe—probably. I'll be right back—again, probably."

Captain Palmer stepped up onto the rail of the ship with her blade drawn, and Finn did the same.

"Go," she booted him in the butt with a laugh.

Finn screamed as he swung across the gap between the two ships. Looking down to the roaring ocean below was a big mistake. He was used to swinging, but dropping a few feet to the ground had nothing on what would be a drop to certain death.

As the rope's momentum stalled over the Blue's ship, Finn let go and landed on the deck. For a moment he worried this was some kind of trick to be rid of him.

A naval officer approached with his sword drawn, but Finn still wasn't ready for a fight. Captain Palmer swung over and kicked the officer in the face, sending him flying into another approaching officer.

She pointed a finger at a female crew member

standing in the middle of the ship's deck. "She's our target."

Something about her seemed familiar at a glance, but there wasn't any time for Finn to think about that. The ship's crew wasn't ready for such a bold plan of attack. It was a large ship, and since there were so few men on deck, they must have been below on the cannons.

That's why it was imperative to end the battle quickly.

Captain Palmer led the attack, parrying three different men's sword strikes at once. Finn did his best to contend with one officer, something that wasn't quite on the captain's level, but he figured his little effort was valiant. He ducked a slash and kicked the officer in the chest. The man flew over the side of the boat, and Finn started to panic.

He had screwed up already.

"Ugh. C'mon, kid," Captain Palmer said.

She pushed back the men she was fighting, ran across the deck, and slashed two ropes near where the man had fallen overboard. Finn peeked over to see the man swimming to the lifeboat that had hit the water.

A female shout sent him spinning around. It was their target, and Finn barely managed to deflect her swing. All he could do was find the time to parry. Her attacks were so swift and fluid, it was as if an opening to strike would never come.

"Fortune's got a young new crew member, huh?" she said between strikes. "That's rare."

"Really?" he asked.

A quick kick from Captain Palmer sent the officer barrelling into the ship's mast. She had handily dealt with three officers on her own and had now taken the ship's lead officer hostage in a matter of moments.

"Tell your men to surrender." Captain Palmer

pointed a sword to the woman's throat. "Now."

"Men, send word below deck to hold fire. We're surrendering. Weigh anchor, now," the target said. "Long time no see, sister."

Captain Palmer clicked her tongue a few times. "You made this way too easy, Penny."

"We weren't expecting two psychos swinging from ropes to drop in and beat us up," Penny said. "Most vessels don't bother putting up a fight with my vessel."

"What if it were those monsters on the Poisoned Rose or the nut-jobs of the Hell-Born Storm?"

Finn had never heard of a ship called the Hell-Born Storm, but as soon as she mentioned the Poisoned Rose he wished he could jump into the conversation. If someone was going to have information on that ship, it made sense that she would.

Penny smirked. "Leaving out Poseidon's—"

"Don't go there," Captain Palmer said.

"Alright, alright."

"Why are you chasing us this time?"

"You got a bit too close to a commanding fleet. They sent me to catch up to you," Penny said as she rose to her feet. "But it's actually a good thing because I have some information you might be interested in. By the way, who's the new lad?"

The relation between the sisters was painfully clear at a glance, but their personalities felt like polar opposites. Every word out of the captain's mouth oozed with either confidence or condescension, while Penny's words were all calm and kind.

He held out a hand. "I'm Finn."

Captain Palmer smacked his hand away. "Stowaway. Hoping he'll grow on me. If not—" She waved a thumb over her shoulder. "What's all this about information?"

"The Royal Navy's discovered the location of one of those ancient treasures you're always on about." Penny rolled her eyes. "Something about an artifact that's been blessed to bring an abundance of good fortune to anyone who holds it."

For a brief moment, Captain Palmer looked like she'd been filled with genuine excitement before she shrugged it off. "Sounds like something Sig'd be interested in."

"I thought so." Penny pulled a map from her coat and pointed at an island. "It's in some temple on an island due south of the Linwood Atoll."

Finn could barely contain his excitement. In just a few minutes he'd joined Captain Palmer's crew, beaten a navy ship in a fight, and now he was learning about an ancient treasure complete with a temple. Forget untold riches, Finn was in paradise.

"Why haven't the Blues simply gone and taken said treasure if you know where it is?" Captain Palmer asked.

"I've told you all I know. I only follow orders— sometimes." Penny gave Finn the most charming wink he'd ever seen, and his face became hot.

"Hm. I'll pass the info on. For now—I have to ruin your ship." Captain Palmer pushed Finn toward a plank that was set on the ship's rail. "Don't head south, so we don't run into this problem again."

"Come on. You don't have to do that."

Finn had no idea what repairing a ship after a volley of cannon fire would be like, but he imagined it wasn't simple. It would be timely and costly, but the Blues had more than enough coin to spare, so it wouldn't be too great of an issue in the long run.

"I do. Need to make it convincing," Captain Palmer said with a cheeky wink of her own back at Penny. "Good seeing you, sister."

"Good to see you, Fortune." She turned her attention to Finn. "Keep her safe, kid."

Finn rolled his eyes. "You two are definitely related."

Captain Palmer kicked Finn in the butt again, this time to hurry him along the plank. "Quiet, you. TRIGGER!"

-BOOM!-

As Finn and the captain made their way across the plank a volley of cannon fire passed by them and took out the sails on Penny's ship. The hole-filled sails reminded him of the cheese that the women of Embar used to make. Once pristine, the ship had become just another ruined vessel.

"Won't they—"

"Relax." Captain Palmer held her hand up. "There's a port town not too far from here. Less than a day's sail, even with that much damage. They'll be fine."

"I guess that was kind of an easy first test, huh?" They hopped down onto the Albatross, and Finn beamed with pride. "There's no way your sister's men would have actually killed us, right?"

"Sure. Whatever you want to tell yourself, kid."

"Shall I continue the course, Captain?" Walker asked from behind the wheel.

"Yes, the plan has only changed slightly." She headed up toward the wheel with Finn in tow. "Stop in Bridger, and then we'll carry on to the capital. Let's head under, shall we? We can show our new friend what the pyrate life is really like."

"Aye, Captain," Walker said as he pressed on the centre of the wheel and spun it with all his might.

Finn pointed to the spinning wheel. "That doesn't seem like safe navigation."

A dull orange glow reflected off the water around

the sides of the ship. The boat started shaking as if it was caught in the middle of an earthquake before it began sinking into the depths of the ocean. It had to be the same thing that the Poisoned Rose had done all those years ago, but it was far scarier experiencing it firsthand.

"Should the boat be doing that?" Finn looked around with wild eyes. "Are we supposed to be sinking?"

Captain Palmer stared at Finn, trying to hold back a laugh. Walker had an amused grin of his own on his face. Even the rest of the crew seemed to be unbothered by their sudden downward trajectory. Unlike all the others, Bug rushed over to Finn, sharing in his fright.

"Is anyone going to tell me what's going on?"

"It's so much more fun if we don't." Captain Palmer taunted.

The ship sunk lower until the floor of the deck became level with the ocean. Finn felt a kind of energy pulse flowing around the ship before the entire thing dropped under the ocean waves.

Chapter 8:

Gliding Under The Sea

Finn closed his eyes and held his breath, expecting water to crash all around him, but the icy water never came. In fact, he was unusually dry for someone who was certain he just went down with a sinking ship. The air was a little cool, but other than that, Finn couldn't complain about anything.

He popped an eye open to an incredible sight.

The entire ship was gliding across the glittering water—under the surface of the sea. There was no telling how fast they were moving, but it felt far faster than any ship should have been able to sail. There was no way Penny's ship would have caught them if the captain didn't want to be caught.

Seeing the water rushing around the strange energy that surrounded the boat, along with all the marine life—it was gorgeous.

"What is happening?" Finn placed a hand on the nearby railing to get a closer look. "What—what am I looking at? Where did we—"

Off in the distance, an enormous creature swam by a huge school of bright fish. Many of the fish broke off and reconvened on the opposite side of the creature.

Finn had never seen anything like it in his entire life. It was a whole new world.

"Beautiful, isn't it?" Captain Palmer asked.

Finn looked at the pulsating energy that surrounded the ship. It was so close that someone could accidentally get pulled into the sea if they weren't careful. He reached his hand out, but took a second to think about what might happen to his fingers.

"Go ahead, kid. It's safe." She flicked some water at him "Might sting a little if you leave your hand out there too long, but it's safe."

Finn reached out, and as his fingers passed through the pulse, the tips of his fingers became wet.

"That's how they did it," he muttered.

Captain Palmer cocked her head. "How who did what?"

The ship passed by another school of fish, giving Finn a bit of a fright. They were so close to his fingers, that if his reaction speed was a bit better, he could have plucked one out of the water for dinner.

"Never mind." He pulled his hand back. "It's nothing."

"The way you said that doesn't seem like nothing."

"It is." Finn headed down to the deck with the captain on his heels. "I'm going to sign that contract and be a pyrate, right? I need to toughen up a bit anyway."

Captain Palmer gave Finn a look he didn't even know she was capable of, a look of understanding. "Being a pyrate isn't being an emotionless brute. You want to do that, you can go join another crew. This ship, this crew—well, most of this crew—we're a family. You're your own person, but if you need to speak, someone is here to listen. I can't guarantee that'll be me, but we'll see how things go."

Finn looked down at his sword and put a hand on the hilt. "When I was a kid—"

"You are a kid." Finn shot her a look and she replied with a finger pointed toward him. "Don't give me sassy looks, stowaway."

He sighed, "When I was a kid, my village was attacked by pyrates. One minute they were sailing away, and the next minute, they were gone. The Poisoned Rose —that's the ship that attacked my village—the crew that kidnapped my mom."

Bug started to paw at Finn's leg so he picked him up and cradled him. The dog wasn't around during the destruction of Embar, but he was great at picking up on when Finn's mood had taken a nosedive. Bug was often all the comfort that he needed, even the lazy dog just wanted to nap in Finn's arms.

"So that's why you want to be a pyrate." Captain Palmer moved beside Finn. "Not the tales of the incredulous Devil's Charm, Captain Fortune Palmer. You want—"

"What's incredulous mean?" he asked.

"It—well, I think it means—" she paused for a moment as if the word had slipped from her brain. "It means, I'm a fantastic pyrate."

There was a brief moment where Captain Palmer's confidence slipped away from her. It was funny to see her squirm for the first time, but Finn already knew that laughing wouldn't be the best idea.

"That doesn't sound right," Finn said.

"Moving on."

"I've just wanted to find her—to know what happened to her."

"Even if that means the answer you get isn't the one you're looking for?" Captain Palmer asked.

Finn hadn't seriously thought about that question before. He wanted to know what happened, but a part of him always believed his mother had escaped somewhere. The harsh truth was that his father could be right.

72

"Yes," he finally said.

She raised an eyebrow. "Aren't you just the luckiest stowaway in the world?"

"What do you mean?"

"I may not know the exact whereabouts of the Poisoned Rose—hell, I bet Sig doesn't even have a clue, but I know someone in Bridger who might—if it's really that important to you."

"You mean, you'd help me?" he asked.

"In between contracts and nights of debauchery," Captain Palmer pulled a bottle of rum from a nearby crate and examined it. "We'll see what we can do. No promises. Savvy?"

"What's debauch—" Finn began to ask.

"We aren't doing that again. Do you understand me?"

"Aye."

Finn could feel his emotions welling up. It meant a lot that his hero would offer to help him. As far as he knew, he was just a kid that hadn't stopped annoying Captain Palmer, but in a way, she was already treating him like family.

"Walker, when you have a moment could you find some material to make a small bed for our new furry friend?" Walker flashed a thumb, and she continued. "Kid, follow me. I'd like to introduce you to some of the crew." The captain headed through the hatch that Stitch and Finn had come through. "Just my favourites really—don't tell them I said that."

Walker cleared his throat. "Yer gonna do just fine, kid."

Finn smiled. "When do I stop being a kid?"

"Whenever she decides."

Finn rolled his eyes and followed Captain Palmer through the hatch. They headed further below to a room where cannons lined the walls. It was dark and dingy, but

Finn had a feeling it was a lot nicer than what other pyrate ships had on offer.

Across the room, a shorter man made of pure muscle was tinkering with a cannon. As he turned around to greet them, it became clear that what he lacked in height he more than made up for in width.

"Kid, meet Edmund Trigger," Captain Palmer gestured to the bald man. "Also known amongst most brawlers as Ankle-Biter."

"I'm Finn. Nice to—"

"Finn. Got it." Edmund wiped his hands with a rag. "Yeh can decide between Trigger or Ankle-Biter. If yeh call me Edmund, I'll toss yeh overboard."

Trigger didn't look like he got out of the ship much. While most of the pyrates on deck were tanned, he was a pale white, similar to that of the noble women.

"Trigger it is," Finn said to placate the strange man. "If I can I ask, what's up with the whole Ankle-Biter thing?"

"Every self-respecting pyrate needs a moniker. When Captain Palmer found me, I was a tavern fighter."

"Still not understanding the nickname."

"I'm gettin' there." He looked toward the captain. "Impatient lad yeh've brought us."

She adjusted her hat. "I'm becoming acutely aware of that." She held a finger to Finn. "Don't you dare ask what *acutely* means."

Trigger laughed, "Long story short, people tend to not fight the fairest against a famed fighter. I wouldn't just let people get away with that, so I'd bite 'em."

Finn turned his head. "You'd bite them?"

"I'd bite 'em."

Every pyrate Finn met somehow managed to be even stranger than the last. While Trigger was as odd as Stitch, he was also the kind of rough and tough person that anyone would be glad to have on their side.

"When Captain Palmer found you, you were—"

"Havin' a big chomp on a dirty ole ankle."

Finn was having a hard time figuring out if Trigger and Captain Palmer were just trying to have a bit of fun at his expense or not. The crazed look in Trigger's eyes gave Finn the feeling that he was all too serious.

"Sounds like you've led an eventful life," Finn said with a nervous chuckle.

"Yeh don't know the half of it, lad."

Captain Palmer slapped a thick cannon. "Trigger is our master gunman. He mans all the cannons himself. I honestly have no clue how he does it."

"Yeh don't need someone beaten down, do yeh?" Trigger asked as he invaded Finn's personal space.

"No?"

"Yeh let me know if yeh do."

Trigger was covered in some kind of black ash, but it didn't cover the scent of a man who hadn't bathed for weeks. The smell brought tears to Finn's eyes and choked out all of his other senses. He had a feeling Bug couldn't have been loving the stench either.

"Trust me," Finn shuffled back. "You'll be the first person I come to."

Trigger nodded as Bug lifted his head and yawned. "What the hell is that thing?"

Finn looked around. "What?"

"Crap." Captain Palmer shook her head. "We'll get out of your hai—out of here. Nice shots on those sails back there. I don't think there was a single wasted shot."

"Be—be on your way, now." Trigger turned his attention back to his cannons but kept glancing back at Bug.

Finn had seen people who feared animals before, but never anyone that feared Bug. The pup was much too small to pose a threat to someone the size of Trigger. It was comical that a man who'd be willing to bite another man in a fight feared a small dog.

Finn snickered. "Are you really afrai—"

"Come on, Finn," Captain Palmer said as she pulled him out of the room.

"You know, for someone who calls me impatient and annoying, I sure don't get to finish sentences all that much."

"What are you complaining about? You just got an irritatingly long one out right there."

Finn ignored the comment and put Bug down. "What was that back there?"

"I forgot to mention that Trigger has a bit of a thing with animals."

"A thing with animals?"

She shrugged. "He's afraid of them."

"He's afraid of animals? All animals?"

"All of them. That's why he's in here. He can't deal with the fish and other sea life while we're under. You should see him come face to face with a turtle. You'd swear a fair young maiden was around with the way he shrieks." She pushed Finn down a hallway. "I'll take you to meet Tobi. If you liked Stitch, you'll probably like him."

Finn thought back to his conversation with Stitch. It was a short while ago, but it already felt as if it had been days.

"She did mention something about a Tobi," he said.

"That's not surprising in the least."

They turned down a few hallways and came to a door that was different from the others. The word *carpenter* was written on it, and rather than just a single door, it had double doors. Finn figured it was to make the movement of materials easier.

"I guess Tobi's the ship carpenter then?" Finn asked.

She pushed the doors open. "He certainly is. You've never seen a man make repairs as quick as he can." Her lips curled into a smirk. "Quicker when he's threatened."

As they entered, the damp smell of the ship changed to a much homier scent. Tools lined the walls of the room and a number of inventions Finn had never seen before were strewn about. At the far end, a bear of a man faced away from them. He was tinkering with something letting off a dull orange glow with Stitch by his side.

"I used to do some carpentry back on Embar."

"Then you two should have lots to talk about." Captain Palmer slapped him on the shoulder a bit harder than he would have liked. "Tobi, come meet our young stowaway."

"Ooh!" Stitch tapped the large man. "You're going to like him."

"Am I?" He turned around and wiped his hands before heading over and nearly shaking Finn's entire body.

His bear-like hands enveloped Finn's hand and with the way he shook it, Finn wouldn't have been surprised if he could have chucked him across the room. His physical presence was so imposing that it was strange he wasn't on deck for the earlier conflict.

"Tobias Wood—or Rough-hands if you'd prefer that." Tobi gave him the kindest smile he'd seen since he made it onto the ship. "So pleased to meet you."

When he finally let go Finn rubbed his shoulder. "Finn Townsend. No interesting moniker."

"We'll remedy that at some point. I'm sure—" Tobi crouched down to pet Bug. "And who's this little fella here?"

"That's Bug."

"Finn and Bug. Those certainly are some names."

"You're the ship carpenter and your last name is Wood," Finn said with a bit more sass than he intended. "I could say the same to you."

Tobi gave him a surprised look at first, but his surprise morphed into happiness. Something about him reminded Finn of his father, of a kind of warmth he never got to experience.

"You're going to fit in just fine. What can I do for you?"

He glanced around the workshop again. "I did similar work back home."

"You don't say? Well, at least I know I can trouble another soul for some help. Stitch won't have to do quite as much heavy lifting." Tobi looked at Stitch, but her stance told him that his sarcastic joke hadn't landed.

Captain Palmer cleared her throat and picked up a tool. "I was just taking him around to meet the crew."

"Ah." Tobi smiled. "The favourites."

Finn never would have expected Fortune Palmer to have favourites amongst her crew, but Tobi was right. If anyone else on deck mattered all that much, Captain Palmer would have stopped them for a moment.

She smirked. "So sure of yourself."

"Tell me I'm wrong."

She narrowed her eyes. "Good thing Stitch is here."

"Awe." Tobi gave Stitch a playful tap. "You hear that? Captain Palmer loves us."

"Love is a strong word." She picked up a tool as if it grossed her out and tossed it aside. "How does *begrudgingly put up with*, sound?"

Stitch ran over and wrapped Captain Palmer in a tight hug. "It's okay, we love you too."

"Yes, very good." Captain Palmer rolled her eyes and gave her a light pat. "Thank you, Stitch."

"Any hull damage from the skirmish?" Tobi asked. "Didn't hear too much commotion."

"Things went even smoother than I could have predicted considering I took this one along with me."

Finn had a feeling that the many backhanded compliments he'd received were all the positive reinforcement he'd be getting from his captain.

"First day, first skirmish." Tobi gave Finn a surprised look. "Not a bad way to make a name for yourself, lad."

Finn glanced toward his captain. "It wasn't exactly—voluntary."

She had a devilish grin on her face. "Yes, enough of that. I still want you to make those changes I asked for when we make land at Bridger, Savvy?"

"Aye, Captain. I'll begin making the necessary preparations. Did you still want those barricades for the heart?"

She nodded. "I think that would be best."

Tobi nudged Stitch. "You got some time?"

Stitch looked like her heart had jumped out of her chest. "Anything for you, Tobi."

He smiled and turned his attention back to Finn. "I'm sure we'll be seeing more of each other soon. I've always got time for a fellow craftsman."

The captain pulled him out of the room as Tobi got to work hammering something. Finn wasn't sure what he expected Captain Palmer's crew to be like, but they were nothing close to what he had imagined.

He figured it would be a big tough crew full of stoic pyrates, but instead it was full of a bunch of friends.

"Where to next?" Finn asked as they rounded another corner, but he stopped in his tracks when a dull glow from behind a door caught his eye. "What's that?"

"This here is the heart of the ship." She led him over to the door and placed a hand on it. "It's of grave importance that this stays safe. If anything were to happen to it—let's just say it wouldn't be good."

Captain Palmer swung the door open and Finn stepped into a cozy room. The darkness reminded him of nights when he'd come home late and the only light would be the roaring fireplace. A warm flame offering warmth and comfort from the cool dark night.

He stared at the bright orange heart. It was beating like the heart in his very own chest. In a way, it was strangely alluring. The heart beckoned him closer, but he wasn't sure why.

Finn took a step toward it, but she caught his arm. "That's as far as we need to go."

"So, that's how the ship—"

"Aye. Marvellous, isn't it?"

"It is." He looked around at the empty room. It would only take an intruder a couple of paces to permanently sabotage the ship. Finn had no idea what would go into repairing something like that. "I can see why you want those barricades."

"Aye. It's rare anyone even makes it below deck, but it would allow me to station someone here with a gun. I'd be more comfortable knowing no one has a chance of getting to the heart of the Albatross. Come—it's time you met Walker properly."

Finn followed the captain to the upper deck. "You and Walker, you two seem close."

"Do we?" she asked with an amused tone. "I'd imagine so. He's been my friend since I was a young girl."

He'd always hoped he'd get to learn more about the life of Fortune Palmer, but he never thought he'd get to learn more from Captain Palmer herself. Most of the pyrates on the ship seemed quite a bit older than the captain, and that included Walker, so it was a surprise to learn they'd known each other for that long.

"That's why he's your second in command?"

"No. There are many I care for that I wouldn't want anywhere near my ship. Walker is my second in command because he is one of the only people I can trust to do his job—and he does it damn well." They reached the hatch leading back to the main deck and each shielded their eyes as they stepped out.

The sudden burst of sunlight was blinding, but it was comforting. As beautiful as it was under the sea, it felt like a lot less could go wrong above the waves.

"When'd we get back above the water?" Finn asked.

"Pyrate business. Stowaways aren't privy."

"You're going to enjoy this as long as you can."

"Absolutely. What is life at sea if you can't have a little fun?" They headed up to the ship's wheel where Walker greeted them. "You've already met Walker, but allow me to reintroduce you to the greatest drunk on the seas."

"Drunk?" Walker burped, and Finn understood. "Should he really be steering the ship?"

"You know, probably not, but it's never been a problem."

Walker laughed, "I'm a better navigator than Captain Palmer could ever hope to be."

She took a long breath. "I'm going to let that one go because we both know it's true."

Finn wasn't sure what to make of the way people conversed with the captain. There was no way she'd put up with a comment like that from the average pyrate, but she hadn't taken much issue with Finn's comments. Either she was going easy on Finn, or somewhere deep down, she liked his spirit.

Walker turned his attention to Finn. "Yeh seem to be bright, and the Captain hasn't tossed yeh. Yeh'll do well 'ere."

Finn smiled. "Everyone here is a lot nicer than I thought a band of pyrates would be."

Captain Palmer scoffed. "Just wait until they get to know you better. You managed to annoy me in record time. Everyone'll be threatening to toss you overboard and forcing you to do embarrassing things for their own personal enjoyment in no time." She turned and her eyes fell on a nearby island. "Look at that, we made it in record time."

Finn turned and looked at the bustling island. Even from the distance, he could see smoke billowing into the sky. On the horizon stood the bustling port city, Bridger.

chapter 9:

The Silver-Tongue of Bridger

By the time they'd gotten settled into the port, the sun had already reached the horizon. As the crew ran around tying things down, Finn noticed Captain Palmer always kept one eye on a pristine ship on the opposite side of the port. The ship could have been ripped straight from Finn's imagination, because to him, it was a true pyrate ship.

Whoever owned it meant something to Captain Palmer.

Much of the crew headed off the ship to enjoy the nightlife of Bridger, but Tobi and a few hands opted to stay behind.

Captain Palmer, Walker, Stitch, Trigger, and Finn all headed off the ship together. Despite it already being the evening, the docks were still bustling with sailors and fishermen.

"Captain Palmer," Finn said as they passed by a group of salesmen closing their stalls. "You mentioned that you knew someone here who could give me some information on the Poisoned Rose."

"Ah, yes. Walker, can you take our stowaway to the fortune-teller beside the tonic shop? Trigger, you're with me. I've some important business to tend to. I'll meet you all at the Clipped Wings Tavern, savvy?"

"Aye, Captain," everyone said.

"We're here for medical supplies, and fresh crew members," Captain Palmer said. "Not to cause any trouble—Walker."

"It was one time, Fortune," Walker said, but he was met with the captain's raised eyebrow. "Captain Palmer."

"Just make sure the lad doesn't end up on the wrong side of someone's sword."

"I thought that was the Albatross that I saw coming into port." A suave voice came from the top of a nearby staircase. "I rushed all the way here just for you."

The voice reminded him of Gord. It was far softer than that giant's, but there was a similar pompous energy that flew along with the words.

Captain Palmer stopped in her tracks, but it was Walker that spoke first. "That's not good."

Bug growled up at the man. Even he knew that whoever this guy was, he was trouble.

The man was covered in red and brown leather, making him look rather expensive. His hair had been slicked back, but that didn't keep a few loose strands from falling into his face. If Finn didn't know any better, he would have sworn the man was some kind of royalty, but if the captain knew him, that meant only one thing.

"Silver-Tongue." She spun around with fire in her eyes. "I'd say it's a pleasure, but every time I see you I want to jump under the nearest passing ship."

Finn leaned toward Walker. "Who's this Silver-Tongue guy?"

"Long story. If yeh enjoy having all yer fingers, it's better to not ask too many questions," Walker said.

"Silver-Tongue? How you wound me." The man headed toward Captain Palmer. "I remember a time when the sultry lips of one Fortune Palmer would only speak of me as Jonas, *my love*."

It was near impossible for Finn to picture Palmer in any kind of relationship. It was even harder to see her linked to someone like that rogue.

"That was so long ago I'd almost forgotten about it." Captain Palmer became red in the face, but it looked like a mix of embarrassment and anger. "You'd think someone as pompous as you would have moved on by now." Her eyes bulged as she spoke under her breath. "I know I have."

Jonas kept moving like she hadn't said a thing. "I see you're still travelling with the classics—although this one's new." His eyes fell on Finn. "He's a handsome young lad. He'd do much better on my crew. How's about it?"

Finn wasn't about to turn his back on Captain Palmer. Even if he hadn't already found a crew to join, he had a feeling he would never find himself joining Jonas.

She tapped a finger on the hilt of her sword. "The kid is fine where he is, thank you very much."

"You're here to find some new crew members aren't ya? Of course, you are. Why else would anyone come to a crappy city like Bridger?"

Crappy wasn't the way Finn would have described Bridger. Even from the docks, he could tell the entire city was packed with people. As they'd approached, he tried to gauge the size of the city, and he ended up guessing roughly five times larger than Embar.

"What do you want? If you'd like, I'll keep a mental note of when you'd prefer me to embarrass you next. Can't promise I'd show up, though. You know, with the whole, you being absolutely insufferable thing."

"Not here to start any trouble? What kind of pyrates are you then? You already know I'd love to take you for a tussle," Jonas said to her with a wink.

Finn leaned toward Walker again. "So they were— they used to—"

"Aye," Walker nodded. "And yeh'd be best to forget this once it's over."

Stitch swooned. "Nothing better than a good love story."

"This certainly isn't a *good* love story, girly."

There was no way the captain would put herself through the suffering that would have been being with a man like Jonas. He must have been a completely different man just a short while ago. Whatever it was that changed him, it must have been massive.

"Final time I'm asking before I try to purge my mind of the disturbing fact that we happen to be in the same port at the same time," Captain Palmer squeezed the hilt of her sword. "What do you want, Jonas?"

"I was at the capital a few days ago, and I gotta say, you are in *trouble*," Jonas said.

"Keep speaking in riddles and I'll—"

He brought a finger to her lips. "So impatient. I'm getting to it. Sig's interested in a meeting with you."

She looked like she was ready to bite Jonas' fingers off. A battle with a pyrate hunter and dealing with a young stowaway never brought a hint of anger to her face, but Jonas was succeeding where everyone else failed.

Captain Palmer twisted his finger and pushed him back. "I'm not worried. I have a lead on some booty that Sig'll be interested in."

"I know what booty I'd like to—"

"I will run my sword through your foot if you even finish that sentence in your head."

"You talking about that treasure off Linwood? The one all the Blues are raving on about? The one I'm planning to pick up myself?"

She prodded his chest. "Sig wouldn't give a screw-up like you a contract like that. Not if the treasure is being guarded by an army of Blues."

Finn stared at the two bickering pyrates. Whether Captain Palmer liked it or not, they did look like a couple of ex-lovers. He wasn't about to mention that to her, though.

"You're right," Jonas cracked his knuckles. "But as they say, it's pyrate's life. I'm doing this without a contract."

"They'll place a—"

"I know what'll happen, but it won't matter once the treasure is mine." A devilish grin crawled across his face. "It's my first step toward reaching immortality."

Captain Palmer looked like she'd been caught off guard. "You've heard tales of the door as well?"

The pyrates were moving at a mile a minute. Sig, treasures, immortality, and secret doors all made no sense. At the very least, Walker looked just as confused as Finn was.

"First the booty," Jonas caressed her cheek. "Then I'll come back for you, my love."

"I think I'm going to be sick."

"Oh, I know," he swooned. "The thought of us being apart makes me sick to my stomach as well."

Finn nudged Walker. "How long ago—"

"Long enough for what Jonas is doing to be pathetic," Walker said.

Stitch cocked her head. "He sure is handsome."

"It's too bad he's insufferable to just about every woman he's ever met."

Jonas waved a hand before he made his way back up the stairs. "I assume I'll be seeing you all again very soon, that is, if I don't get the booty first." He stopped for a moment and looked at Finn. "You may want to rethink your allegiance, lad. Next time we bump into each other at sea, I'll be killing everyone aboard the Albatross."

"Come, Trigger," Captain Palmer said.

Before he could ask one of his many questions, Palmer stormed across the dock.

Finn sighed, "Should have expected that."

"Welcome to Bridger, lad." Walker pulled Finn along by the shoulder. "Let's go find that fortune-teller. Yeh know where we're going, don't yeh Stitch?"

"Aye. The tonic shop is across from the surgeon's shop. I'll keep you company 'till then," Stitch said as she brushed shoulders with Finn. "I need to get more supplies because of a certain someone."

It was clear that Stitch was just teasing him, but Finn couldn't help feeling bad. He hadn't meant to take space from vital supplies, and if things had gone differently with the Blues, the ship might have needed them.

Finn rubbed the back of his neck. "Yeah, sorry about that—again."

"It's fine. I'd rather not spend time around some creepy voodoo man." Stitch giggled. "Bad joo-joo."

Walker raised an eyebrow. "Fortune-tellers are the same as pyrates. Liars seeking coin, and nothing more. We're going to him for information, not for magic."

"What exactly is a fortune-teller?" Finn asked.

"They commune with the spirits of the dead to predict people's futures," Stitch said as she oohed and awed at the various shops.

"They merely say they commune with spirits." Walker snatched a bottle of rum from a cart and tossed a few pieces of gold back to the vendor. "If yeh ask me, it's all a load of crap. Yeh'll see."

The trio came to a large crowd that blocked the road. Finn picked up Bug and they waded their way to the front. A dull orange glow similar to the one on the ship formed in front of them, keeping them from pressing forward.

"What's going on?" Finn asked.

"Been a while since we've been in Bridger," Walker said as brought the bottle to his lips. "Not sure."

A beautiful carriage rolled through the streets of the city. Two jet-black horses pulled the ornate carriage and the driver waved to the interested crowd. Just beside the door, a painting of a beautiful girl decorated the side of the transport. On the side of the carriage just to the left of the painting, the words *Golden Voice* were written in bright gold paint.

Jonas might have had some choice words for Bridger, but it was already far more impressive than anything Embar had to offer. The wealth of the town made it feel like Embar was decades behind them.

"Golden Voice?" Stitch squinted at the carriage. "New entertainer for the tavern? Aw. I really liked those guys with the accordions."

"That lot probably ended up on the wrong side of someone's blade," Walker said. "I heard they liked to ask for far more than they were worth."

Bridger was different, but that wasn't necessarily a good thing. A lot of the people wandering around didn't look like the type anyone would want to bump into. Finn couldn't imagine someone lashing out at a performer with violence, but from the looks of the people, it wasn't out of the realm of possibility.

"I've heard tales of a girl from a land far away with a golden voice." Walker continued. "Must be who's in the carriage."

Finn looked at the dotted windows of the carriage and could have sworn he made out the figure of a woman brushing two distinct tails of hair. "Are we going to see the entertainers at the tavern?"

"I'd imagine they're headed there now to get ready." Walker looked to the sky and watched as a bird danced through the air. "Don't get yer hopes up, lad. You've got a fifty-fifty chance of a Bridger woman being beautiful. If she's hiding her face and known for her voice—it don't bode well."

Once the carriage was at a distance, Walker led the group in the direction the decorated transport had come from. Most people were closing up their shops for the night, but some were still peddling in the streets.

Finn had never seen salesmen so pushy back in Embar. He felt as if a salesman could grab him and start shaking him for whatever coin they could find.

Stitch nudged Finn. "It's a lot to take in, huh?"

He nodded. "It's different. Embar is so quiet, and I don't think I've had a moment of quiet since we arrived."

"Bridger's kinda grimy, but it's a popular spot for travellers. Lots to do here at night."

Finn was able to see the fortune-teller's tent from down the street. It stuck out much in the same way he felt he did. A wrinkled tent was set up right next to the tonic shop as Captain Palmer had said. If her directions weren't enough, the two roaring torches that lit up the entrance made the tent impossible to miss.

As they approached Finn ran his fingers along the fabric. It felt both old and new at the same time. It was one of the smoothest and softest materials he'd ever felt, but the wrinkles and tears throughout gave it a shabby feel.

"Right, I'll be across the street. Don't go forgetting about me, you hear?" Stitch wagged a finger at Walker. "I was cross the last time you left me in port."

Finn raised an eyebrow at Walker. "You guys forgot Stitch?"

"It was one time!" he sighed. "There was a lot going on, and I'd had a fair share to drink. I thought she was right there with us."

Stitch stomped. "Don't you dare go to that tavern

without me or I'm going to get Tobi too—"

"Crush me with his bare hands, aye."

That wasn't the first time Stitch threatened to bring in Tobi against Walker. His response was too nonchalant for that to be the case. Those three had to have been good friends for quite some time.

She shook her finger a final time. "As long as you know the consequences."

Stitch turned and skipped into the medical supply shop. As the door swung shut behind her, Finn could have sworn he heard her let out an excited squeal. Knowing her, there was probably someone in the shop that was injured—someone she could practice on.

"Every time I talk to her she seems stranger than the last time," Finn said.

"That feeling never goes away."

"Was that serious?"

"Stitch's threat? Nah. Tobi and I go even further back than she does. She just likes to think he'd do anything for her since they're so madly in love."

Finn thought back to when he saw them in Tobi's workshop. They seemed friendly, but they didn't seem especially close.

Finn cocked his head. "The two of them are—"

"Not really. Like the old stories of a love that cannot be. Pretty sure everyone knows they love each other, except for them."

"Have you ever thought about telling them?" Finn asked as he set Bug back on the ground.

"No man should ever get involved in another man's love life. Well, unless he wants to cause a spot of mischief on purpose."

"Spoken like a true second in command," Jonas said as he sauntered around the nearby corner accompanied by another man.

Whoever the other man was, he managed to look even meaner than Jonas could ever hope to appear.

"Jonas." Walker scowled at the menacing man that accompanied Silver-Tongue, "Wade."

"Walker," the two men said in unison.

"I didn't expect to bump into you again so soon," Jonas ran a finger along his belt. "But I have promised I'd be a good little lad while in port. It's your lucky day."

"Forgotten the last time we went toe-to-toe have yeh?" Walker asked.

"You only got the better of me because I wasn't prepared for drunken baboonery," Jonas spat back.

"Sounds like the words of a man who can't quite cut it." Walker smirked. "Face it, Jonas. Yeh and yer crew will always be second to Captain Palmer and the crew of the Albatross."

"You insolent—" The man with Jonas started.

Jonas held up a hand. "Wade, that's enough." He turned his attention back to Walker. "I'm sure that's why you're recruiting again, and so young at that. Superior crews change so often, don't they?"

"The heart of a good crew doesn't." Walker pointed his bottle at Wade. "The lad could probably do well against yer mate there."

Helping out against Shad was one thing. Combating the Blues was another. Getting into a fight with a mean pyrate was at the absolute bottom of Finn's to-do list.

Finn's eyes went wide. "Yeah, but we kinda have something to—"

Jonas rubbed his hands together. "I'd love to see that." Sauntering over to a barrel full of mops, he snatched two. After snapping the heads off, he tossed one to Finn and one to Wade. "I'd love to see that right now."

"I don't fight with a staff."

"A pyrate fights with whatever they can find, lad. Don't worry, it's just for a bit of fun. Wade won't hurt you—much. Walker can even step in if he feels you're in any danger."

Wade whirled the staff around his body as if he had been training with one for years. The staff moved so fast, it was clear that he had no fear of accidentally whacking himself.

Finn had no chance.

He stared at Wade. "Are you kidding me?"

The staff felt awkward in his hands. He suspected it was due to him being used to fighting with his grappling hook. That may have been two-handed, but he was able to hold it however he wanted. There wasn't a comfortable way for Finn to hold the long stick.

"Bug, you stay with Walker," Finn said. "I don't want you accidentally getting hit."

Bug replied with a low bark.

Before Finn could get comfortable, Wade rushed forward and struck. He nailed Finn in the leg, and as if instinct took over, Finn blocked a few strikes. Maybe it wasn't as hard as Finn had thought, or maybe his body hated the sting of the stick so much that he barely needed to think about blocking.

Wade spun in a circle, creating some distance between them. "Not bad, kid."

The compliment was nice, but Finn had forgotten to breathe during the exchange. He was gassed.

"Would it get me any points if I said I have no clue what I'm doing?" Finn asked.

Walker took a swig from his bottle. "Hit him with the hard part."

"That's literally every part."

"Exactly, so it shouldn't be a problem."

Wade rushed forward again, but Finn couldn't keep up a second time. A few stiff shots to his body and arms knocked Finn's makeshift staff to the ground. Wade launched a final attack right across Finn's cheek, sending him to the ground as well.

"Ow." He brought a hand to his cheek. "It's becoming clear why Captain Palmer hates you guys."

Jonas reared back and laughed, "Looks like the Albatross is striving for age over quality. Let's go, Wade. If I wanted to be disappointed in someone's meagre performance I would just watch Walker try to talk to women at the tavern."

"Buncha pricks," Walker said as the two walked off.

It had been a long time since Finn had been put in his place like that. If he was going to be facing foes like Wade on a regular basis, he knew he'd need to put in some more practice. If he didn't get some practice, his adventure may not end up being as long as he had hoped.

chapter 10:

Black Heart

Walker held a hand out to Finn. "Y'alright, lad?"

"Why'd you do that?" Finn took his hand. "I didn't want to fight anybody—Captain Palmer asked us to not cause any trouble."

Finn knew that trouble was entirely different for pyrates, and she'd probably be disappointed he'd lost to one of Jonas' crew. He hadn't even been a pyrate an entire day and his record was one-to-one. A silent vow was required, one that said Finn wouldn't be losing any more fights. At least, not when it mattered most.

"Sorry if it caught yeh by surprise," Walker said. "Pyrates fight. It's what we do. Now yeh can be ready for that in the future. At least now we know we aren't giving yeh a staff anytime soon. Let's just get all this business with this fortune-teller over with."

They turned their attention to the tent once more. Finn hoped Walker wasn't right about the fortune-teller being nothing more than a con-man. Anything, any insight at all on the Poisoned Rose was a step in the right direction.

Finn pushed his way by Walker and entered the mysterious tent. "Hello?"

The inside of the tent was far brighter than it should have been, but Finn wasn't sure where the source of the light was even coming from. The small holes Finn could see from the outside had disappeared altogether.

A shirtless man with some kind of sack over his head sat on the ground of the tent which was littered with decorative pillows. On the table in front of him was a series of glass orbs, skulls, and a small cauldron—each with its own distinct orange glow.

"Ah. I was wondering when my final guests of the day would arrive. Come in, take a seat."

"Good sign," Walker laughed. "Shouldn't a real magic man know exactly when someone's coming in?"

Finn tip-toed toward the table and took a seat on a pillow. Bug made himself comfy in Finn's lap, but kept an eye trained on the man across the table. Despite all the strange people he'd met that day, the fortune-teller was the absolute strangest.

He didn't know where to start. "I was told you could help me with information on something—"

The fortune-teller cocked his head. "But it is not a *something* you seek. Your heart is telling me that you're seeking a someone," The fortune-teller groaned, "I can feel your heart is in—it's in pieces."

"What are you talking about?"

As if the final embers of a weak flame had just died, the tent grew darker and darker.

"There are many pieces of your heart here, in this very city." Every time the fortune-teller moved, his bones cracked so loud, Finn suspected his bones were breaking. "Two great pieces—but there are others far across the sea. Two great pieces to the west of the sea, a great piece in a cobbled-together stronghold, and a great piece in a horrible place to the north."

Finn had never left Embar so he was confused as to how pieces of his heart could be all over the world. A part of Finn prayed that one of the pieces was his mother.

"The pieces—who are they?" Finn asked. "Where are they?"

"That, I do not know."

Walker cleared his throat. "We don't need to hear yer mad ramblings. Ask him yer question, lad."

The fortune-teller looked right up at Walker despite there being no way he could see through the sack on his head. His movements were sharp, as if Walker had offended him, but he didn't make a sound. It was almost unnerving as his head slowly turned back to Finn.

"What is your question?"

Finn gulped. "Can you tell me anything about the Poisoned Rose?"

The fortune-teller hummed. "Evil. Barbaric. Animalistic. Monstrous. The Poisoned Rose has caused more bloodshed than any other ship at sea. Why would a mere boy be seeking a band of merciless killers?"

"Yeh're the fortune-teller, yeh tell us," Walker spat.

"Pain." The fortune-teller ran his hand along one of the orbs and its glow pulsed. "Great pain. They stole a piece of your heart, dear boy."

Finn stared at the fortune-teller. "Yes—they took my mother when I was a boy. Can you tell me if she's alive?"

"I do not know."

"Why not?" Finn looked between the fortune-teller and Walker. "You knew all that other stuff."

The fortune-teller held out a hand. Finn delicately gave him his hand. The moment they touched, the magic man's head snapped back, sending him to the floor. It was so sudden that Finn nearly jumped out of the tent.

The fortune-teller started to shake. "Blackheart. Blackheart. Blackheart. Blackheart. Blackheart. Blackheart—Blackheart—Blackheart—"

The man's entire body was writhing like he was in pain. His voice sounded like he'd burst into tears, but it was impossible to tell if that was the case. If he was putting on an act, it was convincing.

Walker sighed again, "Great, yeh busted him."

"Please." Finn leaned closer to the fortune-teller. "Is my mother alive?"

The fortune-teller shook his head to say no. "Yes."

Finn raised an eyebrow. "Is that a no or a yes?"

"No." The fortune-teller nodded his head.

Finn could feel himself getting angrier by the second. "Let's just get out of here." He pushed Bug off and turned to Walker. "This was a waste of time."

Walker looked at the strange man. "Yeh didn't tell the lad anything, we ain't paying."

As Finn reached the exit the fortune-teller spoke again. "There will come a time where you must make a terrible choice. You must choose wro—ng."

Finn turned to look at the fortune-teller, but he had curled into a ball on the ground. The strange man was letting out hushed sobs as he clutched at his own heart.

Finn's annoyance and anger got the best of him and he stormed out of the tent. If his mother really was alive, he was going to have to find out himself.

chapter 11:

The Girl With the Golden Voice

As soon as the door to the tavern swung open, an explosion of shouting, laughter, and energetic music flowed through opening. It could be heard from outside, but nothing could have prepared Finn for the noise he was met with. He'd passed by the tavern back home while the men were getting rowdy, but their noise level had nothing on the Clipped Wings Tavern.

"How's yer face, lad?" Walker asked.

Finn rubbed the spot Wade had whacked him. "Good enough."

They scanned the crowd, but the captain hadn't arrived yet. "Good, then yeh don't need a drink. We've got time to kill. I'll be getting meself another drink by the bar. You two stay out of trouble."

Stitch wrapped her arms around one of Finn's. "Let's go find a place to sit for when Captain Palmer arrives." Stitch pulled Finn through the crowd with Bug in tow. "I'm so glad you guys didn't forget about me. Last time I wandered around town for days. No one had any clue what I was talking about. They probably all thought I was some crazy beggar woman instead of a pyrate. Could you imagine that? Me, a crazy woman?"

Finn replied with an awkward laugh.

The people of the tavern seemed so different from the people of Embar. Some were as dirty as a beggar on the street, while others looked as if they came from some kind of royalty. Regardless of how people looked, everyone was mingling and having a good time.

They passed by a group of women dressed in beautiful gowns who each winked and giggled at Finn. Each of the women had makeup on, something that was considered a rarity on Embar. Most people wouldn't even notice the smaller details thanks to the dusty haze that lingered in the air.

"Maybe I should have stowed away on a pyrate ship earlier," Finn said as Stitch pulled him along.

She looked at the women and scrunched her face. "You don't want anything to do with those girls."

"Why not?"

"Those sorts of girls are for men looking to—" Stitch found an empty table and took a seat. "Crack Jenny's teacup."

"I don't know why anyone would be mad enough to crack one of their cups." Finn gave her a confused look as Bug hopped up in the chair next to Stitch. "Those ladies all look nice."

"That's not what—never mind." She leaned toward him. "Their services cost money."

"Why would you pay for a woman?" Finn took a moment to clue in. "Oh—yeah, never mind."

"Good boy."

Finn's attention was caught by the small show going on, on the stage at the front of the tavern. A man tinkled away on the keys of a piano as a group of women in dresses danced around. As the song came to a close the girls all bowed and danced their way off the stage.

"I love those piano players." Stitch swayed as the musician played a light tune. "Live music is so soothing."

Whenever Finn heard music, all he could think about was learning to play as a child. Embar didn't get anything as intricate as piano, but they did specialize in a unique little instrument.

"Back home it's kind of a right of passage that the men of the village learn to play this little instrument from the far lands. They only make them on Embar in this part of the world. I should have brought it with me," he said.

"Maybe one day we can make port on Embar again and you can play for all of us."

A man with a beard that nearly fell to his feet walked onto the stage. "Attention."

The crowd remained as rowdy as ever.

"Attention!"

It seemed like nothing was going to pull the wild drunken patrons from their night of debauchery.

"ATTENTION!" The man smashed a glass at the feet of the loudest group in the tavern.

The man smiled as the entirety of the tavern fell silent. "Thank you." The man had flipped from scary to pleasant without a moment's pause. "We have a very special talent up next. She comes all the way from the other side of the sea. Ladies and gents, the girl with the golden voice, Madame Kili."

A gorgeous girl stepped onto the stage from behind a small curtain. Her hair was longer than any woman Finn had ever seen, falling into two long tails of hair with a curtain of shorter hair covering her forehead.

She scanned the crowd and smiled, but it felt like she was smiling right at Finn. The girl had to be from the other side of the world, because she looked so different from anyone he'd known—from her skin to her eyes, to the dimples that formed when she smiled.

"You can close your mouth now, Finn," Stitch said.

He'd completely forgotten Stitch was even beside

him. "Sorry, I just—"

"Never seen a girl from the other side of the world before?"

He shook his head. "Like I said, this is the first time I've ever even left Embar."

"Aw, I'm here for your first time. Well, I was going to say you have bad taste, but that lass is one of the prettiest girls I've ever seen, even from the other side."

It was clear that most of the bar shared the same opinion of Madame Kili since everyone had remained fixated on her. Her midsection was visible, but her shirt had long flowing sleeves with lines of fabric that fell to the ground. Oddly, Her pants looked as if there was room enough for three people to walk around and be comfortable.

Everyone held their breath as she began her act.

Every word sounded better than hearing a loved one tell you they missed you after a long time away. The way her body moved around the stage was unlike anything Finn could think of. The entirety of the tavern gave her their undivided attention during her performance.

When she was finished, the bar exploded with applause. After a quick bow and a wink to the happy audience, she headed off-stage. The crowd returned to their previous rowdiness as if she had never even shown up.

Finn watched as she strut up a flight of stairs. He stood up without looking away from where she had gone. "I—uh—I'm gonna go—"

"You don't need an excuse, just go talk to her. I'm sure you won't be the only one." Stitch stood up. "I'll take Bug with me to catch up with Walker."

Finn headed toward the stairs. "Thanks."

"*Good luck.*" Stitch sang as she headed over to Walker.

Finn made his way through the rowdy crowd, bumping into a few drunken villagers as he went. The crowd seemed happy, but each time he bumped into someone, he could tell it wouldn't take much to turn the tavern into a storm of violence.

He reached the staircase, which creaked under each of his steps. When he reached the top, Madame Kili was across the room where the lights from the tavern below weren't quite reaching. Instead, a few candles were scattered around to light the room.

A final creak sent her whirling around. "Who are you? What are you doing up here?"

"Sorry. Am I not supposed to be up here? I—" Finn stammered.

"I'm just messing with you," she said before she removed some of the jewelry that covered her body. "How'd you like the performance?"

"I've never seen anything like it."

"Then you must not be from Bridger."

"It's my first time here actually."

"Well, you picked a good night to arrive," she winked at Finn. "I think I was absolutely wonderful out there—incredible really. You good with knots?"

"I—what?" Madame Kili turned around and Finn studied the various knots that covered the back of her outfit. "Oh, yeah. I'm kind of a pyrate."

"No offence, but you don't look like one. How are you *kind of* a pyrate?"

Finn inched closer and started to untie the knots. "I stowed away on a ship, I haven't officially signed on or anything."

"Signed on? To be a pyrate?" She turned her head until their faces were close. "Sounds like you're getting scammed."

He took a deep breath and tried to remain composed. Finn was having a hard time with basic body functions. Getting nervous around women was never his thing, but something about that girl was different.

"They're good pyrates."

"Good pyrates?" she tried to stifle a laugh. "There's no such thing."

Finn finished a set of knots on one of her arms and a long ribbon fell to the ground. "Well, I'm going to be a pyrate, and I like to think I'm a good person."

"I don't really know you, and you aren't a pyrate yet, so—" Madame Kili trailed off.

"I'm Finn, by the way," he said as he finished the other set of knots.

She turned around, Finn couldn't remember the last time he was so close to a girl. The dolled-up women from the main floor of the tavern had nothing on Madame Kili—and she didn't have a speck of makeup on.

"Kili. Now if you don't mind, I'd like a little privacy." She gestured to the stairs as a rotund man came into view. "Oh, great. Another fan."

She rolled her eyes, which made Finn feel like he'd done nothing but be a nuisance. Everyone he'd ever known was happy to see Finn, but that had become completely different since he'd met Captain Palmer.

The large man was red in the face. "Yeh just might be teh prettiest girl I've ever—" He hadn't noticed Finn at first, but as his sights set on him, his face morphed to one of anger. "Ah see what's goin' on 'ere."

"You're gonna have to clue me in, big guy," Kili said.

Even from a distance, Finn could smell the liquor radiating off of the man. No good ever came from anyone who had drunk as much as he likely already had.

The large man stalked toward Finn. "Yuh go 'round on stage makin' eyes at e'ryone just so yuh'll get a few pieces fer teh night. Yuh make all us tink we're special and ten yuh have yer pick of teh litter."

"You've got it all wrong." Finn held his hands up. "I'm not up here for—"

Kili raised an eyebrow. "You kinda are up here for

that, though, aren't you?"

"Well—I—" Finn got red in the face. "I just wanted to talk to you."

She shook her head. "So innocent."

The man threw the glass over the rail and grabbed Finn. "And ah just want teh talk teh *yuh.*"

Through the noise tavern, Finn could hear the people below yelling about who threw the glass.

He eyed the fist that the man had balled up. "I don't think you know what *talking* means."

"One of those brainy fellas, huh?"

As the man swung, Kili whacked him with a candlestick. The man let go of Finn as he screamed in pain. He had received a face full of hot wax from the still-lit candles. Kili tossed the stick to the ground, extinguishing the flames as they fell, and she booted the man in the stomach as hard as she could. He flew over the railing, still clutching his face.

"Whoops." Kili shut one eye. "That's not gonna go over well."

-CRASH!-

The tavern fell silent again.

Kili smiled and rushed to the railing. Finn did the same and stared down at the drunk man laid out on a broken table. All the people that had been sat at that table were soaked, no doubt with alcohol. The drunken patrons started kicking the man, but others came to his aid. In a matter of moments, the entire tavern devolved into an enormous brawl.

Kili gave Finn a mischievous grin before hopping over the railing to engage in the fight.

Finn stared down at her. "Who is she?"

He scanned the tavern for Walker and Stitch. To his surprise, the both of them were ignoring the brawl and keeping their noses in their drinks. That didn't seem all the pyratey to him. Although, it couldn't be the first time they were in the midst of a tavern during a brawl.

Finn looked down to where Kili was and she had managed to knock two separate men out each with lightning-fast kicks. The problem was that two other men were sneaking up on her with blades drawn.

"Crap." Finn looked around for anything he could use to help. "How the hell am I going to—"

Chairs and bottles seemed like the best options, but all the chaos was going to make having any plan useless.

A frayed rope beside him was all that was keeping the tavern's chandelier hanging. All it would need is one good tug. He set his hook onto the rope and hopped across to the chandelier. A sharp tug did exactly what he thought it would, sending Finn down to the floor of the crowded tavern.

His fall was broken by the two men sneaking toward Kili. As the chandelier tilted against their bodies, he used the momentum to run across a table, scoop a plate into his hands, and block the killing blow a man was about to land on someone laying on the ground.

"It's a bar fight," Finn said in a panic. "Why are you trying to kill someone?"

The grotesque man tried to head-butt Finn, but he slipped out of the way and drove his shoulder into the man's nose. The crack that accompanied the strike was sickening. The violent patron dropped down, clutching his nose as blood trickled through his hands.

Finn looked down. "Sorry?"

"You little brat!" Another man rushed forward ready to strike, but Finn grabbed a nearby chair and held it up.

After redirecting the strike through the chair, he sent the blade out of the man's hands with a twirl. Finn had cocked back a punch, but a bump from behind sent him flying forward. Finn nailed the man in the face, but not being ready for the strike caused him serious pain.

Kili had been grabbed by a wild-haired man and another was headed right for her. Finn grabbed a bottle off a nearby table and whipped it at the man holding her, shattering it over his head on contact. As if she'd told Finn to throw the bottle for a plan of her own design, Kili broke free and nailed the approaching man with a backhand.

Finn could have sworn he heard Walker cheering and laughing from the bar.

A hand on his shoulder sent him wheeling around. On instinct, he lashed out with a hard kick. It landed squarely between the legs of an angry bald man. He sank to the floor and Finn stared wide-eyed. Anything goes in a bar fight.

A few men turned their attention to Finn and he figured that was because he'd just decked their friend. He fled across the tavern and hopped beside Kili as she was being pushed backward by a red-bearded man.

Finn launched a fist into the man's face and shook his pain-filled hand. "I gotta stop punching people."

Kili elbowed Finn in the side. "I was doing fine by myself."

He pulled his blade and blocked a strike that was aimed right for Kili's head. "And now you're doing even better."

Another blade came for Finn instead, but Kili returned the favour. "I could say the same for you." She kicked the man she'd blocked backward, and he sprawled across a nearby table.

The group of men he'd fled from stormed toward Finn, but Kili used her sword to toss a few drinks from a nearby table to the ground. The men slipped on the alcohol as they approached, creating a pile-up in the middle of the bar.

Finn blocked a woman's sword strike, but Kili slipped her way in between them. She locked her leg in between the woman's and gave her a solid shove.

The duo looked around and noticed that much of the bar had turned their attention to them. Kili and Finn pressed their backs together as they held the remainder of the crowd at the ends of their swords.

As far as pyrate adventures go, Finn didn't expect so much conflict right from the jump.

Kili gave Finn another slight elbow. "If I die here because of you, I'm going to haunt your non-pyrate, pyrate-ass for life."

"I have a feeling if one of us is going to die, we're both going to end up dead," Finn said as he glanced at the angry drunks.

"I'll haunt a ghost!" she said. "You don't know me or what I'm capable of. I'll be a real spectre's, spectre."

-BANG!-

A gunshot stopped everyone in their tracks. Captain Palmer stood in the doorway to the tavern with a sword in one hand and a smoking pistol in the other.

Trigger was standing beside her along with two other men Finn had never seen before. One looked as if he'd just received news that his family had died, and the other looked horrified by all the chaos.

Captain Palmer sauntered into the tavern and pointed her sword at Finn. "If you'd all please, I believe that stowaway belongs to me, and I'd like him returned unharmed—the girl is optional."

"Your *good* pyrates, I presume?" Kili asked

One of the men in the tavern stared at Palmer. "Who the hell is this broad?"

"Here we go." Finn beamed.

"The Devil's Charm, Captain Fortune Palmer," she said with a bow. "At absolutely no one's service."

The crowd shifted into a murmur about Palmer.

"How do we know you're the real Captain Palmer?" someone asked.

She smiled. "Would anyone like to come find out?"

A man rushed her with a sword, and with two quick swings, the man was disarmed and on the floor of the tavern. If the crowd had doubts before, there wasn't a single person who didn't believe her after that.

"Anyone else, or are we all square?" Captain Palmer asked.

The tavern emptied out, with every patron being careful to keep their distance from Captain Palmer as they left.

Finn turned to Kili. "Thanks for having my back."

"I only had to have your back because you escalated things." She shoved Finn. "It was all fun and games until you squashed those guys with the chandelier."

"Squashed those guys—I saved you. They were—"

"I don't remember ever asking for any saving."

Finn couldn't believe what he was hearing. Most women would have been grateful that someone rushed to help them. It was shocking that someone could be so ungrateful, especially since she was about to end up as a Madame-Kili-kabob.

"Are the children done squabbling?" Captain Palmer asked as she put away her weapons.

"I'm not a child." Finn and Kili said in unison.

"Oh, good. Now there's two of you."

Walker made his way over. "The girl's a fighter."

"Is that so?" Captain Palmer asked.

"Quite the pipes on her too," Walker said with a nod. "Yeh should see her move. Yeh said we were looking for an entertainer. Yeh've got a two-in-one deal there."

Kili put her sword away. "I have no interest in joining a crew of pyrates."

"And if I told you"—Captain Palmer placed a hand on the hilt of her sword—"You had no choice?"

"There's always a choice."

Captain Palmer narrowed her eyes at the smaller, defiant girl before laughing. "It's a fine few days for new crew members! How'd you like to join the crew of the Albatross for a life of adventure?"

Finn almost felt hurt he hadn't received a reception like that from Captain Palmer. She looked ready to take Kili under her wing. It had been a while since he felt jealous, but this girl just broke that streak.

"The answer is still no." Kili had a confused look on her face. "I don't care about adventure. I care about money."

"And what do you think a band of pyrates are after on all of their adventures?"

Kili considered what the captain had said. "Gold?"

"All the gold your—" Captain Palmer flicked the fabric of Kili's pants. "Strangely baggy pants can carry."

"Fine, I'm in—but I better be treated like a princess." She glanced at Finn and then around to the rest of the crew. "I'm not swabbing the deck or whatever it is you pyrates do."

"Then we'll see you at first light. The ship with the purple sails. We've got a few days of travel ahead of us, so we'll need lots of entertaining." Captain Palmer turned her attention to Finn. "How'd it go with the magic man?"

"Not great." Finn scratched his head. "He kinda— broke. He was talking about pieces of my heart, then he touched my hand and then just started saying—*black heart*

—over and over."

Captain Palmer stared at Finn with an expression that told him something was wrong. She looked uninterested until he mentioned the black heart part.

"What's going on?" Finn asked.

Her tone became cold. "I think it best if you take that as closure. No more looking into the Poisoned Rose. I'd rather avoid a skirmish with those brutes if we can help it."

"But—"

"That's an order," she said, before exiting the tavern without another word.

The remainder of the crew followed her out the door, except for Stitch. She studied Kili and adjusted her glasses. "I don't like her."

"Thanks, glasses. I don't like any of you, so that's just fine by me," Kili said before she headed out the door. "See ya on the job tomorrow!"

"I really don't like her." Stitch repeated.

Finn stared at where Kili had left. "I think—I do."

chapter 12:

Not The Only Nuisance Anymore

Waking up outside of Embar was a strange feeling for Finn. Rather than the light scent of baked goods mixed with the distant smell of the salty sea, he was awoken by man-farts.

He had gotten up before most of the other crew members, and he made his way down to the dock with Bug. The two sat on the edge to enjoy the fresh ocean air, but the longer they sat, the busier the docks became, and the quicker the ocean air was choked out by the smell of fish.

"We really threw ourselves into the thick of it, didn't we, boy?" Finn asked as he pat Bug.

He figured he'd fall asleep as soon as he made it to the crew quarters, but that wasn't the case. The long events of the previous day danced through his mind all night.

A familiar bossy voice caught Finn's attention. "You're expecting me to live on *that*, with all those filthy men?"

"I do it just fine," Captain Palmer said.

Finn headed toward the Albatross and spotted Kili

and Captain Palmer with their noses nearly pressed together. At least Finn wasn't the only one who managed to get under the captain's skin.

"Hey, good morning you—"

Kili held a finger up to Finn. "I bet you only do *just fine* because you have your own private quarters. It's not safe for a lady such as myself to sleep in the same quarters as a bunch of dirty pyrates."

Captain Palmer let out an amused laugh. "Then we'll just have to see to it that you receive your own quarters."

"Wait, really?"

"If it'll allow me to be rid of the incessant whining, certainly."

"What's incessant mean?"

"My sweet go—" Captain Palmer buried her face into a hand. "There really is two of you now. What have I done?"

Finn wasn't sure what incessant meant either, so he was glad Kili couldn't score any more brownie points. The issue was, he wasn't sure if being lumped in with her was a good thing or a bad thing.

Kili scoffed. "And you just *magically* have enough space to give me my own private quarters?"

"You know nothing about my ship or my crew," Captain Palmer said. "You'd do well to stop asking questions while you're ahead, and thank me for my generosity before my patience runs out, savvy?"

"Thank you for the hospitality." Kili looked like a child who'd just been admonished by their parents. "When can I meet everyone? Do you have someone who can carry my things?"

"Of course." Captain Palmer gave Finn a mischievous smile. "You met our young stowaway last night, correct?"

"The not-pyrate, pyrate? Yes."

"What a fun nickname." Captain Palmer looked like she was considering further use of the nickname. "He can carry your things and show you to your quarters."

Kili came complete with a massive ornate case. It looked as complex as the carriage he'd seen her in, almost like the trunk came with the wagon. Finn knew that with his luck, the trunk was going to be far heavier than it looked.

Finn's eyes wandered from the trunk to his captain. "I have no idea where I'm supposed to be taking her. I haven't exactly been on the crew for years."

Captain Palmer waved a hand. "Through the hatch, down the stairs, and at the end of the long hall. Big mostly empty room. Once you're settled in, Finn can take you to see Tobi. He'll make sure you have a proper bed built."

Finn walked over and lifted the trunk. Just as he thought, it was far heavier than it had any right to be. What a travelling entertainer needed that was so heavy was anyone's guess.

"You were riding through town yesterday in a personalized carriage, weren't you?" Finn asked as he found the best way to hold the trunk. "You're just going to abandon it?"

"I don't see how that's any of your business," Kili crossed her arms. "But if you must know, the tavern owner owes me quite a lot of money. I told him we'd be mostly square if he stored my carriage for me."

Kili didn't look much older than Finn, so he wondered how someone so young could have so much influence in such a rough and bustling town. Entertainment had to pay well.

"If there is anything else you require before you board, I suggest you go now. We will be leaving upon my return," Captain Palmer said before heading toward the town.

"I'm all set. Travel light, as they say."

"I don't know who said that to you," Finn lost his grip and nearly dropped the trunk. "But remind me to ask them what they meant by *light*."

"Oh, quit your whining. Aren't you supposed to be a strapping young pyrate? A girl's trunk should be nothing compared to—whatever it is you do on a pyrate ship."

Finn headed up onto the ship with Kili. Her giggling caught his attention and he turned to see Bug walking between her legs. The little traitor was trying to get in good with the pretty lady, probably in the hopes that someone else will sneak him some tasty treats.

"You like animals?" he asked.

"I love animals." Kili picked Bug up and hugged him. "What's his name?"

"Bug."

"I don't love that name."

He shrugged. "It has personality."

"It reminds me of beetles. Why couldn't you have picked a nice name like Leopold or Benji?"

"Leopold the dog?" Finn looked at his furry friend. "That's a terrible name. Bug suits him."

In truth, Finn had named Bug for his beady eyes. Even as a pup, he had eyes that could have rivalled a lizard. If he didn't know any better, Finn might have thought Bug could see in every direction all at once.

"I guess it does kind of suit him." Kili ran her fingers through Bug's fur. "I think it's the huge eyes that do it." She set Bug down and he darted off deeper into the ship.

Finn approached the hatch of the ship, but Kili showed no signs of grabbing it. He wasn't sure why he thought she might, she had mentioned wanting to be treated like a princess the previous night, and clearly, she wasn't joking.

Just what everyone needed. Another nuisance.

"His eyes may be big and beady, but they're good for

scoping out danger." He set the trunk down, opened the hatch, and hauled the trunk back up. "After you, *princess*."

"That's exactly how I should be treated at all times."

Finn followed his captains instructions until he came to an old rickety door. While Kili was impressed by the craftsmanship below deck, it was clear that the shoddy door worried her.

Kili raised an eyebrow. "If the room is in the same shape as the door, I might start rethinking my options."

They threw the door open to a small, cozy room, complete with a small wooden desk. It was surprisingly warm, and it got Finn thinking about what Captain Palmer's quarters were like. Kili stepped inside and looked around at the dusty room.

She brought a finger to her bottom lip. "I can make this work."

"Nicer than what the rest of us have."

"Where do you sleep?"

He set her trunk down. "In a pool of man filth, farts, and snoring."

She put her palms together and shook her hands. "Thank the gods I have my own quarters."

"You want some time to deal with your things?" As nice as Kili was to look at, she'd already been getting on Finn's nerves. "I can come back later and take you to Tobi if—"

"We can go now."

"Are you sure? I could—"

"Now works."

That wasn't what he wanted to hear. Something told Finn that there were few people who could manage spending a few uninterrupted hours with Kili. It was possible that she was the kind of girl that grew on people, but a pretty face wasn't going to be enough to do that.

Finn sighed and opened the door, "After you."

"Keep up this behaviour and we might end up being

friends sooner than you think," Kili said.

"I'm still debating whether or not that's a good thing," he muttered.

She shook her head as she passed by, and one of her ponytails whacked Finn in the face. He'd never met someone who managed to both simultaneously intrigue him, and irritate him to his core.

Her hair caught his attention and he studied the way her long tails of hair fell just below her hips. She had a set of high-end ribbons tied around each tail. It looked wonderful, but it hat to be impractical in a fight.

When Kili turned around, where Finn's eyes were trained must have looked very bad.

"Enjoying the view?" she spat.

"No, that's not what—"

"What should I expect?" Kili said with a sigh. "Welcome aboard the pyrate ship."

For the first time since their meeting, Kili looked like she was disappointed. It was hard to blame her. She was probably leered at by men around the world. Finn wasn't intending to leer at her, at least, he didn't think he was.

He took the lead toward Tobi's workshop. "Don't flatter yourself, I was just looking at your hair. I don't think I've ever seen someone with hair so long."

Kili took one of the tails in her hands and ran her fingers through it. "You like it?"

He felt his face get hot. "It's unique."

"I haven't cut my hair in years. Looks like that's the case for you too."

Finn ran a hand through his own curly hair. "I've never really cared much about hair."

She leaned back and took a look at his backside. "You better be careful or one of these pyrates are going to think you're a girl from behind."

Finn had no idea whether that was meant as a compliment or as a dig.

He turned a corner and spotted the doors to Tobi's workshop. "I think I'll be fine. I have a feeling that after stories of us meeting you in the middle of a bar fight start spreading, people aren't exactly going to want to mess with you, even if you're the only woman they might have a shot with."

"Good. I could probably take anyone on this ship anyway."

Finn felt an amused grin crawl across his face as he put a hand on Tobi's door. "You think so, do you?"

"What would a bunch of random pyrates know about actual swordplay?" she asked.

"What would a random performer know about *actual swordplay*?"

"Just because I like to sing and dance doesn't mean that's the only thing I know." Kili leaned closer. "I know plenty."

The next words out of Finn's mouth weren't the best he'd ever picked. "I'm sure you do."

Kili reared back. "What does that mean?"

"I just mean—I'm sure you do."

For a moment it felt like they were connecting, but Kili had pulled back entirely. All of the sudden, it looked like someone had lit her trunk on fire in front of her. Finn had learned an important lesson, women are confusing.

"You are so annoying," she said.

A commotion from above caught Finn's attention. It wasn't unordinary to hear pyrates shouting on board, but that commotion was different. It sounded like everyone on the main deck was excited. Finn wasn't about to miss out on whatever was going on to keep dealing with Kili.

"That's Tobi's place," Finn said as he started heading topside.

"Where are you going?" Kili asked.

The question had come out so sheepish that Finn stopped in his tracks. Kili shifted awkwardly by the door to Tobi's workshop. It was her first day on the job, and it showed. She had to be nervous to be left on her own.

He shot a finger up. "I'm heading up for some fresh air."

"Could I come with you?"

Finn groaned, but he prayed it was only internally. He had a feeling that due to how close they were in age, Kili would want to be around him out of comfort.

He scratched the back of his neck. "Don't you want Tobi to get started on your bed?"

"I can talk to him later." She caught up to him and tapped his chest. "I'd love for my personal guide to continue showing me around."

"Come on then."

After a few steps, the churning of the boat became a bit rougher, and Kili brought a hand to her stomach. Sailing wasn't for everyone, a fact Finn knew all too well. She was making the same face Diego made the first time he wound up on a boat—right before he lost his breakfast in the sea.

Finn laughed, "There's no turning back now."

Kili rolled her eyes. "Oh, joy."

Once they made it back to the main deck, she took in a deep breath of the open air. Finn half expected her to rush to the rail to throw up, but instead, she set her sights on Bridger and flipped the island the bird.

"Ay, Finn!" Trigger called. "Come over here and meet some of the new guys."

That's what all the commotion was, the deck of the ship was bustling with new crew members. All the people present made the crew Finn had first joined seem like a skeleton crew.

Trigger was chatting with the two men who had been with him and Captain Palmer last night. Neither of them looked particularly happy to be on a pyrate ship, but the scowls on their faces were more of the norm aboard.

One of the men seemed a bit overly eager as he stretched his hand out. "The name's Francis." He gestured with his head. "This here's Smiley."

"Finn."

"No offence, lad," Francis said. "But you don't look like much of a pyrate."

"If you took away the hat and coat, does Captain Palmer?" Finn asked.

"Good point. I was actually going to chat her up until she started barking orders at everyone in sight. It became clear pretty fast exactly who she was."

"She tends to do that."

Francis seemed nice, but both he and Smiley gave Finn a weird feeling in the pit of his stomach. He wondered what Stitch would think of the two of them. A bad feeling about Kili never emerged, despite how annoying she could be, but maybe Finn was just a bad judge of character.

"Finn?" Kili said. "Are you planning on introducing me at some point?"

Finn let out a silent sigh. "Kili, meet Trigger, Francis, and Smiley. Those two are new as well."

Kili waved. "Good to meet some of the other new recruits. Ready for a ton of fun?"

Trigger laughed, "No offence there, girly, but why don't yeh leave the fun to the men? Yeh're here to keep us all entertained."

Finn hadn't known Kili all that long, but he knew that wasn't a smart thing to say. That wasn't a smart thing to say to any woman anywhere.

Kili's expression melted into a glare. "Excuse me?"

"Here we go," Finn groaned.

"All I'm saying is, it'll probably be best if yeh don't

get to know the men too well." Trigger leaned forward. "Yeh're a little young for everyone aside from the lad. We don't need anybody getting confused."

Finn could almost see the steam pouring from Kili's ears. The shade of red that draped across her face was something he'd never seen before. Something bad was coming, and for whatever reason, it felt like the bad thing was coming for Trigger.

"And that's my problem how?" she asked.

"The last thing yeh need is one of the lads trying something on ya—that's all," Trigger said with his hands up.

"I think I'll be just fine." Kili got in his face. "You can mind your own business. I'll be sure to inform the Captain that I won't be doing any performing for you."

"You'll watch yer mouth or yeh're going to have a hell of a time on this here ship," Trigger jabbed her backward with his finger. "Girly."

"Okay, I'm sick of this." Kili balled her fists. "Let's go."

Trigger scratched his head as Kili stepped forward with anger in her eyes. "Uh—what?"

"What?" Kili raised her hands. "Afraid of a girl?"

"Yeh have no idea what yeh're getting yerself into."

As much as Finn wasn't interested in ever getting into a physical fight with Kili, she didn't know anything about Trigger. She handled herself well against a bunch of drunks, but Trigger was a tavern fighter. He made a living beating up people that had to be far bigger than even himself.

"Kili," Finn put a hand on her arm. "Seriously."

"I'm not afraid." She shook his hand away. "Fists or swords? Or are you afraid I'm going to embarrass you in front of everyone?"

Trigger looked around the ship. Most of the crew, new and old, were all watching. Finn followed Trigger's eyes up to Captain Palmer who was looking on with a smirk.

"Well?" Captain Palmer said as she looked on. "Don't keep the lady waiting, Trigger. You made your bed with your foolish comments. Time to lay in it. Do you beat a young girl or does the young girl beat you? Either way, you come out looking like a moron."

Trigger stepped forward and cracked his knuckles.

They really were going to fight.

The tough pyrate was in a tough spot, but Kili could still back out. Unfortunately, any chance of peace was gone when Kili spat in her hands.

She was ready to go.

Francis's eyes nearly bugged out of his head. "You ain't—aren't seriously going to fight a girl."

"Watch and learn newbies." Trigger moved closer to Kili and leaned toward her. "I'll even give her the first shot, just to make things a wee bit fairer-er."

Finn expected Kili to let a bit of fear show through her hard-headed exterior, but she was sturdier than anything Tobi could have hoped to craft. She was focused and had to be debating the best tactic to take against a guy like Trigger.

She wasn't going to back down an inch.

"Well, girly? I'm waiting for—"

In one swift movement—Kili flew under Trigger's arm, flipped him to the ground, and placed her boot on his throat. Finn was thankful she hadn't gotten hurt, and a little more concerned about future comments he may make when she annoyed him.

"I'm sorry, I can't hear you over my *foot* on your *windpipe*," Kili said.

Trigger tried to say something, but she pressed her foot down, turning his words into sputtering.

She lifted her foot a bit. "This is where you apologize and say, *oh, Kili, that was so cool. I hope you'll be gracious enough to teach me how to do that one day.*"

Francis looked like he was ready to spring into action, but he was unsure of whether or not that was a smart move.

"Look at that, our new entertainer is already busy entertaining," Captain Palmer laughed as she slid down the nearby railing. "That's enough from the both of you. Kili, let Trigger back to his feet, please." Kili kept holding on. "Now. He will not lash out. Will you, Trigger?"

Trigger started shaking his head and Kili let him back up. "Wasn't ready—for a move—like that."

Captain Palmer stared at him. "Yes, well perhaps in the future we won't be disrespecting someone because they are a woman, savvy?"

"Aye, Captain Palmer."

"Very good. The two of you, shake hands and apologize." They stared at each other before Captain Palmer spoke again. "I *will not* ask a second time."

Kili held a hand out, this time with a cutesy grin on her face. She was as adept at switching moods as Captain Palmer was, a frightening feat for someone so young.

"I'm sorry about all that, girly." Trigger shook her hand. "Rum for breakfast wasn't the best choice."

"I'm sorry too." Kili stepped back toward Finn. "No harm done."

Finn nudged her. "Where did you say you were from again?"

"I've been telling all of you, you know nothing about me."

"No kidding."

Finn wasn't surprised when everyone rushed to Trigger rather than Kili. She clearly knew what she was doing in a fight, maybe even as well as Trigger, but the men were going to stick with their own.

Kili hadn't intended to alienate herself from the

crew, but that may have been exactly what she just did. He worried that it wouldn't matter to her, which could just mean he'd end up spending more time with her.

More time with that bratty, beautiful, irritatingly fascinating singer.

Great.

chapter 13:

Time to Dance

"You're a natural, lad," Tobi said.

Finn shifted his gaze from the task at hand to Tobi. "Glad someone thinks so." He peeked toward the churning waters below. "You know, being dangled over the ocean feels a lot different than it does being dangled a story or two above the ground."

Finn had been in his fair share of less-than-ideal circumstances before, but hanging off the side of a pyrate ship was easily the least ideal. There was enough goodwill in his heart to trust a piece of rope for a few moments or when he knew a drop wouldn't lead to certain doom, but that goodwill was gone.

Tobi shrugged. "You get used to it."

"Hopefully sooner than later." His hand slipped down the soggy rope, and he re-gripped it as tight as he could. "Couldn't we have just waited until we made port?"

Tobi shook his head. "You know how the Captain can get. Besides, we need to be ready for a skirmish at any moment, and that means constantly making sure the ship's in fighting shape."

"Not that I don't trust you know what you're doing,"

Finn finished pounding a section of rope into another crack in the hull. "But what exactly is all of this accomplishing?"

A wave shook the boat enough to send Finn into a panic. Being on a ship could get a bit rough, but Finn wasn't exactly *on* the ship. If that wasn't bad enough, a wave of water splashed up and soaked his legs.

Tobi looked down and laughed, "The rope is going to help us keep the pieces of the hull in place, all while stopping any additional leaking from those kinds of waves. Just thank your stars that I don't have you doing anything more complicated. This is rather simple—common even."

"You do this often?"

"After most skirmishes, aye." He finished banging in another section of rope. "It's been a while since I've come out here, so it's nice to have help for once."

Finn was regretting having ever mentioned his minor carpentry experience. Unlike Finn, Tobi wasn't having any issue with the task, in fact, it looked like he was loving every minute of it.

"Well if it isn't my two favourite strapping men." Stitch swooned as she leaned over the railing.

"What can I do for you, missy?" Tobi cracked a warm smile. "You looking to dangle over the side of the ship too? I'm sure Finn could use the moral support."

"As much fun as that looks—and it really does look fun." Stitch adjusted her glasses. "Let's actually do it sometime—I'm going to have to pass."

"You sure? Your *surgical precision* could help this fly by."

Stitch looked as if she had everything she needed in life whenever she was speaking to Tobi. "As right as you are, I don't think the Captain would take too kindly to dangling the ship's only doctor over the endless sea."

"You were just a tailor, right?" Finn chuckled. "Couldn't be that hard to replace you."

He worried that his sarcasm would fly over the head of someone like Stitch. She could be a bit spacey at times, so something like sarcasm might have been a foreign concept. All his worries were put to rest when he spotted the hint of a smirk on her face.

"Just a tailor? Replace me?" Stitch feigned offence. "I'm one of a kind. I bring a much-needed air of uniqueness to the crew"

"That's for sure," Finn said under his breath.

Tobi raised an eyebrow. "Not so unique the more women we let aboard."

She waved her arms. "Oh, whatever. I just wanted to see if we were still going to have dinner and look at the stars tonight?"

Even though he couldn't see Tobi's face, he knew anyone could tell he was blushing. His whole body stiffened as if he was embarrassed Finn had overheard their plans. Stitch may have had some mastery of sarcasm, but when it came to Tobi, subtly may as well not exist.

Finn gave Tobi a cheesy grin. "How cute."

"Shut up, you." Tobi glared back at him. "How's the girl?"

"What do you mean?"

"You know exactly what I mean."

It had been a few weeks at sea, and Kili had hardly left him alone for a moment. They had been getting along better, but Finn was always a more independent person, and Kili could be a diva if things weren't going exactly how she liked. Still, Finn couldn't help finding himself wanting to be near her, even at her worst.

"The entertainer?" Stitch chimed in. "Still don't like her."

"We know," the dangling duo said in unison.

Tobi looked up. "That sounds lovely, Stitch."

She flashed a mischievous smile. "Can't wait."

As she disappeared, Finn climbed up until he was in line with Tobi. "You two make quite the couple." He pounded another piece of rope into the hull as he snickered. "I think that's all the cracks in this section."

"Excellent lad," Tobi flipped his hammer in his hand. "We'll head up and prepare for the next section. Just a couple—"

"Where is the nuisance we refer to as a stowaway?" Captain Palmer's voice came from overhead.

It was hard to tell if Captain Palmer was warming up to him or not. She spoke with him most days, but that could have just been part of her job. Still being labeled as a boy or a nuisance didn't give Finn much hope that he and the captain would ever be swapping life stories anytime soon.

"Looks like you're needed elsewhere." Tobi sighed, "Thanks for the help, lad."

"Anytime," Finn said, hoping Tobi would never ask for assistance with that particular task again. "If you're still working away at this by the time I finish with—whatever it is the Captain needs," He and Tobi made the climb back to the main deck. "I'll come back and help you finish up."

Captain Palmer strutted up to him. "What a good little lad. Unfortunately, you won't be helping Tobi for the rest of the day."

"No?"

"No. Walker is going to start with that training we talked about." She rubbed her boot over a spot of grime on the deck. "I don't need you getting your blood all over my—supposedly clean deck."

"What about—"

"The girl? She'll be training with me."

Finn wasn't even going to bother hiding his

disappointment. "I won't get to train with you at all?"

"If I think it's worth it, then sure."

Finn was ready to pipe up, but Captain Palmer was ready for it. One quick finger right in front of Finn's face was enough to stop his incoming idyllic rant. Without another word, she headed below deck.

The journey to the pyrate capital had been a long one. Admittedly, both Finn and Kili had grown restless, much to the rest of the crew's dismay. They had managed to annoy Captain Palmer enough to get them some specific training on disarming an opponent.

Tobi tapped Finn's back. "Best show her what you can do then, lad."

As Tobi disappeared below deck, Finn headed toward Walker. He had pulled out a barrel full of wooden swords—reserved for teaching children the basics of swordplay. Quality weapons seemed to be a rarity on the ship, so the simple practice weapons made sense.

Walker tossed Finn one of the swords. "Don't you go complaining about not using a real sword."

"I'm not going to complain." Finn got a feel for the weight. "I have no problem not potentially dying over some practice."

"Good. Where's Francis? I told that moron we'd be training today, but I've yet to see him once. If he keeps shirking from what he's told, he's not going to be on this vessel very long."

Francis came barreling out of the hatch. "Sorry, I'm late. Was assisting—with inventory."

Walker raised an eyebrow. "Is that so?" He tossed Francis a wooden sword and grabbed one for himself. "How much do each of yeh know about disarming an opponent?"

Finn looked at the sword. "Pointy bit bad."

He had been trying to keep things light during his time on the ship, but he'd also been learning that pyrates aren't in love with his brand of humour. Walker gave him a dull look that he'd wound up seeing at least once a day since he joined.

"'Bout that much," Francis said.

"Disarming yer opponent is about more than hitting them with the sharp end of yer sword." Walker gave the sword a few fluid swings. "It's about technique, speed, and anticipation. Knowing how to handle a blade will be the difference between life and death."

Captain Palmer surfaced with Kili and chuckled. "Walker doing his technique speech again?" She pulled two swords from the barrel and tossed one to Kili. "We'll keep it simple, and then we'll let the lot of you practice on each other."

Walker and the captain led the trio through a series of drills to disarm an opponent. The techniques seemed simple enough, but Finn had a feeling it would be much harder in a fight against a seasoned opponent.

He watched as Kili whirled around a strike from Captain Palmer. Every time he watched either of them fight, it was like he was in a trance. They each fought with an elegant wrath, a wrath he never wanted to be on the receiving end of.

"Yeh paying attention, lad?" Walker asked as he tapped his sword against Finn's.

"Sorry." His attention snapped to Walker. "I'm just a little—"

"Mesmerized? Looks like dancing actually is good for something after all."

"No offence or anything," Finn's eyes wandered back to his childhood hero. "But I was kind of hoping I'd get to train with Captain Palmer."

"We'll switch shortly, not that she can teach yeh anything I can't."

Something about the way the words left his lips was different from the usual Walker. It sounded like he was putting out a challenge more than he was making a statement. To no one's surprise, the captain picked up on that very thing.

"You sure about that?" Captain Palmer asked as she rolled under a swing from Kili. "I'm sure I've still got quite a few tricks you're yet to pick up, my old friend."

"How's about a wager then?" he asked.

"I'm game."

Walker whirled the sword in his hand. "Two rounds. First is the two of us. Second is the girl up against one of mine."

"I like your thinking. Prize or punishment?

"Aren't they the same thing to different people?"

"Aye."

It was moments like the small challenge between Captain Palmer and Walker that may it clear they'd been lifelong friends. There was a competitive energy radiating off of the both of them, and there weren't many people ever willing to go toe-to-toe with Captain Palmer. Either Walker was truly confident, or he didn't mind losing to his old friend.

Finn stepped forward. "Do we get any say in this?"

"No," Walker and Captain Palmer said together.

"Let's say, loser steers the vessel through the night for the remainder of our current voyage. If it's a tie, we'll call it a wash." Walker continued.

"Then it's a bet." Captain Palmer nudged Kili. "Time for the ladies to *once again* show the men why they shouldn't mess with us. Everyone stand back and try to visualize yourselves in the place of myself and everyone's favourite drunk. Picture what you would do."

They all stepped back as Walker and the captain circled each other with wooden blades at the ready. Captain Palmer examined her practice sword and tossed it to the floor. Walker did the same and they each drew their very real, very sharp blades.

Kili leaned toward Finn. "Why am I not even slightly surprised?"

He couldn't keep a smile off his face. "Because you've been on this ship for more than five minutes."

The two clashed blades with immense speed. Finn was shocked by Walker's skill since he had never seen him in a fight. If he didn't know any better, he might assume Walker was just as much of a threat as Captain Palmer.

Smiley was swabbing the deck, but even he was held in a trance by the fight before him. "That's really something."

Kili nudged him. "Any good with that mop?"

Smiley looked at the deck. "I think so."

"I meant in a fight. It was a joke."

"Oh. No, I'd rather not fight."

Finn looked at Smiley's lanky frame. He was incredibly tall, but he wasn't particularly muscular. Maybe it was his body, or maybe it was his demeanour, but it didn't surprise Finn to hear he wasn't interested in fighting.

Captain Palmer slashed Walker's sword clean out of the way and whirled around for a strike, but he pulled his sword back just in time to block it.

Francis rubbed the back of his neck. "Walker's defence is incredible. See the little adjustments he's making?"

Kili crossed her arms. "That's what she wants him to do."

She was right.

Finn had heard stories of how Captain Palmer was able to strike her opponent in such a calculated way, that they'd strike back exactly the way she wanted. To her, a sword fight was a game of chess, and she was a master.

Walker blocked a strike, but he was left in an awkward position. The captain whirled the blades around and knocked his hand with her sword.

Walker's blade fell to the ground, and Captain Palmer chuckled. "Round one goes to me. Not that I'm all that surprised."

Walker even joined in and had a laugh. "It was a good try, though. Wasn't it?"

"Much better than last time. You're improving," she said as she turned to the group. "Your turn."

Kili stepped forward and twirled her sword around. "Which one of yeh would like to give it a shot?"

Finn and Francis looked at each other, but Francis spoke first. "You're probably the better of us two, lad. I don't know much about fighting."

The captain had her classic mischievous grin taking residence on her face. "How about they both take a crack at her?"

"Are yeh sure?" Walker asked.

"Well, they don't need to work as a team. It can be a free battle, but if one of your two lads beats my lass, you'll win the round. I don't think the girl's going to have much trouble either way."

"Both of yeh, get to it."

After seeing how Kili had handled Trigger the other day, Finn was a little nervous of being made to look like a fool. He didn't have the kind of weight that Trigger had, so Kili would probably be able to repeat exactly what she did with little issue. Finn wasn't looking to get embarrassed in front of Captain Palmer.

He looked toward Kili. "How hard do you guys want to go?"

"Full force." Kili launched forward into an attack on Finn.

He blocked the strike right before it landed across his neck. It was a much closer call than he would have liked.

Francis rushed in with a few pathetic swings. Both Finn and Kili had no trouble pushing him back. A grown man who had no clue what to do with a sword seemed like a rarity, especially if that man was willing to join a band of pyrates. He figured even someone who had never held a sword could do better than Francis.

Kili kept on smacking his sword hand with her blade to knock it away, but he kept a tight grip. Finn could see Francis growing angrier the more Kili smacked his hand.

"C'mon, boys. Is that all you got?" she said.

Finn started pressing the attack, but when Francis rushed in, Kili met his hand with another hard whack. He shoved Finn to the floor, and by the time he looked back, Kili's sword was on the floor.

"I guess that makes the bet a wash." Walker clapped his hands. "We'll call it there."

"No, we won't." Captain Palmer still had that strange expression as she held up a hand. "Finn and Francis will continue until one disarms the other."

Finn got to his feet, but the captain's eyes never left Francis. Francis had shifted from being ready to kill a man to mousey like Stitch in an instant. That had to be why he had a bad feeling about him, Francis had a dangerous mean streak.

Finn raised his sword. "You didn't need to shove me like that."

"I had an idea," Francis raised his sword as well. "And you were in the way."

Kili still looked stunned by what happened. "Get him, Finn."

Finn had an idea.

If he could get Francis angry again, maybe he could take advantage of his emotional outburst.

"You fight like an old man." Finn taunted.

Francis parried a strike. "I've never done this before."

He looked like he was intently focused on every movement, but something felt off. Finn blocked a strike and smacked Francis hard across the ankle. When Francis looked at Finn again, there was an angry fire in his eyes.

Finn raised an eyebrow. "You alright?"

Francis started pushing the attack, and Finn was having a hard time keeping up. For every strike he managed to block, Francis managed to whack him hard across the body.

"Take it easy, this is supposed to be friendly training," Finn said as Francis snapped back to his mousey persona.

Finn took the opportunity to slash at his ankle again, sending him right back into a rage.

Francis telegraphed a huge strike with his body, and as he swung—Finn rolled out of the way and brought his sword down hard across his hand. Francis's sword fell to the deck, but he stormed toward Finn.

He looked like he was ready to kick the crap out of him. For someone who wasn't comfortable with a sword, he sure took his training seriously.

Bug had rushed over from wherever he had been napping and he put himself between the two. His hair was on end as he barked and snarled at Francis. The fuzzball wasn't all that scary, but Finn appreciated his little buddy's attempt to protect him.

Captain Palmer rolled her eyes at the fat dog and stepped over him. "That's enough for you today, Francis. Get back to—whatever it was you were doing before this."

Francis clicked back to his calm demeanour. "Sure thing, Captain Palmer." He tossed his practice sword back in the barrel and headed back under without another word.

Kili came over and started to poke Finn's body

where he'd been hit. "This hurt? How about this?"

Finn jokingly slapped her hands away. "Quit it."

"That Francis guy is really weird."

The captain brought a hand to her chin. "Aye, but he may be useful in a fight. Anger leads to sloppiness, but he struck your sword so hard it dropped out of your hands before you even knew what happened."

Kili hung her head. "I wasn't expecting it."

"Always be ready for anything. Now then, you two, more drills."

Kili readied her sword. "Ready to dance?"

"Not if you're going to throw lines like that at me," Finn said.

They each launched at each other with a flurry of attacks before clashing blades. They pushed against each other, but Kili almost looked distracted. Like she didn't want to hurt Finn. He wasn't quite sure why, but Finn figured he probably had the exact same expression.

Finn?

Wake up.

Chapter 14:

The Ship In The Mountain

After a few days at sea, a large mass of land came into view on the horizon. Bridger was unlike anything Finn had ever seen, but wherever they were about to make land, it had Bridger beat by miles. The entire mass was dotted with pyrate ships, but the thing that caught Finn's eye was the mostly intact ship planted firmly into the side of a mountain.

"LAND HO!" Walker shouted.

Finn made his way up to the wheel where Captain Palmer and Walker were speaking. "Why didn't we do that cool underwater thing? Couldn't we have gotten here way faster?"

The captain handed the wheel to Walker. "It's not just something we can do whenever we want. There are a lot of different things we need to keep in mind before we travel that way. Distance, depth, speed, supplies—"

Walker scoffed. "The fact that we're out of the materials to even travel in that manner."

"That as well," she said with a smirk. "Go check on our new friends, make sure they're ready to land. They need to watch their tongues on the island, Kili especially." Captain Palmer seemed more serious than

Finn had seen her before. "Savvy?"

"Aye." Finn headed to the stairs and paused. "Captain Palmer, what about my contract?"

"Do the job I assigned you. New crew members means lots of new contracts, and we only have one that can be signed. We'll pick up more on the island. Oh, and before you go—leave Bug on the ship. He'll probably be safer here."

He nodded and headed off to deliver the captain's warning. Francis and Smiley were each swabbing the deck, and neither seemed all that impressed by the ship taking residence on the side of a mountain. Finn hadn't had much of an opportunity to talk to them since Captain Palmer had kept him running all around the ship with Tobi.

"Hey, you guys ready to make land?" Finn asked.

"Aye," they said in unison.

"Captain Palmer wants everyone on their best behaviour. She said to watch our mouths, so knowing her, it probably means we're at risk of losing our tongues."

Francis gave Finn a wide-eyed look. "If that's the case I think I'll hang back—watch over the ship."

"Finn Townsend!" Kili screeched as she swung the hatch to the main deck open.

Her shrill shout was one that Finn had grown accustomed to. It would be a surprise if he went a day without hearing it at that point. There was always something to complain about, and he was always the one to complain to… apparently.

"What'd you do this time, lad?" Smiley asked as he stuck his mop into a bucket.

"Isn't that a good question," Finn said as he turned to meet Kili. "Everything alright?"

"No, everything is *not alright*. I was told I would be treated like a princess while aboard this ship. It's been weeks and not a single person has cleaned my quarters yet."

"Didn't you say you *packed light*? How did you already make a mess of your quarters?."

"Does that matter?"

"I'm sure a pyrate's version of a princess is very different from your version of a princess."

Smiley and Francis shuffled away before they got dragged into the situation. At that moment, they were smarter men than Finn.

He brought a hand to his face as he continued. "Who do you want going into your private quarters? Francis?"

They both looked over to Francis as he dug for some manmade gold.

"That'll be a no from me." Kili shuddered. "Why don't you do it? What exactly is your job on here anyway?"

That was a good question.

Finn still hadn't been given any kind of official job. He just did whatever it was that Captain Palmer asked of him. His close work with Tobi made him feel like some kind of a carpenter's apprentice, but that wasn't what he had hoped for after years of dreaming to get out on the sea.

"I'll help you, but I'm not doing it for you." Finn began muttering to himself. "I'm doing it so they'll stop dangling me off the side of the ship."

"Works for me."

After what felt like an eternity of cleaning, the ship pulled into the dock of one of the strangest cities he'd ever seen. Even though Finn hadn't seen many different cities in his life, he knew this one was unlike any other. It lacked the polish of a civilized world built under the empire.

All the buildings looked thrown together with

whatever scrap and old wrecked ship parts people could get their hands on. The entire place reeked of booze and body odour, something Kili was destined to complain about.

Most of the crew had already hopped off to go about their business. Finn, Kili, and Walker were all waiting on the dock when Captain Palmer hopped off the ship with Trigger, Smiley, Tobi, and Stitch.

Walker looked around. "Francis ain't coming?"

"He offered to watch the ship." Captain Palmer walked around him. "Would you prefer that privilege?"

"No, Captain."

"Good. Everyone, come along," she said as she headed deeper into the strange island. "We've got an audience with the king."

Kili nudged Finn. "A king?"

Whenever Finn thought about kings, he thought of golden throne rooms, tables filled with exotic foods, and the fattest stomachs possible. None of that would have fit in on the island. The only people in sight looked like they hadn't eaten for weeks.

"I'm just as in the dark as you." Finn shrugged. "I don't even know where we are."

Captain Palmer turned around. "We are in the pyrate capital of the world. A safe haven for any who have signed a pyrate contract. Smiley, Kili—kid—don't let anyone know you haven't signed a contract."

The group followed along behind her, and Finn tapped her shoulder. "What happens if someone finds out?"

"Just means you aren't protected under the code of the seas. There can be no violence between crews on this island, regardless of the animosity they hold."

"Does that mean the Poisoned Rose could—"

Captain Palmer glared at him. "I told you we're done with that ship. They aren't allowed to set foot in this place. They are renegades—outlaws, even to us pyrates."

They turned a corner and the group found themselves on a beautiful red carpet that stretched on for what seemed like miles. If there really was a king, that was exactly the kind of path to one Finn expected to see.

Kili had a confused look plastered on her face. "So there's normal drunkards, the navy or—Blues, regular pyrates, a king, and now there's *evil pyrates*? Why did I agree to come along?"

Walker pointed to the solid gold lanterns that lined the walkway. "That's why."

"Who is this king? You've all met him before?" There were bags of coin in her eyes as she asked her questions.

Tobi scoffed. "The larger-than-life pomp isn't for all of us. Stitch and I always end up finding a niece spring to relax by. Once we reach the palace, you're stuck with the rest of 'em."

Why everyone on the Albatross assumed they were in love was becoming clearer every day. Finn was willing to relax near a spring with someone like Kili, as long as she could promise to not shout at him or complain about bugs.

Captain Palmer turned back to Tobi. "Since you two will be going off on your own—little adventure—would you be so kind as to stop by the fuel depot and get two crates of cells sent to the ship?"

"Two crates?" Tobi raised an eyebrow. "That's going be of hefty cost."

"Just inform them it's for me. Jonas may think I'm in trouble here, but I'm owed a debt. They won't ask you for any payment—if the people at the depot know what's good for them."

There had been a few times since Finn made it onto Captain Palmer's ship that it seemed like everyone was speaking a different language. Things were never more confusing than when they started talking about cells. As far as Finn knew, cells were where you kept the worst of the worst, not something you stored in boxes.

Finn cleared his throat. "I'm sure even asking this is going to get me bombarded with ridicule, but crates of cells?"

Captain Palmer shrugged. "Now why on earth would we ridicule you for something like that when we have so many other options?"

"Can't wait for the promotion from village idiot."

"*Ship* idiot," she corrected. "Don't forget, you can't be promoted higher than captain."

Finn glared at her. "Mmm-hmm."

"You asked about why we hadn't travelled through the sea. It's because we are out of cells. We feed the cells to the heart, and it charges its energy," Captain Palmer said as she continued her strut through the city. "Enough cells means we can travel through the sea for a long, long time. Outside of your sleepy little port town, much of the world has access to certain advancements."

"Advance—"

"We're done with the questions."

Finn turned his attention to the surrounding buildings. Nothing about them seemed particularly advanced. The sights around were beautiful and on the stoop of every house was a different group of pyrates playing games that he feared he'd never comprehend. Nothing all that different from Embar.

He looked at Smiley, but it looked like he didn't care about the marvel in front of them. It was as if someone glued a frown to his face as a child, and he never managed to take it off.

Finn fell to the back of the group to walk next to him. "How're you feeling about all this?"

"Meh," Smiley said.

"Meh?"

"Meh."

"You don't think this is incredible?"

Smiley glanced around. "I've seen better."

"You have?"

"I have."

Finn narrowed his eyes. "Good chat, Smiley."

"Yep."

It's possible that he was used to Kili's never-ending chats, but it's also possible that Smiley didn't like Finn all that much, regardless the guy was weird. Seeing a sight stranger than the island must have meant he'd already spent plenty of time travelling the world, but doing what?

Finn caught back up to his captain and Kili. "Fun guy you picked to join the crew there."

Captain Palmer laughed, "He may not be a ray of sunshine, but he's a damn good cook."

"He's the one who's been cooking?" Kili asked.

"Cooking and cleaning. Don't pass judgement on someone before you learn their value."

"Not many people are going to agree to come onto a pyrate ship purely to help keep it clean." Walker chimed in. "Yeh gotta scoop people like that up whenever yeh get the chance."

They followed the red carpet all the way up to the old boat shipwrecked in the side of the island. How it could have gotten that high was anyone's guess. Nevertheless, it was impressive. To Finn's surprise, as he got closer he was able to see that there were actual guards waiting at the entrance.

"Everyone on your best behaviour in there." Captain Palmer turned to the group as Tobi and Stitch broke off on their own. "If you disrespect him, Sig'll probably just have you killed. If his daughter is kicking around, try to avoid saying anything to her. She's—something else."

One of the guards by the doors laughed, "Yeh got that right."

"So why do pyrates need a king?" Finn asked.

"It's the way it's always been," Captain Palmer ran her hand along a solid gold post. "All contracts for crews come through him. If one learns of a treasure, they must first bring the request to him, and he must approve it. Do otherwise, and you may become a renegade crew."

"Being a renegade crew is bad?"

"The worst." She pulled out a gold coin and started flipping it. "Sig gets a cut of all contracts, whether it be a specific artifact or just some of the spoils."

Finn was well-aware of the captain's personal rules for her crew, but he also knew that most pyrates didn't have rules of any kind. Learning that there were far more rules for the average pyrate than he had initially thought was fascinating. He wasn't going to admit that to anyone, though. Finn didn't need any more exciting nicknames.

"That seems kind of unfair," Finn said.

"You just gotta know how to deal with him," Captain Palmer said. "The benefits outweigh the drawbacks. Especially with all the things he has access to." She nodded to the guards and they opened the doors.

Walking into the back of a pyrate ship shocked Finn, but the decor was beautiful. Everything looked way too expensive to call that island home, and various artifacts laden with jewels were on display. He started moving to get a closer look at a jewelled sword.

Captain Palmer cleared her throat. "Don't even think about trying to touch a single thing in this room. You'd be dead before you laid a finger on anything."

He looked around until he spotted a balcony running along the entirety of the room. Without a single gap, pyrates lined the balcony each with long guns pointed down at the crew. Finn let out a nervous laugh and waved to them as he fell back in line with his captain.

She pushed the set of doors open and Finn was— underwhelmed by what he saw. It wasn't the room itself, the room was beautiful, complete with a solid gold throne.

The appearance of the great Pyrate King was the most underwhelming thing. He'd built this image in his head of this burly man with a long thick beard, teeth made of gold, and an intricately designed coat.

Instead, at the end of the room sat a greasy-haired man in dirty grey clothes. He looked bored, and almost offended that people would enter his throne room. The closer they got, the faster his look of disapproval morphed to one of arrogant amusement.

He had dealt with Captain Palmer more than once in his life.

"Well, if it isn't the crew of the Albatross. Palmer, Walker. Who are the new recruits?" Sig asked.

The king's smooth voice threw Finn off. He had figured the king would speak similar to Walker, but with even more authority. He sounded like his lavish lifestyle had been spoiling him for quite a while. In a way, he sounded even more proper than the captain.

"Good to see you're in one piece, Sig." She flicked the gold coin from earlier toward him, and he caught it out of the air. "All of you, introduce yourselves to King Sigourney."

Kili stepped forward and curtseyed. "My name is Kilala Saelim."

Finn didn't know that Kili was a shortened version of her name. He had liked Kili, but he liked Kilala even more. A name like that was a solid signifier that she hailed from the other side of the world, something that could be dangerous when confronted with the wrong person.

"I'm Finn." He bowed. "Finn Townsend."

Captain Palmer leaned toward Finn. "You guys don't need to be so formal. He thinks it's weird."

Smiley didn't move an inch. "Smiley."

Sig narrowed his eyes. "Interesting group you've found here, Palmer. I must say, we have much to discuss."

"Do we?" she asked.

"We do. You're in quite a lot of trouble."

"Not when you hear about the lead I got on a new piece of treasure." The captain waved her hand. "It's on a little island—"

A door beside Sig's throne burst open and a girl whose hair trailed right down to her feet stormed out. "FATHER! WHERE ARE MY PAINTS? YOU SAID I'D HAVE THEM ALREADY! WHERE ARE THEY?!"

Everyone cringed at the piercing shrieks of Sig's daughter. She was a pretty enough girl, but her lack of volume control made it hard to view her in a positive light. Unlike Sig, his daughter was exactly what Finn had pictured a princess to be like.

"I TOLD YOU, THEY'LL ARRIVE WHEN THEY ARRIVE, DAUGHTER!" Sig buried his face in his hands. "I'm a little busy at the moment. Could we—"

The princess stomped her feet and shouted something completely unintelligible. She almost made Kili look like a saint.

Finn leaned toward Walker. "She seems cheery."

The princess snapped toward Finn. "Quiet, you dirty little twerp."

Everyone started snickering, even Smiley.

Finn looked at him. "Oh, *now* you do something other than frown."

"My dear, just hold on a little longer." Sig stood up and took his daughter's face in his hands. "The crew I sent out gave me their word that they would be back today, so they will be back today."

"And if they aren't—you'll cut their tongues out, won't you?" the princess suggested.

"And if they aren't, I will personally cut their tongues out."

"Yay! Thank you!"

That was one princess Finn never wanted to cross. With how nonchalant Sig had been about cutting out multiple people's tongues, it probably wouldn't be his first time dishing out such punishment.

Sig rubbed his head. "What were we talking about?"

Captain Palmer stepped forward. "I have a lead on an artifact that's said to bring great fortune to the one wearing it. Seems to be a diadem of sorts."

The princess got wide-eyed. "A diadem?" She turned to her father. "I want it."

"Princess, please, I—"

Captain Palmer threw herself back into the conversation far faster than Finn would have expected. "It isn't the sort of diadem you'd be interested in."

"QUIET!" Everyone plugged their ears from the brat's wicked shout. "You said I could have anything in the world and *I* want *that.*"

"Palmer you owe me a debt," Sig said. "If you retrieve this diadem for me, I will not only wipe it away, but I will think about not punishing you and your crew. Is that clear?"

"Aye, Sig," Captain Palmer said through gritted teeth.

"Then you have one moon to return to me with the diadem." Sig turned to his daughter. "How does that sound?"

She clapped her hands. "Perfect!"

Captain Palmer adjusted her coat. "I have reason to believe that not only will there be multiple waves of Blues nearby, but also the crew of the Poseidon's Deceit."

Sig cocked his head. "I don't remember giving Jonas any contracts."

"I thought that was the case."

Finn continued to enjoy the surprises of his new life as a pyrate. There was a certain level of politicking at play amongst the various crews. He couldn't help but wonder if Captain Palmer could be considered to be near the top of the food chain.

"He will be dealt with accordingly." Sig paused a moment in thought. "Is any of that going to be a problem for you?"

The comment caught her off guard, but she recovered like always. "The more crews the merrier, sir. The Blues involvement just might make things more complex."

"Complex or not, you *will* return to me with the diadem. Is that understood?"

"Aye." Captain Palmer flashed him a cheeky grin. "So long as you throw in two crates of cells for the ship."

"Two crates?" Sig glared at her. "You know full well how expensive two whole crates are."

"Sure, but just think of all the favours I'm doing for you here. Grabbing the diadem for your daughter, getting some treasure, dealing with Jonas, and making the Blues look like idiots. Nothing but wins for you, Sig." Captain Palmer examined her nails. "That's all without mentioning those other times you shorted me."

One of Sig's eyebrows twitched. "You will watch the way you speak to me, Fortune. That arrogance is best saved for those beneath you, and you'll do well to remember that."

"Sorry, sir."

Finn had never seen Fortune appear so small as a person. Whatever power a Pyrate King might hold, it was enough to spook Captain Palmer into submission.

"Be off with you," Sig said with a dismissive hand

wave.

As they turned to leave, that's when it hit Finn. If anyone was going to be able to give him any information on the Poisoned Rose, it would surely be the Pyrate King.

Finn stepped forward. "King—sir—Sig, can you tell me anything about the Poisoned Rose."

Sig's face melted into one of anger. "Palmer, why is your boy asking me about this?"

"I don't know, Sig." The captain slapped a hand onto Finn's shoulder and spoke through gritted teeth, "I told him to keep his mouth *shut.*"

"I'm sorry, I—" Finn started.

Sig held up a hand. "We do not speak of those barbarians. You want some information about them? Stay away from them. The only person lucky enough to clash with them and get out alive is standing right next to you."

Finn stared up at his captain, but she just shook her head and walked away.

She knew more than she had ever said.

Why hadn't she told him?

And what else was Captain Palmer hiding?

Chapter 15:

Lies Amongst Friends

Finn made his way to the main deck of the ship with a bowl of fresh stew. He was happy to have Smiley aboard as a cook. The stew was better than anything he'd ever had back on Embar. That wasn't too hard, as his pop was never the best cook. Just how the ingredients all tasted so fresh was a mystery Finn wanted an answer to.

The past few days, Finn had been feeling dejected. After his screw-up at the pyrate capitol, Captain Palmer still hadn't even bothered to speak to him. He couldn't tell if she was angry, disappointed, or ready to give him the boot over the whole situation.

What little sword-play practice Finn managed to get in with the captain had been completely replaced solely with Walker. The old drunk was a great teacher, but he had nothing on Captain Palmer.

He spotted Trigger, Francis, Smiley, Tobi, and Walker all sitting around a lantern. "You guys mind if I join you?"

Walker pulled out a box for Finn to sit on as Trigger smiled and gestured to the open spot. "Always room for another one of the lads."

"The real men of the Albatross eat topside," Tobi

said. "Where's Bug?"

Finn pointed towards the wheel with his spoon. "Pretty sure he's asleep up by the wheel—or steering the ship. Who knows?"

He wasn't sure how important it was to ensure that the wheel was fully manned, but the Albatross was being steered far less often than expected. Finn knew better than to ask too many questions while people were being nice to him.

Smiley watched Finn take a seat as Francis stuffed his face. "You lot enjoying the stew?"

"Actually, yeah." Finn moved the stew around a bit. "It's fantastic."

Smiley almost actually smiled.

There were a lot more potatoes in the stew than Finn would have liked, but he had a feeling he couldn't be too choosey. Food options were probably fairly limited on the ship. It was a good thing that they could sail around in no time at all to pick up fresh food when needed.

"We were just telling Francis about all the insanity he missed at the capital," Walker said.

Finn stared into his stew. He knew he'd screwed up, but he meant well. He figured the crew would end up talking about it at some point. His real worry was whether or not Captain Palmer would ever cool off. She hadn't even looked at him since they got back on the sea.

"Don't worry a single hair on that head, lad." Trigger tapped Finn's arm. "Everyone's had some kind of fluff up like that—and if yeh haven't yet, yeh will eventually." Trigger finished by pointing his spoon at Smiley and Francis.

Francis let out a nervous laugh. "Well, if what you guys told me is true, I'm going to do what I can to hold off on that."

Finn popped a spoonful of stew into his mouth and then pointed it amongst the men. "You mean, you three all screwed up big at some point?"

Trigger held up a hand and pointed toward Walker. "Some of us have been screwing up with the Captain our whole lives."

"Keep it shut." Walker tossed a piece of potato at Trigger and he caught it in his mouth. "I'm happy to share some stories, so long as I'm the one to tell 'em."

Finn smiled. "I'm all ears."

"I'll give yeh a pick of the story, lad." Walker tossed his empty bowl onto the box in front of everyone and pulled out a bottle of rum. "Aboard the Albatross, or before the Albatross."

Finn took a moment to think. He would have loved to hear a first-hand story about Captain Palmer from an old friend of hers. On the other hand, hearing what Captain Palmer was like before her life of piracy sounded just as intriguing.

"Before the Albatross."

Walker raised an eyebrow. "Interesting choice. Probably heard one too many stories of the Captain's adventures already, huh? Let's see here——"

"Give him a minute." Tobi wiggled his spoon at Walker. "Takes a while for his brain to get in proper order—you know, old age."

Walker frowned at Tobi. "There's just too many stories to choose from yeh goon. When we were about yer age, just before all this piracy business began, I got into a heap of trouble."

He wasn't about to say it out loud, but Finn wasn't surprised by that.

"What kind of trouble?" Finn asked.

"Quiet, and I'll tell the story," Walker said. "See the Captain came from what is the equivalent to royalty in most pyrate's eyes. Her pop was one of those high-command people in the Royal Navy."

Hearing that blew Finn's mind. One of the most

famous pyrates of all time came from a Royal Navy background. Her sister taking the exact opposite path made sense. It wasn't the opposite path, it was *the* path.

"I was a foolish boy." Walker continued. "Hard-headed and brash. I'd pick a fight with just about anyone I could. One night, I picked a fight with the wrong group of men—Royal Navy men. Long story short, I whooped their asses. As punishment the next day, they tossed me behind bars. To tis day, I don't think I've ever seen Captain Palmer as angry as she was when she spat at me through those bars."

Trigger laughed, "I always pictured yeh as a man on the run."

Walker smirked when he noticed how enthralled everyone was. "So late that night, the Captain returned and broke me out of jail without anyone finding out. I thought I'd never see her again since, at that point, we were headed in very different directions. Jump forward, and here we are now. I'd hate to see the poor soul who gets her screaming again like she was that night."

Finn knew he'd be bugging Walker a whole lot more to hear even more stories from his youth. Having an inside look at what Captain Palmer was like when she was his age made his hero seem so much more human.

He looked at the other two. "Trigger, Tobi?"

"Much less intcresting stories." Trigger waved a hand. "I accidentally got us into a skirmish once when I snuck up on the enemy."

"How is that a problem?"

"They weren't really an enemy at that point. More like a trade partner. That all changed real fast."

"Tis pretty funny now, though." Trigger laughed, "Tobi's is boring."

Tobi scoffed. "I think that just makes me the best veteran crew member. Captain Palmer got mad at me when I lied to join the crew."

"You lied?" Finn asked.

"I wasn't always a carpenter. That changed really quickly once the Captain found out I lied about my qualifications. My options were, learn carpentry or learn to swim. I picked the first option and now I'd wager I'm a better carpenter than any man you'd find at any port."

Two female laughs caught the group's attention. Captain Palmer and Kili were making their way into the captain's private quarters. Kili looked back at all of them as they reached the door and stuck her tongue out.

Finn could just barely see inside the quarters and it was as spectacular as he expected. While much of the ship felt drab, her quarters were filled with rich colours that he'd never seen before. A trip inside to examine all of her many treasures would have been heaven.

Walker laughed and slapped Finn on the back, "That young lady there is going to be a world of trouble for yeh."

"What do you mean?" Finn tried to avoid eye contact. "She's—something else."

"Yeh don't need to do the stoic hero act. We've all caught yeh two giggling and making eyes at each other."

Everyone put their empty bowls in a pile, and Trigger tossed his down on top. "She's a cute one, lad. Nothing to be ashamed about. She's too young for any of us anyhow. Seems only right our annoying stowaway should be the one to be with our equally annoying entertainment."

Finn leaned back. "You all sound like a bunch of girls talking about the boys they fancy."

"Looks like the lad can fight back after all," Francis said.

For the first time since he'd joined, Finn felt like he was really bonding with someone other than Tobi or Kili. It felt like he was becoming one of the lads, something that he assumed came with a few additional perks. Being close with someone like Walker was never a bad thing.

"All we're saying is you've got the blessing of all the lads on the ship." Tobi pulled out a handful of small cards. "Well, the lads that matter."

Finn narrowed his eyes at Tobi. "And when are you and Stitch planning on getting hitched?"

"How's about a game of cards?"

"Nice dodge," Finn said with a wry smile.

Francis rubbed his hands. "Now you're speaking to me heart."

Walker handed the bottle to Smiley for a swig. "What game are we playing tonight?"

"What's that one from a couple nights ago?" Smiley handed Trigger the bottle. "The lying one."

Francis perked up even more. "A Cheater's Bluff."

"Aye, let's play that one."

Finn looked around. "How do you play? I've never played cards before." They all laughed at him. "What's so funny?"

Francis got the bottle and took a swig. "When you've travelled the world—even on merchant vessels, you often forget what the young folk have and haven't done."

"Teach me."

The game was unlike anything Finn had played before. They had to go around the box taking turns laying down cards. Each person had to say exactly what cards they were laying down and how many, but they could lie about anything. If someone picked up on a lie, they'd have to slam their cards down and call the liar out.

Anyone who got caught in a lie was out of the game. The punishment was that the first one out had no choice but to do any one thing the rest of the group asked.

The first was a practice round that, as far as he could tell, went well. He managed to lie a few times, despite him thinking he was a terrible liar. The actual loser of the practice round was Smiley and the winner ended up being Francis of all people. Smiley was a good sport and took a punishment even though it was a practice round.

"Smiley, finish the bottle," Walker laughed. "I'm going to grab another quick."

Smiley sloshed back the remainder of the liquid and let out a burp. "Easy."

Kili came out of Captain Palmer's quarters and waved to Finn. "What are you rowdy bunch getting up to?"

"Just a game of cards. You want to join?" Finn asked.

"I've got my daily fill of sweaty man-energy. I'm going to bed."

"You're missing out. Loser gets a punishment."

"What kind of punishment?"

He stuck a thumb toward Smiley. "He just had to finish a bottle of rum."

"Kids stuff—Tobi?"

Tobi lifted his chin. "Aye?"

"Kick his butt, and give him the most wicked punishment you can think up." Kili headed down into the hull of the ship, but as she went, her eyes lingered on Finn.

"Oh, we will." When Finn turned his attention back to the men, their mischievous grins gave him the feeling that he needed to win his next game.

Finn let out an awkward laugh. "I'm feeling confident, Tobi. How do you feel about being forced to ask Stitch to marry you?"

All the guys oohed, but Tobi thought fast. "I don't have to win, I just have to beat you. Ain't that right, lads?"

Everyone let out a sinister laugh and Finn knew he was screwed.

He did his best, but as if they'd all conspired against him, the first time Finn had to lie—they called him out.

"How'd you guys know?" Finn asked.

Francis laughed, "You're a terrible liar. We were just being nice in that practice round."

Finn looked at Smiley for some help, but he shrugged. "He's right. You're a terrible liar."

"So, Mr. Confident," Tobi leaned forward. "How do you feel about paying the young lady a late-night visit?"

Everyone burst into laughter again as it was now Finn's turn to become bright red. "I don't know if that's a good idea."

He'd thought about asking Kili to hang out after supper a number of times. Never in any overtly romantic way, Finn just thought it would be nice to take in the sight of the night sky with someone like her.

Walker shook his head. "Rules are rules, and we pyrates follow the rules—when we're goofing off at least." He leaned closer to Finn. "All yeh have to do is pay her a visit."

"More is always an option." Trigger smirked. "You'll just have to share the details."

"Gross, Trigger." Finn stood up. "Alright, alright. Fair is fair. I'll go pay her a visit, but then I'm heading to bed."

They all waved and Finn started toward the hatch. "Ay, lad," Walker said, causing Finn to spin around. "Yeh're welcome to eat with us anytime."

Finn smiled and headed below deck to see how his punishment would go. He was nervous, though there wasn't any pressure to do anything other than talk. Finn kind of considered Kili a friend—about as much as he would have considered Minerva back home a friend, that is.

Of course, Kili was far easier on the eyes.

Finn came to her old run-down door and knocked.

"Kili, you still up?"

"Finn?" she called through the door. "Come on in, I'll be one second."

Part of him hoped she was already fast asleep. It was pretty late, and by her own admission, she had a habit of falling asleep as soon as she hit her nifty new bed. He wondered if Kili had purposely stayed up, but there was no way she could have known he'd have to visit.

Finn pushed the door open and saw Kili slip behind a divider she had set in the corner of the room.

"Is everything okay?" Finn's question was answered by Kili's silhouette through the shade. "Oh—uh."

"Just getting changed."

Finn covered his eyes and whirled to the side of the doorframe. "Ah—Uh—I'm sorry. I shouldn't have—"

Kili laughed at Finn, and he pulled his hand away to see her in a robe. Her usual two tails of hair were combined into one massive ponytail.

"There's a shade, you didn't need to cover your eyes."

"I know. I just—you know—" Finn stammered as his face got hot all over again.

"You're so uncomfortable."

"I really am."

"It's kind of cute." Finn's embarrassment started to fade as Kili continued. "So what can I do for you at this hour?"

Finn really wasn't sure what he was supposed to say. The whole situation was out of his depth. He hadn't even thought through what he even could say. What does one do when they go see someone that late at night?

"Well, I—you see—huh. I lost the game with the guys. My punishment was to come and pay you a visit."

"I should have known." Kili crossed her arms. "And what kind of *visit* is this supposed to be?"

Her tone reminded him exactly of what a late-night

visit like that could mean.

Finn nearly gasped, "No, not that kind of visit."

Kili raised an eyebrow.

"Not that I wouldn't want that kind of a visit." He continued. "Anybody would be lucky to have a visit like that with you."

She cocked her head.

"I—uh—I don't know where to go here." He took a flustered breath. "What I'm trying to say is that it's just a friendly visit. I'm here—visiting." Finn waved a hand. "Hello."

"Hello, Finn," she stifled a laugh before falling silent.

Finn couldn't tell if she wanted him to stay and chat or leave her alone. The way she was looking at him said she wanted to talk, but her lack of words said otherwise.

"Well, thank you—for the visit," she finally said. "Have a good night."

"You too." She shut the door and Finn stared into the wood regretting having ever gone down there. "You have a good night—too."

"Oh, and don't be weirded out if the boys give you funny looks tomorrow." Kili called through the door. "I'm definitely going to make up a fun story for *your visit*."

Finn nudged himself with the base of his palm as he headed to bed for the night. "Smooth, Townsend. Real smooth."

chapter 16:

Magic Cubes, Witches, And Purity

Finn had spotted a lush green island in the distance and knew it was go-time. The chance to spend some time in the crow's nest was nice, but it was probably so that he couldn't keep on bugging Captain Palmer. To his delight, he got to deliver the news to her personally.

"I'll only be taking a small crew with me," Captain Palmer said. "I have no idea how long this will take so the rest of you, split yourselves into two groups and have the ship ready to go at a moment's notice. We may need to make a hasty exit."

Finn had trouble containing his excitement. He'd seen Captain Palmer ready to go before, but something about the island felt different. Rather than hearing a tale of the great Captain Fortune Palmer discovering treasure, he was going to be a part of it.

"Tobi, Trigger, Smiley, Kili, Francis, the kid, and—" She gestured to a group of men on the side. "You five, with me."

They all piled into two separate boats and rowed to the shore of the island. There was no telling if they had enough people to carry whatever riches they'd manage to find. Finn had never seen actual treasure before, but the stories that Vi had told him back on Embar made treasures seem grandiose.

Finn caught the captain staring at him and hoped to break the tension. "I'm surprised you wanted to bring me along."

"Figured it would be best to keep you near me. Wouldn't want you to speak out of turn and get yourself killed." Her usual cool tone had turned dark by the time she finished speaking.

"I was just trying to take a page from your book and be spontaneous."

"Well, you picked quite literally the worst time to start. You could have been killed right there in that throne room. All it would have taken was a single snap of his fingers."

It was a necessary risk for Finn. He knew that, like a parent, Captain Palmer would get over her anger at some point. Once she was back to her normal self, that was when Finn could learn everything she knew about the Poisoned Rose. Still, he knew better than to open his mouth for the rest of the ride.

As they reached the shore, a group of native islanders came out to meet them. They had fewer clothes than any of the crew, but what they lacked in clothes they made up for in paints of strange colours and beautiful jewelry. They all either carried spears or bows, but they didn't feel primitive.

They felt prepared.

"Friend or foe?" The eldest of the islanders asked as they made land.

"The Devil's Charm, Captain Fortune Palmer," she said with a bow. "At absolutely no one's service."

The islanders weren't enthused.

Not at all.

"Friend or foe?" the elder asked again.

"Wouldn't anyone with half a brain say friend, even

if they were a foe?" she asked as she hopped out of the boat.

One of the islanders turned to the elder. "She raises a good point."

He smacked the young man. "Quiet, child."

"If we were going to attack you, we already would have." Everyone made their way out of the boats as the captain approached the islanders. "No offence, but the sticks probably wouldn't stack up against our blades."

"You would be surprised by our weapons—and our resolve," the elder said.

A long pause fell over the groups. The island's elder never broke his gaze on the captain, and she never broke her gaze on him. There was a thick feeling in the air, but it wasn't one of tension, it was one of respect.

Captain Palmer grinned. "I like your confidence."

"And I like yours." The elder waved a hand and the others lowered their weapons. "I am the village elder. Please, come with us. We'll provide your crew with food and drink while you explain what your purpose is in our homeland."

Kili grabbed Finn's arm and gave him a concerned look, but Finn knew to trust his captain. If she was confident she would be fine, she was confident her crew would be too. They all followed the islanders a short way inland to their village that looked out toward the sea.

"Uh, excuse me," Finn tapped one of the islanders. "Do you all speak Common?" The islander nodded. "Does your whole tribe live right here along the shore? What if the weather gets bad?"

Finn looked out toward the waves. For an instant, he could have sworn he spotted a familiar orange glow. It wasn't the same as on the ship, it was just a faint shimmer just a short swim from the island.

"Our gods protect us," the islander said as he gestured all around. "We witness great cyclones out at sea, but they never come near our island—unless we anger the gods. We don't all live here. More of our people live inland. Many villages."

Gods or not, there was more to the island than Finn originally thought. If his eyes weren't playing tricks on him, the islander's homeland was possibly even more advanced than Embar ever had been.

"AAAAAAHH!" A woman's scream came from deeper in the village.

Without a word, the islanders rushed toward the source of the scream. Kili had to have had her worries eased since the entire village had no fear leaving the crew unattended.

There wasn't any time to think, and Finn's gut was telling him that whatever was happening, they needed to help out. As it turns out, he wasn't the only one with that gut feeling.

"Come on." Captain Palmer waved an arm. "Let's see if we can help them."

Every time they made land, Finn was surprised by something new. He never imagined he'd be out trying to help local populations. The thought that pyrates might do a bit more ignoring when it came to the cries of helpless people wasn't a pleasant one.

The source of the scream came from a beautiful islander girl. She was laying on the ground shaking as if she were caught in the midst of an earthquake. A group of men with spears surrounded her, and it looked like they were more than ready to skewer her.

The eldest islander started shouting in a language Finn had never heard before, but it didn't seem like it was helping. The men replied, and it looked like the situation was about to get a lot worse. Unlike the previous standoff, this one filled the air with tension.

A strange glowing idol resting on a stone shrine caught Finn's eye. If he didn't know any better, he'd say they were in the middle of the village, making the idol a likely place of worship. It reminded him of the heart of the Albatross with the way it pulsed.

"Anyone know what they're saying?" Captain Palmer asked.

Smiley stepped forward and held out a box that glowed with an orange hue Finn knew all too well. An orange light shot out of it and he started to read what looked like a floating letter.

"The elder asked them what they think they're doing, and the men said that this woman was caught placing a spell on the women of the village. Enticing them to the devil or something." His eyes bugged out. "Then there's a lot of salty language coming from them directed at the pretty girl in the middle."

Everyone stared at Smiley. He hadn't ever mentioned a device like that, but then again, Smiley didn't ever say much without being asked first.

Captain Palmer pulled her sword. "We're going to have a long conversation about the skills and items you have in your possession at some point. Does that thing let you speak to them?"

"Aye."

"Good, ask the elder if they need us to handle this mess of a situation."

Smiley began talking into the box and it repeated his words in the language of the islanders for the elder, who turned around in surprise. The elder started nodding as he responded and everyone pulled their swords.

"The elder asks for our help to disarm the men— without killing them."

Captain Palmer smirked. "That's our speciality."

Finn rushed in front of her. "We don't need to fight everyone we see!"

"And what do you suggest we do then?"

He had an idea, but it was one that could end with

him on the wrong end of the spears. If the islanders feared things like witchcraft and the wrath of gods, Finn could use that to his advantage.

He held up a finger to Captain Palmer and jogged over to the idol on the shrine. It looked even more delicate than Finn had originally thought. Perfect. After lining his sword up with the idol he whistled as loud as he could. Everyone stopped what they were doing and stared at him.

Captain Palmer raised an eyebrow. "This is your plan?"

Finn didn't need to answer, the islanders spoke for themselves. They'd all started screaming at Finn, filling the air in front of Smiley with words. From his reaction, the words weren't anything too kind.

Finn grinned as everyone approached him. "Smiley, tell them to lay their weapons down or I'll destroy this idol and find someone to curse the island and their gods."

Smiley relayed the message and the angry islanders complied. The elder didn't look thrilled by Finn's methods, but the plan had worked. The crew rushed in and took the weapons from the islanders, and Finn lowered his blade.

Captain Palmer had a shocked expression. "I suppose you can use that brain of yours for something other than irritating me with smart-ass comments." She turned to Smiley. "Ask them if that will suffice."

Smiley held up the box and the islanders began talking. Again, a small piece of orange parchment drifted into the air. As the they spoke, words appeared as if written in fresh ink.

"They aren't exactly pleased with the lad, but they said thank you." As Smiley spoke, a group of islanders with spears rushed over and hauled the attackers away. "The men will deal with this violent group for what they were about to do."

The elder held his hands out toward the captain. "Thank you for your assistance. I am surprised to learn one of your own speaks our tongue." He glared at Finn. "And one is aware of our customs."

She took his hands. and they engaged in a strange shake. "I'm just as surprised as you are, but that's not quite what was happening."

"What is that idol?" Finn interjected.

The elder gave him a confused look. "You mean you don't know? That is the heart of this island. It seeks directly to our god and gives us protection from the harsh weather." He shook his head. "If it were to have been destroyed—"

Captain Palmer turned her attention to Smiley. "Those translation cubes are quite rare. How'd you come into possession of one?"

Smiley looked as if he had just recalled a painful memory. "I received it from someone very dear to me."

It was impossible to tell how the captain would react to the new facts she learned about her crew. Hearing a sarcastic comment in response to Smiley wouldn't have been a shock. Instead, the captain's expression softened as if she had gone through whatever Smiley had.

"We will speak privately about that then." She walked over to the woman who was still on the ground and held out her hand. "You alright?" The woman stared up at Captain Palmer, silent. "I won't hurt you. Do you speak Common?"

She took the captain's hand. "Yes—thank you."

"Happy to help."

The elder put a hand on the woman's back. "Why don't you go and make preparations for our new friends to stay the night? Food, drink, and a mighty fire."

The woman locked eyes with Captain Palmer again before heading off with a smile. Everyone watched her as she went, and Finn couldn't blame any of them. The last time he'd seen someone so beautiful was the day he met Kili.

"Now that all is calm," The elder turned back to Captain Palmer. "Please, what is your purpose here?"

"We've heard tales of a treasure on this island. Specifically, a diadem, which is said to bring great fortune to the one who wears it." Captain Palmer sheathed her blade and the rest of the crew followed her lead. "Your people wouldn't happen to know anything about that, would you?"

"What you seek lies in the temple above." The elder turned his attention to a temple sitting atop a hill in the distance. "You are welcome to try, but it is not for the likes of you to claim."

"Excuse me?"

"The trials within must first be conquered, but even if you manage that, only someone pure of heart may lay claim to the riches within."

The elder delivered each word more serious than the last. Finn was eating up every moment, but when he glanced at Captain Palmer, he was surprised. Rather than a look of determination or seriousness, she gave the elder a dull look.

"Every treasure I've claimed can only be claimed by one that's pure," she said as she rolled her eyes. "I'm not worried about that temple's purity test."

The elder moved closer and took one of her hands in his. "This is no joke. You know which of you are pure enough to claim the treasure." As he finished speaking, his eyes fell on Finn and Kili.

They looked at each other and blushed while Captain Palmer laughed, "Our pure little babes."

Finn wasn't really sure why he was embarrassed. There wasn't anything wrong with being pure. It was a bit odd to be singled out like that, but if what the elder said was true, Finn would be the one to claim a treasure for his childhood hero.

"I'm with Captain Palmer." Finn cleared his throat. "The whole purity thing is dumb."

"Yep. That whole purity thing is probably fake anyway." Kili chimed in. "What makes someone pure in the first place?" Everyone stared at her. "I know what they mean by purity! I'm just saying it's stupid!"

"Well, while you make your decision of who will go to claim the treasure, please rest and join in the festivities of our village," the elder said.

The crew settled in with the tribe like they'd been life-long friends. They laid out a large feast for supper that they cooked on the biggest bonfire Finn had ever seen. It felt like the flames flicked high enough to burn the very clouds overhead.

Something caught Finn's eye, just in the corner of his view. It was the rustling of leaves from within the dense jungle off to the side. Any number of animals could have been watching from a safe distance, so Finn put the disturbance out of his mind.

Of all the mistakes Finn had made up to that point, that might have been the biggest one.

chapter 17:

The Tale of Kilala Saelim

Once everyone had gotten some food into them, some of the crew took part in a special alcoholic drink created only on the island. Everyone was having a great time, maybe a bit too good of a time. Even Captain Palmer was busy learning the culture of the islanders from the girl the crew had saved.

As the night went on, and the air grew cooler, people slowly started turning in for the night. The islanders had cleared out a massive hut for the crew to stay in. It was similar to the size of the Albatross, so the crew likely felt right at home.

The best part was that they had beds to sleep in. Actual beds. It was going to be so much nicer than old sacks and hammocks.

Finn snuck away down the beach for a little quiet time with Bug. It was next to impossible to find any peace and quiet aboard the Albatross. Someone was always shouting something at someone else. Being able to sit and enjoy the sound of the waves hitting the shore was exactly what he needed.

He heard the shifting of sand under boots from over his shoulder. It was Kili. The moonlight bouncing off the ocean lit her in a way that managed to compliment all of her features. Finn found himself thinking things like that more and more the longer he knew her.

"Mind if I join you two? I need yet another break from the horrible, raw essence of male pyrate." Kili asked.

"Pull up a sandy seat," he said as he brushed the sand.

"Don't mind if I do."

There was a moment of awkward silence between them. Finn wasn't sure what to say, and he could feel that Kili was in the same spot. They hadn't had many chances to just sit and get to know each other. Finn was usually great at talking to girls, but he felt nervous talking to Kili.

"So—what's the other side of the sea like?" Finn asked, but immediately regretted it when he saw Kili's reaction to the light-hearted question. "I'm sorry. Too personal. Forget I asked."

Kili shook her head. "No, it's okay." She took a breath and looked out across the sea. "It's absolutely beautiful—but completely horrible."

"Horrible? How can something be beautiful and horrible at the same time?"

"It's not so different over there. There are more colours, and it smells much, much better. Maybe it's a bit more *advanced* than things seem to be over here. My parents were poor, so poor that they were on the brink of starvation."

Whenever people spoke about advancements, it always made Finn picture powerful men in society. It was odd to hear Kili call her home more advanced, and yet people were still starving. People were poor in Embar, but no one ever went hungry, and that seemed to be the case for people everywhere they went.

"When I was a young girl—" Kili looked like she had to prepare herself before she continued. "My parents sold me into a life of slavery. That's when I started singing—to have a way to push away my problems, even for a few moments."

Finn's attention shifted from the sand in his hands to Kili. She kept her eyes trained on the reflection of the moon in the sea. At that moment, all he wanted was to reach out and comfort her.

"How bad did things get?" he asked.

"It depended on the man, the day, my screw-ups." She ran a hand along her arm. "I took my share of hits. The only silver lining was being taught to use a sword. One time I screwed up bad—" Kili pulled the back collar of her shirt down to reveal a nasty burn scar on her shoulder blade. "My entire existence was to serve men. Fetching food, fetching water, running baths, and then when I came of age—I was told I would be expected to serve—in other ways."

Bug felt the emotion radiating from her, so he moved to cuddle into her leg. The two of them had become fast friends, and while Bug would never turn his back on Finn, the pup would often ditch him to sleep in Kili's comfy bed.

Once again, Finn found himself at a loss for adequate words. He said the only thing he thought he could. "I'm so sorry."

"No one was ever going to lay a finger on me without my say-so." She faced Finn with tears in her eyes, but she didn't let a single one fall. "No one. So one night, while everyone was sleeping, I snuck into each of their rooms—and I killed them."

Finn had a feeling that hearing something like that would change most people's opinions of the person who had said it. Maybe he'd view her as a murderer or a bit crazy. Instead, he had a newfound respect for her. She did what she had to do to protect herself, even if it was horrific.

There wasn't an inch of pride on her face. All that lingered was sadness and remorse.

"I killed them all." Kili continued. "I didn't have any possessions, so I took what I could and left before anyone knew anything had happened. I stowed away on a boat headed across the sea, and here I am."

"You were a stowaway too, huh? Looks like we aren't completely different," Finn said, trying to lighten the mood.

"I guess not."

"The travelling entertainer thing—" Finn said, trying to choose his words carefully.

Kili looked at him as if she'd read his mind. "Why would I leave a life of servitude to men for—another life of servitude to men?"

Finn nodded.

"I don't know." She started using her foot to fiddle with the sand. "Maybe—It's something that's become ingrained in who I am. Maybe—it's because I know that singing and dancing is something I love, and I can do it on my terms." She let out a weak grin. "Maybe it's because I like taking money from those kinds of foolish men."

He had so many questions, he just didn't know which ones were appropriate to ask. Her quick-to-violence nature made so much more sense to Finn, and he wondered if things had gone different her first day if Trigger had known all of what she was telling him.

Finn thought back on his life, and how caring his father had been to take in a young boy after losing his wife. He wished Kili had someone like that in her life. Someone to step in and be her hero.

"Did you ever want to go find your family?" he asked.

"No. Family doesn't just throw each other away like garbage." Kili ran her finger along Bug's back. "Family finds a way, even when things feel hopeless. Those people were never my family."

"You have a family now." Finn put a hand on hers. "It may be a weird one, a smelly one, and a rowdy one—but it's a family. We're always going to protect you—or at least I am if that counts for anything."

Kili looked into his eyes and he felt his heart begin to race. The way she was looking at him, it was like she was asking for something without saying a word, Finn just didn't know what. There was another moment of quiet before Kili pulled her hand back.

"You're right." She took a breath as she stood up. "I think it's time for me to get some sleep, you coming?"

"I think I'm going to spend a bit more time out here. No yelling or snoring. It's nice to have nothing but the sound of the waves for once."

Kili smiled. "Good night, Finn."

"Goodnight, Kili."

For the first time since he'd known her, Finn was filled with a new sense of appreciation rather than more frustration.

Kili was one tough lady.

After a while of basking in the moonlight, he patted Bug. "C'mon, bud. Let's do a wee before bed."

Bug had a long stretch before following him. As Finn pushed through the brush, the snap of sticks beneath heavy feet gave him pause. Bug let out a low growl, but Finn tapped his back and brought a finger to his lips.

The jungle around him was foreboding, it was too dark to see anything, so why anyone would be traipsing through it was a mystery. Thanks to the dull glow of fires from inside the large hut, Finn managed to make out a couple of people creeping toward it. He wasn't sure if he should call out to the figures, or to the crew inside the hut.

Captain Palmer appeared in the doorway with a yawn, and that's when the shadows struck. The figures all darted forward and held her at the ends of their swords.

Someone had set a trap.

Chapter 18:

There Had To Be A Traitor

Finn peered through the brush, doing anything he could to make out just who the people who had taken the crew captive were. One by one, the crew was hauled out of the hut and tied up. As one of the men leading the ambush came through the door to the hut, his face was lit by the bright moon.

It was Francis.

"That bastard," Finn whispered.

"Looks like someone is missing," Francis said

His voice had changed completely. His usual soft-spoken demeanour had morphed to reflect the Francis that Finn had seen during their training exercises. He seemed like just another crude pyrate.

"Who?" one of the men said.

"They've got another young one—a lad," Francis said as he looked around. "He isn't here."

"Must've gotten scared and run away."

"He doesn't seem the type. Might as well ask the fearless leader."

They crouched toward Captain Palmer, and their voices faded into the night.

Finn looked around for any type of advantage he

could get. It looked like there were only five of them. There was a chance he could handle one or two on his own, but he needed to get at least one of the crew members free to help out.

CaptainPalmer's voice picked up. "I don't know where the kid went. He probably went to relieve himself and got picked off by an animal. That sounds about right for that nitwit. Why don't you go take a look for yourself, while I escape, beat your men within an inch of their life, and leave your fate up to the island's inhabitants?"

Finn wasn't sure if he should have taken what she said offensively or as the captain protecting him. With how strained their relationship had been, it was entirely possible that's what she really thought.

"Yeh might think of yerself as some mighty pyrate lord," Francis stood up. "But yer looking at the most successful band of pyrate hunters this side of the sea."

"Really?" Captain Palmer seemed more amused than scared. "Pretty sure I would have recognized you if that was true. Who've you caught?"

"I don't need to justify meself to a lady. I caught yeh, didn't I? Enough of this." Francis pointed to his men. "You two, check the area. The kid's probably hiding in the bushes somewhere soiling himself."

Two thugs were a lot more manageable than five. Finn tapped Bug and they headed deeper into the trees as quietly as they could. He needed to think of a way to knock both those guys out without alerting anyone. If he had more time he could probably set up some kind of trap, but with no tools and no knowledge of his surroundings, it was going to be difficult.

Finn found a large tree, one big enough that his climbing it wouldn't create too much movement, and snatched up a few rocks. The additional weight of the stones made the climb a pain, but there wasn't any time to complain. If he failed, the entire crew was done for. Even from a great distance, Finn could see the hunters each with a bright lantern in hand.

He pulled out his grappling hook and looked back down at his trusty companion. "Okay, Bug. You're the distraction. You just wait here and be your awesome self."

A part of Finn was worried that Bug would run off now that he was on his own. Bug was letting out a bit of a nervous shake, but he was still there, loyal as ever. If things went well, that dog was going to be getting half of Finn's food for a week.

The hunters had spread out, so he picked the nearest one to start with. A perfectly tossed rock struck a tree near the hunter and Finn watched as the lantern shifted. A few more rocks drew the hunter closer until he was in the right spot.

"Come to master pyrate, Finn Townsend."

The hunter looked down at the dog and scratched his head. Bug growled and let out a bark, so Finn knew he had to act fast.

He whirled the grappling hook and swung it sideways down into the hunter's head as hard as he could. The hunter fell to the ground, but the other one was on his way in a hurry. Finn pulled the hook back up and inspected it for any blood, but it was clean.

"One down, one to go." He looked down at Bug "Good job, boy."

He felt bad leaving Bug. It was plain to see how scared the pup was. There was no telling what animals were lurking in the dark waiting for a chance to hop out and have a late-night snack.

The second hunter arrived sooner than Finn thought he would. He bent down to check on his comrade as Finn threw the hook. It was just Finn's luck that the hook narrowly swung over the hunter's head. To his dismay, the swing made enough noise to clue the second hunter in.

As he backed up and turned his attention to the tree, Bug started peeing on the man's leg. The man lashed out with an angry kick and Bug let out a yelp. The poor fat dog went flying into the darkness.

That bastard.

Messing with Finn was one thing, but no one could mess with Bug.

Without a second thought, Finn launched out of the tree at the hunter. He nailed him with a tackle and they rolled to the ground. Finn recovered, and it was clear that the hunter had no clue what had hit him. As the hunter went for his sword, Finn whirled his grappling hook and smacked it into the man's head, knocking him out.

He rushed to check on Bug. "You okay, bud? Everything still working how it's supposed to?" Bug shuffled around, careful to put weight on one paw. Finn picked him up for a hug. "Glad you're okay, boy. Let's go deal with the rest of these guys."

He made his way back to where he was watching the hunters. Everyone on the ground had their legs bound and their hands behind their back. All of their weapons were just off to the side, but even if one of them were able to grab a blade, they wouldn't be much help in a fight.

Finn needed to cut them free.

"The boys must have gotten pretty deep into the jungle," Francis said. "I can't see the lights anymore."

"They'll turn around any minute. Those two hate doing more than their fair share—always trying to get off the hook," another man said.

The grappling hook.

Finn freed the hook free from the end of the rope. The hook's point was sharp enough to at least fray a rope, if not cut it outright. He just needed to get it to any of them. The only way that was going to happen, was with the help of Bug. Finn looked down at his faithful companion.

"I need you to be brave, Bug." Finn crouched down. "You gotta take this and run as fast as you can. Take it to Captain Palmer, okay?" He wagged a finger. "Captain—Palmer. Only when I get out there."

Bug looked up at him with his big eyes. He often spoke to the dog like he could understand all of Finn's words, but he knew that wasn't the case. If he understood anything, now was the time to show that off. All Finn could do was pray that his desperate plan would work.

"I really hope you understand me." Finn rushed out of the brush and the light of the pyrate hunters' torches revealed him. "You're gonna need a lot more than two of those morons to deal with me."

He circled away from where Bug would be running out and hoped to pull the hunters away. They probably wouldn't pay him much mind even if they saw him, but no one needed to spot the hook.

"Make this easy, lad," Francis spat as he and the remaining hunters stepped forward. "If yeh don't, we'll have to kill yeh."

"Wasn't that what those other two guys were for?" Bug darted from the bushes, so Finn pulled his sword. "What do I know, though, right? I'm just a kid."

Francis' voice morphed into a growl. "Last warning. Put the sword down, or we'll gut yeh."

Bug made it to the crew undetected, but instead of running to Captain Palmer, he ran to Kili. Not exactly the plan, but at least she had the hook to free herself and the others.

"At least let me ask," Finn said to buy time. "How the hell did you even set this ambush up?"

"Yer Captain isn't exactly a subtle lady. She told me exactly why and where I'd be going if I joined, so I tipped me boys off to meet us here."

It looked like Kili was having some trouble shredding through her ropes. It couldn't have been easy to drive the hook through the ropes with her hands still tied. The look she gave Finn wasn't one of panic, something that put his mind at ease.

"You know, I never really liked you, Francis," Finn said.

Francis rushed toward Finn, ready for a fight. There was no telling just how much he'd been hiding back when they trained. All Finn had to do was survive long enough for the others to get free.

The entire plan was thrown for a loop when Trigger hopped up and head-butted one of the hunters. As if they'd come up with their own plan, Captain Palmer followed suit with a jumping kick to another hunter.

"We'll do what we can, kid." Captain Palmer blew a streak of her hair out of her face. "Kick his ass."

He dodged a strike. "Doing what I can here."

Finn had his hands full with Francis, so there was no way he'd be able to protect the others. The two hunters had recovered and were closing in with swords drawn. The others would have to fight while they were still bound.

As Finn parried a few slashes, Trigger and Captain Palmer each narrowly avoided strikes of their own. "Hold on, guys!"

As Finn and Francis clashed blades, Kili, free from her bonds, rushed for a weapon. Finn wasn't the only one that had noticed her—the other hunters were right on her heels.

Without wasting a movement, she snatched a pair of swords and blocked the incoming strikes from the two men. She pushed them back and tossed the hook to Captain Palmer.

Finn made his way toward her and as he parried a strike, he tossed the hook's rope down to her. "You may want to get good with a grappling hook."

She scoffed. "I'll have you know I'm quite good with one."

Finn blocked a strike and pushed Francis away from his captain. "That so?"

"I'm quite good at everything I try." She snatched the hook and started prying at her bindings. "A grappling hook should be no different."

Kili held her own against the two hunters, but it was clear they weren't quite as skilled in a fight as Francis. She kept twirling between the two, leaving each man confused as to where to strike next.

Finn tried some unconventional strikes of his own. Slicing toward Francis' feet, he managed to throw him off balance. Two quick steps closed the distance and Finn threw an elbow into his head. It sent him reeling, but Finn couldn't capitalize, because the strike had done a number on his elbow.

"How we doing Kili?" he asked as he rubbed his elbow.

She kicked a bunch of sand into the hunter's eyes. "I seem to be doing a lot better than you."

She wasn't wrong, but he wasn't going to admit that. "Leaders are supposed to be more skilled than grunts."

"Two grunts have to equal a leader, though."

"Do you think you and I could take Captain Palmer?"

"No!" Captain Palmer piped up before Kili could respond.

Trigger, still entirely bound, pounced onto one of the hunters Kili was engaged with. He got him to the ground and lashed out with a series of head-butts that left the guy laid out and bloody.

Kili focused on the lone hunter and whirled each sword in her hands. "Thanks for the assist, Trigger."

Trigger was muffled by the gag in his mouth. "Think about it as a proper apology, girly!"

A flurry of slashes sent the man she was fighting on the back foot. Her quick movements managed to make even Captain Palmer look novice in comparison. She wasn't sword fighting, she was dancing with swords in her hands.

The hunter had no clue how to deal with her. "Francis, this girl don't fight natural!"

"Quit yer moaning! Kill her!" Francis growled.

Francis inched toward Finn yet again, but something was different. It felt the same as when Shad had started to pull back against Captain Palmer in Embar. Francis had something planned, but Finn had no idea what it might be.

"What's wrong, Francis? Getting tired?" Finn said.

Francis smirked. "Tired of yeh."

He pushed his blade against Finn's, but he was moving in a strange way. The traitor wasn't trying to push his sword toward Finn, he was trying to angle his wrist. Trigger launched into Francis from behind, sending all of them sprawling to the floor just as—

-BANG!-

The scent of fresh gunpowder filled the air, but Finn had no idea who had taken the shot, or even where the gun was. Tobi was free now, but he was busy untying the others. For a moment, Finn could have sworn he spotted that islander girl they saved earlier dash toward the other huts, but there was no way she had a gun.

Finn nodded to Trigger. "I guess I gotta thank you

too, Trigger."

"No problem, lad!"

Francis made it to his feet and prepared to strike Trigger, but Finn blocked it. That's when he spotted Francis's torn sleeve and the smoke trailing from it.

He had some kind of gun on his arm.

He took a few more swings at Finn as Trigger rolled away from the conflict. They clashed again, but Francis started angling his other wrist right toward Finn's face.

He closed his eyes—

-BANG!-

—but he wasn't dead.

Francis' arm had been pulled toward the ground by Finn's grappling hook. A grappling hook that was held in the hands of Captain Palmer.

"Told you I knew what I was doing." Captain Palmer smirked as she pulled the rope hard, sending Francis to the ground. "Now you can't hold our encounter with Shad over me, savvy?"

Kili placed a foot on the hunter she'd been fighting. She flashed Finn a thumbs up as she tried to catch her breath. "Looks like the losers are all tuckered out."

Finn pointed his sword at Francis. "So what do we do with them?"

The hunter that Trigger had taken out was back on his feet with his sword in hand. "Unhand them, or—or I'll—"

The hunter stopped when he felt the slight jab of a spear. He turned to face many of the inhabitants of the village with a series of glowing spears in hand.

They really did have access to more tech than Finn could have ever thought. He had a feeling the crew was feeling pretty lucky they had befriended the islanders.

"You five are going to tie all the men up," Captain Palmer pointed to the five additional crew members she had brought along. "Take them back aboard the Albatross, and then come on back. Each of you will take turns on lookout."

The elder stepped forward from the group. "We will give you some of our people to keep watch with your men. We apologize for allowing such violence to befall you on our land."

The fight wasn't the fault of the islanders, but they all looked as if it was. It was wonderful that they were so welcoming, but Finn couldn't help worrying about someone more manipulative paying them a visit. It was possible that they were too trusting, but maybe that was just another misconception he held.

"We thank you, elder. The rest of us are going to get some rest now." Captain Palmer turned to her crew. "The elder has been kind enough to provide us with beds and we will make sure we use them. We'll need the rest for what tomorrow holds."

"Aye, Captain."

When Finn tried to follow everyone into the hut, Captain Palmer put a hand on his chest. "Nice job there, kid. I owe you my life—yet again. That's an accolade not many can claim."

"You would have done the same."

"No." Finn cocked his head in confusion, as the captain smiled. "I would have done it better."

"I'll take what I can get." He gave her a final look as she headed toward the group of islanders that still lingered. "Good night, Captain Palmer."

chapter 19:

Crocodiles are Jerks

"Finn—Finn!" A sudden shake roused him from his short sleep. "Get up, we've got a problem."

Kili was leaning over him, a sight that he would have welcomed most days, but her face told him something was seriously wrong.

"Kili? Another one?" Finn rubbed his eyes and roused Bug. "Already?"

There wasn't enough sleep in the world to make Finn feel well-rested. He was lucky that he wasn't all that banged up from the previous night, but it had still taken a lot out of him. Despite worries of any other issues, Finn was out as soon as he hit his bed.

"I said the same thing." She handed him a canteen. "Apparently, it's just the life of a pyrate or something like that, that's what Fortune said."

"It's Captain Palmer." He took a sip of the cool water and his gruff voice smoothed out. "She'll get mad if she hears you calling her Fortune."

"She told me I could call her that. Hurry up and let's go."

"You sure you don't want to join me for another five minutes of shut-eye?"

His face get hot as soon as he finished speaking. He hadn't meant anything by the question, in fact, it was really just Finn trying to get more rest. There was nothing he could do, so he braced himself for the taunting he assumed was coming.

"As tempting as that is—purely because I could use more sleep and absolutely no other reason—it's a big problem."

"Thank you for that very specific clarification." Finn rolled out of bed. "When don't we have big problems?"

"Not a morning guy, huh?"

Finn and Bug followed Kili out of the hut and caught up with the rest of the crew. They were looking out toward the ocean. The big problem was apparent right away.

Off in the distance, two ships were headed straight for the island. It looked like there was a third ship even further at sea, but it was impossible to see if it was headed his way without a scope.

"Yeah," Finn pointed a finger. "That looks like a problem."

Captain Palmer gave him a side-eye. "Nice of you to join us, stowaway. That is indeed a problem. Our problem." She pulled a scope from her belt and peered through it. "Just as I thought, it's the Blues and—"

The captain's pause sent a feeling of unease around the crew. "What is it?"

"It's the Blues—alongside Poseidon's Deceit."

"I might just be tired still, but Poseidon's Deceit? You mentioned them to Sig, right?"

Captain Palmer sighed and shut her scope.

Trigger nudged Finn. "Jonas."

"That Silver-Tongue jerk from Bridger?"

"That's the one."

One night of excitement was more than enough. Finn had barely managed to rescue the crew when it came to one threat. Two additional threats weren't going to make getting the diadem any easier, especially if Finn was stuck fighting Wade again.

"Great." Finn turned toward the temple in the distance. "What's one more asshole thrown into the mix?"

"That's enough." Captain Palmer turned to face the temple as well. "The kids are with me. You both more than proved your worth last night. The rest of you will remain here and buy us time. Trigger, Tobi, Smiley, you up for it?"

The three men couldn't have been any more different from one another, but they got along like they'd been lifelong friends. Smiley didn't strike Finn as the kind of guy to fight in, but he melded into the crew with ease. None of them looked concerned about what was likely an impending battle.

"Yeh picked the right men to come ashore with yeh." Trigger smiled and punched Tobi's arm. "I can't speak for the ironically named one, but the two of us can take a hundred men each, easy."

Tobi cracked his knuckles. "I was gonna say fifty, but that works too."

"You guys are animals." Smiley stared at Tobi and Trigger. "I like it."

Captain Palmer turned around with a smirk on her face. "That's the confidence of the Albatross, but I'd like you to send someone to the ship to get yourselves some reinforcements. One of the groups Walker will have separated the crew into, savvy? We have no idea what kind of mood our guests will be in."

That seemed like a strange decision, as then the ship would have fewer people guarding it. Finn knew better than to question her, so he assumed there had to be some reason behind her thinking. Perhaps the ship had defences he didn't know about, or maybe there was some strange pyrate code against attacking unmanned ships.

Trigger and Tobi nodded. "Aye, aye."

"Smiley, talk to the islanders and see if they'll help. Inform them that the ships on the horizon will be coming to harm the people of their island. The more hands we have, the better."

"Aye, Captain."

She looked at Finn and Kili as the others rushed off. "Oh, fair and pure ones, This could be dangerous. Do you want to leave Bug here, or have him brought back to the ship?"

"He proved his worth just as much as either of us last night." Finn gave Bug a proud nod. "He sticks with us."

The poor dog had finished the night with a bit of a limp, but he seemed to be back to normal. It was a moment where Finn wished he could hear his friend's thoughts. Bug could have been in pain, but was just too much of a tough pup to show it. His biggest issue just looked to be the island heat.

"If we aren't careful, the little guy's going to become the ship mascot." Captain Palmer nudged him with her boot. "Come along."

The islander woman the crew had saved rushed toward them. "You are leaving for the treasure?"

Captain Palmer studied her. "Ximena. Aye, we are."

Kili may have come from the other side of the world, but her name wasn't anywhere near as foreign as Ximena. It was a unique name that fit with a unique woman. Finn hadn't had the chance to speak to her after the commotion, but he was glad to see her up and well.

"Please allow me to come with you—I will guide you. The jungle is not safe if you do not know the way. We are all surprised this one came out of it alive last night," Ximena said as she gestured to Finn.

"Oh, good." Finn looked toward the nearby jungle.

"Not only could we have been killed by a bunch of pyrate hunters, but we also should have been killed by some animals."

"Or one of the many poisonous plants."

Finn blinked a few times. "So, we're bringing her, right?"

It would have been so easy for him to have stepped into or touched a poison plant while stumbling in the dark. All he could think about was just how close he or Bug had come to being done in by a patch of flowers.

Captain Palmer put a hand on her shoulder. "I can't promise your safety within the temple, but we would appreciate it if you showed us the way."

Ximena put a hand on the captain's shoulder in return. "Then I will show you the way. I am not worthy of setting foot in the temple anyway."

Kili looked up the hill. "No one told me I'd have to go on an uphill trek through the jungle."

Usually, Kili's complaints would have annoyed everyone around, but it was a fair complaint. The heel was steep, almost like a miniature mountain was erected just for the temple. The incline mixed with the heat wasn't going to be an ideal combination.

Finn put the dreaded trek out of his mind and shrugged. "Just think of the gold."

By the time they crested the first hill of their journey, every one of them, save for Ximena, was dripping with sweat. Everyone breathed a sigh of relief when they came to the top of the hill, and then nearly fell over when they realized it was only the first of two huge hills.

"*Join the pyrates*, I thought—*there'll be gold*, they said. I just forgot to think about the journey *to* the gold." Kili looked down at her sweaty figure. "A lady should never have to sweat like this."

Ximena giggled. "You start to get used to it."

"Remind me to ask for one of your outfits when we

get back to the village."

The thought of Kili in the skimpy outfit Ximena had on distracted Finn for a moment. The clothes suited Ximena, but on someone like Kili, it might look more like a costume she might don for a show.

The pull of danger brought Finn's sight back toward the shore. "We need to pick up the pace if we even want to have a crew to bring the treasure back to."

"If you want to run the rest of the way, feel free." Kili slapped his back. "We'll meet you there."

Captain Palmer looked toward the shore. "He's right. Everyone, pick up the pace."

"Okay, but," Kili moved ahead and held a hand out toward a wide river with raging waters. "How the heck are we supposed to get through that?"

"Very carefully." Ximena didn't waste any time. "Dangerous river."

She waded into the rushing waters and made her way to the opposite side. Whatever made the waters dangerous didn't seem to be much of an issue for Ximena. She looked back for a moment and waved for the rest to follow before she headed through the trees.

"We aren't going to do that are we?" Kili asked.

"If we can find a way across that won't soak us, no," Captain Palmer replied.

Finn looked on either side of the river, one side looked like it dropped off, and the other side went on for who knows how long without thinning out. Going around wasn't going to be an option.

He was caught off guard when Bug rushed toward the riverbed. His hair was on edge and his barks were mixed with vicious snarls, but there wasn't a thing in sight.

"Bug, get away from there. Last thing we need is you slipping in there." Bug ran back to Finn, but it the fur on his back was still on end. Finn pulled his grappling hook from his belt. "Glad this thing is getting its fair share of use. You guys see anything for me to hook this on?"

"No way." Kili stepped back. "We are not relying on a flimsy piece of rope to hold us while we cross the river."

The way Kili reacted, Finn would have guessed she had a secret fear of water. Her concern was too much for her to only be worried bout wet clothes. It was the perfect time for some teasing, but Finn was more concerned with the rival vessels.

"We need to cross somehow." Finn looked at the approaching ships and then back to Kili. "It's either this or you can wade through the river and do the rest of the hike with soggy boots. We'll go one at a time."

Captain Palmer had already approached the riverbed and she rose a finger toward the other side. "See if you can hook onto that root sticking out there."

Finn approached and spotted the curled root of a tree jutting out near the edge of the opposite side of the river. It looked thick enough to not snap but thin enough for the hook to latch onto.

"Worth a shot." He whirled his grappling hook around and after a couple of attempts, he got the hook to latch onto the root.

Captain Palmer crossed her arms. "You need to work on your aim."

"That's a long toss. I got it didn't I?" Finn pulled the rope tight and tied it to a nearby sturdy tree branch. "Kili, you first. You're the lightest."

"As much as I trust you," she said. "I am not going to be the first one to climb across the river."

Captain Palmer took her hat in hand and hopped up onto the rope. She wrapped her arms and legs and shimmied across. It took a little while, but she managed to make it across without any issue. The branch held well, and so did the root on the opposite side.

She hopped down to the other side. "Not a problem. Kili next, bring Bug if you can. I'm going to scout ahead a bit—see where Ximena got to. I'll make sure we don't have any other fun little obstacles."

Kili gave the rope a nervous look before she hopped up and wrapped herself around it. "Put Bug on my stomach."

Finn gave her a look as he picked Bug up. "Go slowly."

"I'll keep him safe."

"Or will he keep you safe?"

"Shut up."

Finn put Bug on her stomach and Kili began her slow shimmy. A strong breeze rushed by, shaking the rope, and sending her into a panic. After a moment to compose herself, she tightened her body around the rope.

Bug had no idea what was going on. He kept turning his attention from growling at the river to licking Kili. Whatever was bugging him, it wasn't enough to keep him from providing a bit of moral support.

Kili made it to the other side and took a deep breath. "Alright, your turn."

"I'll do it in record time," Finn said as he hopped up onto the rope.

He had no problem shimmying across, but Bug was unsettling him. Kili picked him up to try to calm him, but he kept barking. The further along he got, the louder and quicker Bug barked.

Finn paused for a second. "What is going on, Bug?"

He found out what was up when a huge crocodile jumped out of the water and snapped at Finn, sending him and what was left of the rope to the waters below.

For a moment, he had no clue what had just happened. Kili screamed, but what she was saying was muffled by the rushing water. A dip in the river would have been refreshing after the stifling heat, but the sudden splash shocked the air out of his body. If he didn't find the shore quick, he was going to drown.

When he tried to get out of the water his foot was stuck on something. He prayed it was wedged under a rock, and not the mouth of a crocodile.

Finn reached a hand out of the water, hoping Kili would take it. Someone grabbed Finn's hand and yanked him up onto the shore. He gasped for air as he looked toward Captain Palmer and Ximena. They must have come back when they heard Kili scream.

"Thanks." Finn managed to squeak out as he reclaimed his now shortened grappling hook.

"I'm not letting you drown on my watch," Captain Palmer said with a wink. She stood up and looked toward the temple. "I don't think there's anything else between us and that temple—besides that last hill."

Ximena nodded. "You are correct."

"Oh, great." Kili rolled her eyes. "Another hill."

The loud hiss of a crocodile followed by the gnashing of teeth came from behind them. Finn turned his attention back to the river in time to see a crocodile barreling toward him.

He scuttled backward on all fours, but there was no chance he was escaping it in time. His hand met the hilt of his sword, but his awkward position prevented him from pulling it. The crocodile snapped inches from Finn's face, but it stopped completely and let out one of the most pained screeches Finn had heard an animal make.

The hot sun was glinting off of two steel blades, now covered in crocodile blood. The creature whipped back around and rushed into the water while the trio scrambled away from the water.

"Did you guys—just stab a crocodile?" Finn asked.

Kili's lip curled. "In both eyes. Poor thing."

"Poor thing? That *poor thing* almost had me for breakfast."

Captain Palmer scoffed. "Probably would have given him gas. Everyone up. We need to keep moving."

Ximena tip-toed toward the riverbed with her hands raised. "Everyone be quiet. We must back away slowly."

They turned toward the river and spotted five different crocodiles, two still in the water, and three on the edge of the shore.

They were giving the group a look more unsettling than anything Finn could have imagined. He wasn't sure why Bug had stopped barking, but he had a feeling that Bug could sense the danger of the situation.

It felt like a lifetime had passed as they took slow steps backward. The crocodiles didn't move an inch, but Finn knew that if they wanted to, they'd be on the group in seconds.

Once the small lip of the shore separated them from view, Ximena turned around. "We should be okay. They won't follow us far from the water."

Now, Finn was thankful for the burning sun. His clothes would be dry in no time. "Maybe we should have just done what Ximena did."

"Are you kidding?" Kili's eyes went wide. "Did you see how many of those things were back there?"

Ximena shrugged. "I told you—very careful. Very dangerous."

Having a bit of clarification on what made the river dangerous would have been a big help. Complaining wasn't going to do much, but that didn't mean Finn didn't want to. The crocodile-infested waters were probably common on the island, and Ximena must have just assumed everyone was aware of the threat.

Finn sighed, "We know. We know."

"Everything turned out okay in the end. We don't have far to go." She pointed to what looked like a rarely travelled path. "We follow that up the hill, it keeps us away from poisonous plants."

"What about *more* crocodiles?"

"No more creatures."

"Would have been good to know about the creatures before," Finn muttered to himself

Kili tapped Finn. "If you whined like this when you first met Captain Palmer, I'm not surprised by how she treats you."

"How would you like to swim with the crocs?"

"Oh, stop it. You're completely intact." She flicked his forehead. "Aren't you supposed to be saying how it wasn't a big deal? You know, the typical macho act?"

He rubbed his head. "Aren't you supposed to be dancing and singing for people? Not being a constant pain in my butt?"

"You take that back. I am an absolute joy—"

Captain Palmer groaned, "Children. You are deeply and profoundly annoying me. Let's play a game where neither of you speaks until we reach the temple, savvy?"

Ximena turned to Kili and Finn. "I like that game."

What goodwill Ximena had left with Finn was dissipating. He had an image of her in his head, an image of a friendly island girl. Now, she was becoming more like a copy of Captain Palmer with her indirect sass.

Kili leaned into Finn's ear. "That traitor."

"Whispering counts!" Captain Palmer called.

Finn turned his attention back down to the shore. He was confident the crew could handle the Blues if they were anything like the ones he fought on Penny's vessel.

Jonas and his crew were a different story.

If every member was as skilled as Wade, they might be in for some trouble. Whether or not they made it to the treasure, a fight was coming fast.

chapter 20:

Man's Best Friend

The temple was a lot bigger up close, but not nearly as big as Finn expected. He figured that the ancient home of the diadem would be the size of a massive coliseum. Instead, it looked a lot more like a grand mausoleum, though it didn't have doors. Eventually, there'd come a time when he'd stop getting his hopes up.

"There better be—a hell of a lot of gold—in there," Kili said between deep breaths.

"We aren't here for the gold, remember? We're here for the diadem. Any gold we find is just an extra reward," Captain Palmer said as she removed her hat to use it like a fan. "Now how the hell do we get inside? Ximena, any ideas?"

Ximena shook her head. "I only know the way. I know nothing of the temple itself. I am sorry."

"No need to apologize, a guide that can't get us in is better than us being bested by nature on our own before we even get a chance at the diadem."

Captain Palmer had been kind to people before, but never to the degree that she was with Ximena. In most circumstances, she would have had more than a few snippy comments to toss at someone who forgot about the existence of crocodiles. Instead, she spoke to her as if the two had been friends in a past life.

"This is where I must leave you. I am not allowed to even look within the temple. My soul has been deemed impure and wicked. I would only taint the treasure within."

"Those people have filled your head with lies in the name of tradition and religion. It's not right."

Ximena hung her head. "A witch is the last kind of person allowed inside the temple."

Captain Palmer looked agitated, but not in an angry way. She didn't seem annoyed by Ximena at all. The fact that her people had filled her head with such a strange worldview is what was really bugging the captain.

"Witch or not, my crew would be lucky to have someone like you aboard, savvy?"

Ximena smiled again and cocked her head. "Savvy?"

"Oh—do you understand me?"

Ximena nodded. "Thank you, Captain Palmer." She turned to Kili and Finn. "Thank you, pure ones. May the Gods bless the remainder of your journey."

Ximena started back down the hill as if she hadn't just gone on a massive hike. Someone like her may not be allowed near temples, but she must have had plenty of practice getting around the island on her own. How she planned to get past the angry crocodiles was a mystery, but Finn had a feeling she'd be just fine.

"Let's have a look around, shall we, pure ones?" Captain Palmer laughed as she turned her attention back to the temple.

Kili rolled her eyes. "Let's not make that a thing."

Captain Palmer bowed. "Whatever the great, pure ones command."

Kili groaned and muttered something under her breath. Finn couldn't quite make out the words, but it almost sounded like she'd learned to complain to just herself.

The trio examined the stone walls of the temple. Intricate carvings flowed into a large crack between two huge stone blocks. It had to be a door, but the way to open it wasn't clear. Finn traced the carvings from the doors to two small openings on each side of the doorway. He bent over and looked in, but the hole housed only darkness.

"I have a horrible feeling we're going to need to stick our hands in these," Finn said.

"It's worth a try." Captain Palmer brought a hand to her chin. "Alright you two, get to it."

That was exactly what Finn had grown to expect from Captain Palmer.

Kili scoffed. "Why does it have to be us? Why can't you? Shouldn't you be willing to risk your life for your crew?"

"Risk *my* life for?"—Captain Palmer laughed— "You'll do it because I told you to."

"This temple better make me rich." Kili stomped to the opposite hole. "If I lose a hand, You're replacing it."

The thought of what might happen when they stuck their hands in the holes was what first jumped to Finn's mind. In all the stories he'd heard about the captain's exploits, one common theme was always found, traps. A dark hole could have had all manner of traps. Spikes, snakes, even simple crushing were all possibilities.

"I'd get you one of our finest hooks." Captain Palmer pull a hand inside the sleeve of her coat and wiggled it around. "Hell, if we do find some treasure, you can have one of solid gold. Who doesn't love a hook hand?"

Finn slid his hand in the hole. "Can we please stop talking about this, and just do it?" He felt a small handle and wrapped his hand around it. "You feel that?" Kili nodded. "Okay, pull."

They each pulled the handle and yanked their arms

out as the temple started shaking. Earthquakes weren't unheard of in Embar, but they were rare. The small ones they did have had nothing on the tremors radiating from the stone.

Kili fell onto her butt. "Did—did we break it?"

The doors glowed orange as they inched their way open. There could have been anything inside, but it looked to be nothing more than an empty room.

"Not broken,"—Captain Palmer peeked in the temple—"Opened. Let's get that diadem."

When the doors came to a halt the trio entered the temple, the only light aside from what leaked through the doorway shone through small holes near the ceiling. Like the outside of the stone temple, the inside architecture was intricate. If it weren't for the dull grey lining the walls, the room might almost look pretty.

Finn took a moment to study the room.

Something wasn't right.

The ground looked like it was sectioned off into groups of tiles, all raised slightly from where they ought to be. The carvings on the ground ran every which way, but they all led to the opposite side of the room where a small idol sat.

"Where's the treasure?" Kili asked.

"Last night, Smiley told me that one of the islanders mentioned trials which must be overcome to reach the diadem." Captain Palmer brought a hand to her chin. "This room must be one of those trials."

"Well, what are we supposed to do?" Kili tapped on the stone walls. "The room's completely empty. Nothing but stone."

Captain Palmer started toward the other side of the room. "That idol is the only thing out of the ordinary—" As she stepped on one of the raised tiles, it sank slightly. "Hmm."

Finn rushed forward and yanked the captain by the

back of her coat, pulling her to the floor.

"What was that for?" she asked.

-THUD!-

Captain Palmer got her answer when two stone blocks from opposite sides of the room smashed right where she had been standing.

"Eek."

The blocks bashed into one another with such force that Kili struggled to keep her footing. The loud clap of stone just about burst Finn's ears. The blocks didn't crumble when they met, meaning the trap was likely ready to be sprung a second time.

"You can't just rush into every single situation," Finn said, still wide-eyed. "We need to think this through."

"I'm a pyrate." Captain Palmer stood up and brushed her coat off. "Rushing into situations without thinking is the very definition of what I do."

"Wouldn't robbing and pillaging on the ocean be the definition of what you do?"

She looked like she had another witty retort loaded and ready to fire, but she somehow stopped herself from letting it leave her lips. "Quiet, stowaway. Let me try this *thinking*."

Now that Finn was back in her good graces, he had no issue prodding back. She'd always call him a nuisance, but somewhere deep down, it seemed like verbal sparring was even more fun than swordplay for Captain Palmer.

"A *thank you for saving my life—again* would be appreciated."

"You can't pass judgement on a person based on one bad day."

Finn pulled his attention back toward Kili. She had a horrified look on her face. None of them liked the idea of being smushed in an instant, but she looked like she hated it more than the others.

"The floor is pressure sensitive," Finn said as he inched toward the trapped floor. "Maybe there's a way across without stepping on the ground?"

"Like I said, the room's empty." Kili took a small step away from the trap. "Are there any little spots for us to step? How did someone even make this room without dying?"

Finn shrugged. "Fixing up boats is more my speed nowadays. I don't know much about stone."

"Is it possible that once you've set a trap off once, it won't trigger again? Then we could just throw something onto the triggers until we have a path to the other side, right?"

"Be my guest and step on that plate again if you want to test your theory out." He grinned at her. "I'll pull you back."

"My hero." She glared at him. "Fine. I'll try it. Same deal as at the tavern—you let me die and I'm haunting both of you."

Captain Palmer shared Finn's grin. "A spectre following me around would make for even more interesting tales."

Kili moved to the edge of the floor and stepped on the plate. Finn recognized the slight churning of the walls and pulled her back hard. She swung into Finn's arms, and the two few as the trap triggered once again—

-THUD!-

Kili puffed her cheeks. "So, my idea didn't work."

"No." Finn stared at the spot that was almost home to a Kili pancake. "No, it did not."

"Alright, *pure ones*—unhand each other before we suddenly run out of purity," Captain Palmer said.

They separated from each other, each a bit embarrassed. He didn't want to let Kili go, but he didn't know if it was from the fear that lingered in the room, or something else. With how tight she was holding him, the feeling was mutual.

Finn tried looking for anything he could catch his grappling rope on, but Kili was right. There wasn't even any form of decoration save for the carvings. The high windows might have been an option, but the first problem would be getting up to one, and the second problem would be moving to another one without falling.

Captain Palmer was staring at Bug with a hand on her chin. She gave Finn a mischievous look, and he knew precisely what she had in mind.

"No," Finn said before she even had a chance to speak.

Captain Palmer clicked her tongue. "You said the ground seems to be made up of pressure plates—"

"Captain Palmer—*absolutely not.*"

She sauntered toward Bug. "Clearly, each of us are far too heavy to make it across without setting off a trap."

Kili grabbed Finn's arm. "What are you two talking about?"

Captain Palmer crouched down and pet Bug. "This pup might be able to get across the floor without setting off a trap."

Finn shook his head. "No chance."

"What other options do we have?" she asked.

Finn took another look around the room, but the captain was right. The only hope they had at moving past this first trial would be to hope that Bug wouldn't trigger the traps. There had to be an answer, and someone light enough to travel through the room had to be it.

"Why don't we just test it?" Kili started to pet Bug as well. "You had enough time to pull me and Captain Palmer out of the way before the blocks hit. Let's put Bug on one of the plates, pull him off, and see if anything happens."

Finn stared down at his best friend. The fat little pup had no idea what was going on. He'd been spooked by the loud slams, but it already looked like he'd forgotten about the danger. Making him run across the room didn't feel right, but it seemed to be the only way to proceed.

"This has to be your call." Captain Palmer stood up with a softer expression and placed a hand on his shoulder. "He's your dog—your best friend."

Finn took a breath and then crouched down toward Bug. "The big blocks were pretty scary, huh?" Bug replied by licking his hands. "I need you to help us. We aren't going to get through here without you, but I need you to stay calm and trust me, okay?"

Bug let out a little bark. Whether that was his way of expressing he understood Finn or not was still undetermined. He was doing well the previous night until he ran to Kili instead of Captain Palmer.

"Okay. Here we go." He scooped Bug up and moved toward the raised floor. "If you sink, you come running back right away. Try to go slow and those big scary rocks shouldn't come out again." Finn hugged Bug tight and Bug showed his love with slobber-filled licks to Finn's ear. "I love you, buddy."

After crouching down, Finn set Bug on the first plate. He held on as long as he could, but there was no movement.

He needed to let go and hope for the best.

The silence in the room drove Finn's anxiety even higher, but he knew the others were feeling the same. Everyone had gotten attached to Bug.

Finn let go and leaned back.

The plate didn't move.

"I think we're in the clear," Captain Palmer said.

Finn's eyes darted back and forth from Bug to the walls of the temple. "Okay, boy. Back up." Finn stared at the second plate, but it didn't dip as Bug put his weight on it. "Bug, see the big shiny over there?" Finn pointed at the idol, and Bug looked at it with his ears raised. "Go get it, boy."

Finn stood up, his eyes darting all over the room to make sure everything stayed where it was supposed to. Kili stepped forward and placed her hand in Finn's. If every part of Finn's brain wasn't focused on the task at hand, he would have been grateful for the attempted emotional support.

Captain Palmer crouched down with a hand clenched. She'd never admit it, but she was cheering him on in silence. Everyone really did love that dog, whether they wanted to admit it or not.

"It's going to be okay," Kili whispered.

Bug happily trotted across the floor without a single hiccup.

As he approached the idol, the thought that the idol itself may be boobytrapped in some way crossed Finn's mind. All three of them held their breath as Bug hopped up and knocked the idol to the ground.

Arrows launched from the walls on each side of the idol—arrows that flew right over Bug. He had no concept of the danger that just flew over his head. He just sat there with a goofy grin on his face before letting out a bit of gas.

Kili squeezed Finn's hand and jumped up and down. "He did it!"

"Stay there, Bug. You are such a good boy," Finn said as he caught his breath.

With the idol knocked off its pedestal, the room started to glow a familiar orange. The pressure plates on the floor sank down. After a moment, they all raised up in unison to line up with the rest of the floor. The orange glow dissipated, and over by Bug, a stone wall slid open, revealing a new passage.

"So who's going to test the floor now?" Finn asked

"I think us ladies would do best to hang back and let our strapping young man take care of ensuring the room's safety," Captain Palmer said as she nudged Kili.

"Can't argue with that," Kili said.

Finn scowled and lined his feet up with the line where the pressure plates began. He took a breath and put his weight onto the first plate, but it didn't sink. He brought his other foot onto it and did a little hop, but nothing. He stepped onto the next plate and nothing happened once again.

"I think we're clear," Finn said. "The idol must have disarmed the traps."

The women waited for him to make it to the opposite side of the room before each making their way across one at a time.

Finn took the opportunity to wrap Bug in an even bigger hug than before. He knew Bug had no idea how much danger he was really in, but he was proud of his little hero nonetheless.

"Wait a minute," he said as he approached a plaque beside where the idol had been resting. He brushed away some dust. "To all seeking the treasure, light feet, a mighty sword, and pure faith are what you'll need to succeed."

"They really should have placed that plaque by the entrance or something," Kili stomped her foot. "That's so unfair."

"We figured it out, didn't we?" Captain Palmer slipped toward the passage. "Maybe not the intended solution, but the pyrate method is always best."

They all crowded around the dark opening. It was some kind of slide leading to the depths of the temple, and what would likely be the second trial.

Finn leaned forward, but he couldn't make out anything. "Let me guess, I should go first, because—" Before Finn could finish his sentence, a push sent him flying down the slide.

Between his shouts, he could hear the captain at the top of the slide, "What are *you* doing here?"

At first, Finn thought that the push had come from Captain Palmer volunteering him to be the first to go, but after hearing her words, he wasn't so sure.

His surroundings only grew darker as he slid further down. A slight lip in the slide caused him to tumble into what he assumed was the second trial.

Finn was in total darkness, but before he could do anything, an orange glow washed over the room. Torches that lined the walls started lighting, revealing a dusty room filled with cobwebs.

Finn whistled. "I need to get me some of whatever this orange stuff is."

The glow started to fade away when he realized that the walls of the room were lined with decaying corpses, each clutching a sword and an axe.

chapter 21:

A Face Full Of Ancient Dust

Finn knew he'd seen corpses before. Flashes from the night his mother was taken often popped into his head, but something deep inside had always kept that imagery hidden. The bodies in front of him were much creepier than any ordinary corpse. He couldn't pinpoint what it was, but something about their features didn't feel totally human.

"Creepy." Finn drew his sword as he surveyed the chamber.

"You alive down there, Finn?" Kili's voice echoed down the slide.

"Yeah, but it's pretty nasty down here."

Kili's sudden scream was followed by another female shout, and the sound of two bodies sliding on stone rushed toward Finn. The shout didn't sound like Captain Palmer. Similar, but not quite the same. He figured a stone slide wouldn't be enough to get the captain shouting if a near-death experience from two enormous stone blocks couldn't.

Kili landed hard on her butt, with Bug in her lap. Finn laughed at Bug's wide eyes as he put his sword back in its sheathe. "Nice of you guys to drop in."

Bug got one look around the room and rushed to a corner to cower in fear.

Kili rushed to her feet as she drew her sword. "Not now."

He re-gripped his blade. "Not now?"

The second person reached the bottom of the slide, sword already drawn.

It wasn't Captain Palmer.

It was her naval captain sister, Penny, and she didn't look thrilled to be in a dark cavern.

Rather than taking a tumble, she used the momentum to stride forward and point her sword right at Finn's throat. It was the kind of thing he expected to see Captain Palmer pull off, so the athletic talent and grace must have run in the family.

"Penny?"

"Hello again, Finn." she replied with a sly smile.

He let go of the hilt of his blade, and rolled his eyes. "Oh, so someone in your family actually can remember my name."

Penny looked back up the slide. "We don't have a lot of time. They're coming to—"

"You know her?" Kili cut in.

"Beat her and her crew up once. She's Captain Palmer's sister." Finn shifted his attention from Kili to Penny. "What do you mean? Who's coming?"

"You're Fortune's sister?" Kili asked, still more interested in Penny than their current situation.

"What's going on down there, honey?" An irritatingly familiar voice called from the top of the slide.

"All good down here," Penny twirled her sword in her hand before looking back up the slide. "Come on down."

He wasn't really sure what to expect from Penny from their brief meeting, but she seemed like she had a good heart. Despite being at odds with her sister in terms of life choices, the two cared about one another. That was why it was so odd to come to understand that she was working with Silver-Tongue.

Finn pulled his blade back out. "Don't tell me, is that jerk from—"

"Finn, listen." Penny moved as close as she could without getting stuck by the pointy end of a sword. "We need to hurry. The crew—"

Wade came barrelling down the slide next. He landed less elegantly than Penny had, but he avoided a hard tumble. Next down was Captain Palmer, followed close behind by Jonas. Everyone looked unhappy for entirely different reasons.

"I knew it was you," Finn said. "Captain Palmer would have made fun of me before she shoved me."

"Quite right." Captain Palmer confirmed.

Jonas took a step back as Finn moved in.

"Whoa. Easy there, lad." Jonas swirled his sword in the air. "Thanks to the Blues here, my men have the order to not kill any of your mates. If the three of us don't leave here with you, that is a *very* different story."

Penny didn't look like she was thrilled about the arrangement. It was possible she knew of Jonas' past with her sister, but then again, Finn had a feeling most women had an issue being near Jonas for more than five minutes. Finn gave her the benefit of the doubt and assumed Penny made a deal to avoid any loss of life— just like her sister would have.

Finn looked toward his captain, her furious eyes trained on Jonas. "Stand down, lad."

"So what are we looking at here?" Jonas did a circle of the room. "Looks like you did a great job with the first trial. Why don't you all get a move on figuring this one out while I spend a little quality time with Fortune?"

Captain Palmer shuddered as those words left his mouth. "You know this is only making me hate you more, right?"

"You can't have hate without a hint of love."

Captain Palmer blinked. It looked like her brain was about to start smoking. "I—you—that is—quite possibly —the stupidest thing I've ever heard."

"Denial," he scoffed. "Typical woman."

"I can only hope a trap somewhere in this temple absolutely decimates you."

"How crude."

"Total body destruction." She was in her own world. "Maybe a little decapitation or—ooh, maybe some castration."

Some people might have seen the way Captain Palmer spoke with Jonas and thought it was two old friends joking, but Finn knew better. Everything she was saying, she meant with every inch of her body. Jonas was as good as the dust that lined the chamber they were in.

Wade stepped toward the far end of the room where something akin to a shrine was set up. "Captain, there's something written over here."

"Hold on, Wade." Jonas poked one of the corpses with his sword. "Let's let the young ones check it for traps. Not like we need to do any heavy lifting here."

Wade turned and pointed his sword at Kili, but responded with a sword of her own. She had no idea who Jonas was and what his crew could be capable of. Finn didn't exactly know either, but he had a feeling it wasn't anything good.

Finn reached out and pushed her arm down as he stepped toward the shrine. "I've been the lamb for everything else, why not this too?"

The shrine broke the trend of the solid grey of the previous room by being covered in gold. It looked like Kili might get the treasure she was after, after all. There was a set of carvings on the wall above the shrine, but they were covered in dust. As Finn brushed it away, he could see that they weren't simple carvings, but instead simple words.

"The way to the treasure—is beyond your reach— prove your worth—against hell's greatest warriors." Finn read as he followed a line down to a skull resting on the shrine.

"The lad can read," Jonas said in surprise. "My crew could use some folks with some real brainpower. Maybe we'll snag him from you after all. A good-looking kid like that could be my protégé."

Kili scoffed. "Trust me, yours is the last crew he'd be willing to join."

Finn was compelled to move the small skull, thinking it would have a similar effect as the idol from the previous room. As he reached a hand toward it, he started shaking. The thought that anything at any moment could be a trap aimed to end his life lingered in the back of his mind.

When he knocked it to the ground, all was quiet. "Huh."

"What was that?" Jonas asked. "I've changed my mind, lad. Fortune can have you. Probably shouldn't disrespect the dead."

"Shut it, you moron," Captain Palmer snapped. "At least the kid's actually trying things. Brave pyrate Jeremiah Jonas has to send a boy to check if it's safe for him to advance. Imagine the tales told about you."

For the first time, it looked like the captain had struck a nerve. Before he could respond, a wave of orange light washed over the room.

Jonas' face scrunched. "What the hell was that? A temple like this has advancements?"

The snapping of bones and scraping of steel filled the room. The decaying bodies that lined the walls each sprang to life, their eyes all glowing a dark purple. Each warrior had a jagged sword in one hand and a rustic axe in the other. It was zombie creatures covered in moss and broken-down armour as far as the eye could see.

"You've gotta be kidding me," Kili said as she slid to the centre of the room.

Finn stared at a warrior that was double the size of all the others. It was still tucked within the wall behind the shrine, dormant. He counted his blessings that the enormous warrior hadn't come to life along with the others.

Each person backed to the centre of the room and held their swords out toward the warriors.

Finn bumped Captain Palmer. "Does that no-killing thing extend to ancient undead warriors?"

A warrior lunged toward the captain, but Jonas deflected the strike. Captain Palmer whirled under Jonas' sword and deflected a second sword strike before plunging her sword into the warrior's heart. After a brief screech, it burst into dust.

Captain Palmer smirked. "Send these bastards to the Locker."

The warriors screeched and rushed forward.

A fight was coming fast.

A fight Finn wasn't sure he was ready for.

It would have been easy for Finn to act as if he were brave at that moment. If he couldn't feel the fear radiating from the others trapped in the chamber with him, he probably would have. It was a different kind of fear from the last trial. They had control over the pace and could think things through. There was nothing they could do here except to react and push the attack.

Moving toward an approaching warrior, Finn deflected a sword strike. The warrior followed up with a sweep of its axe and it sent Finn's sword across the room. After ducking a series of swings, he rolled around the warrior and pulled his grappling hook from his belt.

"Anyone have any ideas?" Finn called, but all he

heard in response were the grunts and shouts of battle.

He tried to see how the others were dealing with the ancient warriors to find some kind of weakness, but his own warrior was back on him in no time. The attempt at seeing the others fight almost resulted in him losing his head, but he rolled out of the way again.

Finn threw the hook around the warrior's axe hand, and he dove behind the warrior, pulling the top over its opposite shoulder. It struggled against the rope, nearly sending him to the floor. When he got his footing, he pulled the rope as hard as he could, causing the warrior to drive its own axe into its head. The warrior crumbled into a pile of dust.

"These guys aren't so tough." Finn fell back to his butt to catch his breath.

Kili danced around a warrior. She twirled and dipped around each strike before sliding through the warrior's legs. Each time she would avoid a slash, she would return with a shallow cut of her own to the enemy.

"If anybody could help—that'd be great!" Penny called as a warrior backed her into a corner.

Finn rushed over, picking up his sword in the process, and drove it into what he hoped was the warrior's heart. As it turned out, striking something in a specific spot from behind was a lot harder than it looked. The warrior turned, one arm still pushing against Penny, and stared at Finn.

The warrior pulled an arm back and Finn knew what was about to happen. "EVERYBODY DOWN!"

An axe flew from the warrior's hand and everyone in the room hit the ground. Once the sound of steel on stone rang out, everyone jumped right back into their fights.

Jonas was the first to hop back to his feet, and after the quick parry of an incoming blade, he brought his blade through the heart of a warrior.

Finn had his own problems to deal with. A warrior was now standing over him, ready to land a killing blow. As it raised a sword, a segment of steel pierced through the warrior's chest and it exploded into dust, covering Finn. He coughed as he wiped the ancient dust from his face.

Penny stifled a laugh. "That's actually the grossest thing I've ever seen."

Finn puffed far too much dust from his mouth. It was as if he dove mouth-first into a farmers field and taken the biggest bite possible.

"Stitch is going to have a field day treating me." He rubbed his eyes. "What's the remedy for ancient creature dust?"

"Knowing how pyrate doctors operate, probably leeches." Penny prodded Finn's stomach. "She'll use them to get the remnants of the warrior's soul from your body."

"Great."

The chamber started to shake, and Finn's worst fear came to life. That huge warrior on the other side of the shrine was starting to get up. It was creepy enough, but once the creature's eyes snapped open, the purple glow was more menacing than any of the other warriors. As it stood up, it claimed each of its massive weapons.

Penny brushed shoulders with Finn, each with their swords held toward the warrior. To his surprise, Jonas did the same on the opposite side.

He bumped Jonas. "You're actually going to help for once?"

"What?" Jonas held his arms out. "If you die, who's going to be the first to try whatever other trials are in this place? I sure as hell am not."

"That sounds a lot more like the Jonas I've quickly come to hate."

"Careful, lad." Jonas gave him a playful elbow.

"You're almost starting to sound like a woman."

Finn took a look back at everyone else. They were either dealing with two warriors alone or struggling against just one. The big guy was going to be a problem, so Finn was glad to have some backup.

Penny raised an eyebrow. "Yeah, Jonas, I think your comment says more about you than it does about—"

The warrior let out a huge shriek before barrelling toward the trio. It swung a sword down, and despite Jonas and Finn blocking the strike, both of them started to slide back from the force of the attack. Penny ran along the warrior's opposite side, narrowly avoiding a huge slash from its axe, before disappearing completely.

"Climb the arm!" Jonas said.

Finn stared at Jonas with gritted teeth. "What?"

"Someone's either gotta get up to the head or the heart. I'll keep it busy down here."

Finn nodded and dipped underneath the warrior's sword. He hopped onto its arm and prayed it wouldn't sacrifice its own appendage to take one of them out. Inching his way up, he watched Jonas dodge a handful of vicious slashes.

Jonas wasn't amused by how long it was taking Finn. "Hurry up and get to its head, lad!"

"Do—you—want—to try?" Finn said as the warrior waved an arm around. Finn shimmied until he made it to the warrior's shoulder, but as he made it, Penny came into view as she climbed on the warrior's back. "What are you doing?"

"What are *you* doing?" she asked right back.

"Going for the head."

Penny pulled her sword and tried to push her sword through the back of the warrior's head, but it wasn't going through. Finn pulled his sword and tried, but he was having the same problem. If this warrior was once a person, no one would have made it out of a fight with it.

He looked down at Penny. "What now?"

She looked at Finn's grappling hook. "That."

She had the right idea. If he wrapped the hook around the warrior's neck, he could at least try to bring it to the ground. As if she read his mind, Penny hopped back to the ground and readied her sword. Finn straddled the warrior's shoulder and wrapped his hook around the thick neck.

Once it was secure he took a deep breath and hopped down toward Penny. "Coming at you!"

With one hard tug, the warrior fell off balance. It wasn't enough to tip it over until Jonas slashed at the warrior's ankles. Finn fell to the ground and looked up at the large warrior that was about to tumble on top of him.

Penny stepped forward and pointed her sword right where the warrior's heart would be. Before they were squished by the huge undead creature, her sword met the heart and it exploded into dust, once again covering Finn. She shuddered from suffering the same fate Finn had just moments ago.

Finn coughed. "Pretty gross, right?"

She started wiping the dust from her deep blue uniform. "Really gross."

"You two look like you need some maid service," Jonas said as he pretended to dust the air.

"Shut up, Jonas," The pair snapped at him.

Finn watched Wade jam his sword into a warrior he had wrestled to the ground. Unlike everyone else, Wade relished in the violence. He almost looked disappointed when the warrior turned to dust.

The group all looked around for more warriors, but all they found was a mix of dust and cobwebs. Finn tried to catch his breath, and he was glad he wasn't alone as everyone did the same. Every one of them needed a breather after an intense battle like that.

"You alright?" Captain Palmer asked Finn.

"I think so."

"We get 'em all?" Wade asked.

"I hope so," Penny said as she wiped sweat and dust from her brow.

Finn looked to the corner Bug had been cowering in to see the pup staring back at him with a goofy grin on his face. With how small he was compared to the warriors, they probably just assumed that the small furry creature was a big rat and left him alone. With the danger gone, Bug rushed in between Finn's legs.

"Good work on that big guy, Captain," Wade said before pointing his blade at Finn. "Those two wouldn't have been able to take it out without you."

"Aye," Jonas smirked. "That does tend to be the case, doesn't it?"

Finn cocked his head. "Is this guy for real?"

A stone wall by the shrine began sliding open. It was nice to have confirmation that they were done battling the undead. Still, if that was just the second of the trials, what the third might entail worried Finn.

"Looks like we're done here," Jonas pointed his sword at Finn. "Let's keep moving. You first."

To everyone's surprise, light flooded in from the new passageway. Finn sheathed his sword and led the way through the new passage. The musty smell of dust and death shifted to the clean scent of a jungle after a storm. The reason why became clear once Finn approached the edge of a cliff.

The details of the room didn't matter to Finn—not at that moment. What mattered was what sat right in the middle of the room. Across from him, on a lone stone pillar was a beautiful golden chest.

Chapter 22:

The Maelstrom Cave

"Well, ain't this a pretty sight?" Jonas said as he peered through the opening.

The room was a huge circle with an enormous water-filled pit. On one end, a waterfall poured from overhead into the water below. In the centre of the room was a thin stone pillar with a small ornate chest. That had to be the chest housing the artifact they were after.

Kili stepped beside Finn and looked up. "You mean we could have skipped all that if we had just found that opening and climbed down?"

Wade came up behind them. "And how would you expect to climb down from all the way up there?"

"I don't know," One of Kili's eyebrows twitched. "Why don't you mind your own business?"

"Watch your tongue," He wiggled his blade. "Or I'll cut it out."

"Try it." Kili stepped up to Wade and looked him straight in the eye. "I'm not afraid of you."

"You should be."

Kili had more than proven her ability to beat up a fully grown man, but Finn didn't need to see her go toe-to-toe with Wade. He'd dominated Finn with a staff back in Bridger, and something told him that Wade was just as capable with a sword or even his fists.

"Clearly we know who the hot-heads are here, huh?" Jonas laughed and pushed them apart, "Cool it. We've still got to find a way to get the chest."

"Nice to have some fresh air again," Captain Palmer said as she inched toward the cliff's edge. "I feel like breathing in ancient warrior dust is going to leave all of us with some kind of curse."

Penny made her way over to her sister. "I need to—"

Captain Palmer held up a hand. "I don't want to hear another word from you.

"I already told you, I'm only doing this because—"

"I don't care what that bag of bones wants." She stormed around the cliff. "You being a Blue is one thing, this is an outright betrayal."

Captain Palmer's words had stung Penny, anyone could have seen that. It probably would have taken a few giant warrior dust baths to replicate the look she had on her face. Dejected, she moved back toward the wall of the cave and looked out toward the chest.

"What was that all about?" Kili turned her attention back to Finn. "Any ideas on this one? Think your hook could reach?"

"No way." Finn put a hand on his grappling hook and looked out to the centre pillar. "It's way too short after that croc attack. Even if it could, there's nothing for it to catch onto."

"Whatever we do, we should push the big guy down there." Kili peered down to the swirling water below.

At first, Finn suspected that the sound of rushing water was coming from the waterfall. The more he inspected the cave, it became clear that the sound of the water was coming from the churning waters below. Vi had told Finn stories of Captain Palmer battling in the midst of a maelstrom, and the water below is exactly what he pictured.

"I'm not so sure that would be keeping with the no-killing rule."

"The water's gotta be going somewhere. He'd be fine —probably."

"That plaque in the first room mentioned faith. Are there any religious markings anywhere?" Finn asked as he looked around. "Another shrine?"

Kili pointed to Jonas and Wade on the opposite side of the room. "If there were any, someone would have said something by now. We're going to be stuck here all day aren't we?"

Penny rushed over with panic smeared across her face. "That is not an option."

Finn didn't know her well, but he could have told anyone that Penny was terrified. She'd seemed to be in a rush when she first landed in the second chamber, but all the action must have caused it to slip her mind. Whatever was wrong, the worry was back to the forefront of her mind.

"Why?" Finn asked.

Penny's voice morphed into a whisper. "No doubt, you spotted us on our way to the island, correct?" Finn nodded, and she continued. "There was a third ship. A ship full of violent killers. I don't know how they found out about the diadem, or why'd they'd even want it, but they were gaining on us as we made land."

"Between three crews, they shouldn't be a problem," Finn said. "Would they even risk weighing anchor near three other ships?"

Penny shook her head. "These aren't normal pyrates. The crew of the Poisoned Rose is something else."

Finn's eyes bugged out of his head at the mention of the Poisoned Rose. A run-in with them seemed like a once-in-a-lifetime opportunity, but if Penny was telling the truth, he'd have a chance at getting his answers.

"You've heard of them?" Penny asked

"They attacked my village when I was a boy."

Penny averted her gaze. "I'm sorry to hear that."

"Let them come. Like I said, three crews shouldn't have any issue, especially when we've got Captain Palmer."

"Finn, you don't understand." Penny grabbed his arm. "No one fights against the crew of the Poisoned Rose and survives. No one."

"No one—except your sister."

"She's not exactly typical."

The scraping of steel on stone echoed from the doorway they had come through. One of the most disgusting men Finn had ever seen stepped into the cave. The man reminded him of the villainous pyrates from Vi's tales, down to the silver fang that jutted up and hugged his top lip.

The man's yellow eyes scanned the room, his sight falling on Penny. "I'm glad someone thinks so highly of teh crew. We'll be sure teh make dis quick." He raised his sword. "SLAUGHTER 'EM ALL, YEH SCURVY DOGS!"

From behind the pyrate, other grizzled men with yellow eyes rushed into the room. Every one of them had axes and swords in hand. They were human, but somehow, they unnerved Finn more than the ancient warriors could have ever hoped to. As they ran toward Finn, they looked more like demon than men.

"Mendez." Penny readied her blade. "The crew— their weapons are poisoned. Whatever you do, don't let them cut you."

Chapter 23:

Finn Can Float

In a matter of seconds, the room had been flooded by bloody, yellow-eyed pyrates. Finn was thankful when the nastiest looking one, the one Penny called Mendez, rushed toward Captain Palmer. If anyone was going to be able to handle someone like that, it was going to be her.

The issue with Captain Palmer's famed rule became apparent as Kili and Finn struggled to knock out the twisted pyrates.

"Any tips for dealing with pyrates like these?" Finn asked.

Penny scowled. "Don't die."

Not being held back by the captain's rules, Penny launched forward and got to work cutting down the waves of the pyrates. They were tough opponents, but they were also wild savages. Penny was far more skilled than any of them. If that's how well trained the higher-ranked Blues were Finn wondered what would happen if the crew of the Albatross came up against multiple high-ranking captains.

Finn dodged around a few slashes and spotted Wade and Jonas tossing pyrates clean off the cliff. They all screamed as they dropped into the swirling waters below. Those two weren't showing off quite as much skill as Penny, but they looked like they were having way more fun than anyone else.

The clashing of Kili and her opponent grew closer until she set her back to Finn's.

"Mind if we switch?" she asked.

"Not at all."

They locked an arm together and spun, each slashing toward their new opponents as they went. Both of the enemies jumped back in order to avoid the slashes, but that was all Kili and Finn needed to turn the tide of their fights. They each started pushing the pace and pressured the pyrates back against the wall of the chamber.

Finn heard the approach of another pyrate and ducked a swing. The pyrate's sword cut through his crewmate, killing him without a second thought. He caught the ruthless pyrate with an elbow and stared at the death in front of him.

It was horrific.

Seeing the life leave someone's eyes.

He had a family at some point.

A brother?

A mother?

A father?

None of that mattered.

He was gone.

Finn spun around and clashed with the pyrate, but he was stronger than the last. In just a few strikes, he had pushed Finn to the edge of the cliff. There wasn't enough time for anyone to make it over to help him. He was about to take a plunge into the swirling waters below.

The pyrate slashed Finn's sword away and kicked him square in the chest, sending him sprawling backward over the pit.

He closed his eyes and waited for his watery fate.

"FINN!" Kili screamed.

Something didn't feel right.

Finn had fallen, but he hadn't fallen very far.

"What the—?" Finn muttered.

He opened an eye to see the pyrate who had struck him staring at him in shock. There was nothing below Finn, but he felt a slight stone ramp below him. The pyrate took a careful step forward and he too was walking on air.

That had to be what the plaque meant by faith.

Finn looked back and realized he was in a perfectly straight line from the open passageway to the chest. He tapped his sword on either side of him, and sure enough, the invisible bridge only ran wide enough for two men to stand side by side.

"Evil magician," the pyrate spat. "Die!"

The pyrate stabbed at Finn, but he parried it as he got back to his feet. The two clashed blades once more as Finn inched his way toward the chest.

Out of the corner of his eye, he spotted other pyrates from the Poisoned Rose taking note of his fight. One tried sending a foot out onto what he must have thought was some kind of invisible ground lining the pit. He barely managed to catch himself, but Bug came bounding up behind him and jumped at him. Bug bounced back to safety as the pyrate fell into the swirling waters below.

"Atta boy, Bug," Finn said under his breath.

The pyrate Finn was locked in combat with outclassed him in every way. Whoever he was, he'd been living the life of a pyrate for quite some time. The flash of his yellow eyes between each strike terrified Finn. It was the most scared he'd ever been, but he wasn't planning on dying until he knew what happened to his mother.

Finn blocked a strike and hopped backward to the centre pillar. As the pyrate ran toward him, he reached a hand back and grabbed a handle on the chest. He prayed it was locked as he swung it at the pyrate's face. It smashed right into him, sending him sprawling off the cliff and to the waters below.

"He'll—be okay, right?" Finn looked around. "I really hope Captain Palmer didn't see that."

He snapped the chest open, and as they were told, it housed a beautiful golden diadem. That wasn't all, it also housed a hefty share of gold and jewels. He shut the chest and looked out to the fight.

A few pyrates were trying to figure out where to step to get to the centre, but none of them had paid enough attention. They might have been vicious brutes, but they sure were dumb. Not a single one thought to use a weapon to find the ramp as Finn had.

"What's wrong? Afraid to jump?" Finn taunted.

In response, the pyrates trying to make it to the centre pulled their pistols and started taking shots at him. Something caught him across the face, and for a second, he thought he was going to die. Finn ducked around the other side of the pedestal for cover and tried to control his breath.

His face was bleeding, but he hadn't been hurt bad. A shot must have just grazed the side of his face. It was way too close for comfort.

He wiped the blood away with the sleeve of his shirt. "I had to open my mouth."

The entire room started to shake, and enormous boulders began falling from the opening above. Moving the chest must have triggered it. Finn barely managed to catch himself from falling, and from the looks of it, that was the case for many of the others. The shaking caused an entire section of the far wall and floor to crumble into the pit below.

Captain Palmer was able to rush to safety before the ground beneath her crumbled. A large crack was forming, so she must have taken that as her cue to move to steadier ground.

Finn's attention shifted back to his own footing as a huge boulder crashed through the invisible ramp, revealing it in the process.

"How the hell am I supposed to get out of here now?" he asked as avoided a few smaller falling rocks.

Finn looked down at the small pillar. It seemed to be well-crafted, but there was no way it was standing upright without any additional support, not after all the shaking.

He had to be missing something.

Finn put the chest under his free arm and started walking along the edge of the pillar, dangling his sword. As he fell in line with the newly formed exit, his sword bumped into something.

Another invisible bridge.

He ran his sword across the ground to the opposite side. There was no telling how far the bridge would lead, but it looked like it led to the cliff face on the outside of the chamber. With his sword on the ground in front of him, he inched his way across the bridge.

"Captain Palmer, Kili, this is our way out!" Finn yelled.

Kili pushed a pyrate back and made a break for the section of the room that had crumbled away. The chaos provided her enough cover to make it over to Bug on her way.

She snatched him up as she ran. "This better work."

She hopped right into the centre of the gaping hole in the cave and landed on the invisible bridge. Finn could see her taking heavy breaths, even from near the centre of the room.

Captain Palmer did the same from the opposite side

of the gap, and they each held a sword out to keep the pyrates from jumping. Penny, Jonas, and Wade all made their way across the gap as well, taking some pyrates out in the process.

Everyone held their breath as the pyrates of the Poisoned Rose closed in. The monstrous crew stared daggers into each of them, looking for a way onto the bridge without getting skewered.

"What now?" Penny asked.

"I'm thinking," Captain Palmer said.

Finn wasn't sure why the pyrates hadn't pulled out their pistols, but he wasn't about to ask. He just hoped all the shots that were directed at him were the only ones they had available.

As Finn continued across the bridge, Wade and Jonas both moved toward him, putting themselves in between him and his friends. Even if they hadn't already been assholes to Finn, he would have known they were up to something. Wade grabbed Kili, sending both her sword and Bug to the floor of the bridge.

"Hey! What the hell?" Kili said as her sword tumbled to the water below.

"This couldn't have gone any better." Wade held a knife to her throat as Jonas pulled his sword and sauntered toward Finn. "Gimme the chest, lad. I don't want to kill you. It'd get my clothes dirty, and then I'd have to find someone to clean them—I might have to buy a whole new set—it'd be a whole thing."

Finn lifted his sword as Jonas approached, the tips of their blades touching. "Do we really need to do this now?"

"Yes, we do. You can't take me in a fight, lad." He jutted a thumb toward Wade. "You couldn't even beat him. Put your sword away, hand me the chest, and you'll all have a chance to live. That is—if you can get away from those nut-jobs."

"I think I could take you."

"Doesn't really matter, does it, Wade?"

"No, Captain." Wade brandished his knife. "Not one bit."

"Don't, Finn," Kili said. "We'll get out of this."

Finn looked at Kili's pained face, and then at Jonas' smug grin. There wasn't anything he could do. He set the chest on the ground, pushing it slightly with his foot.

"That's a smart, lad." Jonas snatched the chest. "No shame in losing, except you'll have to remember how badly I defeated you for the rest of your—" He looked toward the crowd of pyrates. "Short life."

Jonas started moving back toward Wade, and Finn inched toward them. All he needed was a single opening to help Kili and take back the chest.

Captain Palmer looking down at Bug caught his eye. Bug's hair was standing on end, his teeth were bared, and Finn knew what was about to happen.

Nobody messed with Bug's humans.

He started barreling toward Jonas—

Ran right through Wade and Kili's legs—

It was time for Bug to pounce.

"Captain, watch out!" Wade shouted.

Jonas started to turn, so Finn slashed at him. He parried the slash with ease and stuck Finn in the shoulder with his sword.

"AAARGH!"

Getting stabbed wasn't fun, but Finn had bought Bug enough time.

He wrenched his body down, pulling the sword out, and sending Jonas off balance. Bug hopped up and threw his weight into the pompous captain. It wasn't enough to send him off, but it was enough to send him reeling.

Finn launched another slash, giving Jonas no choice, but to take his chances in the swirling waters below. He managed to control his fall, and he hit the water in an elegant dive. It felt good to get some payback, but now the diadem was gone.

Captain Palmer launched a wicked punch into the back of Wade's head, sending both him and Kili forward. Kili tumbled over the side of the bridge but managed to grab onto the ledge.

Wade looked down to the pit. "Captain—" Without another word, he launched himself into the water below.

Finn rushed to where Kili was hanging, just in time for her to lose her grip and fall. Finn threw half of his body over the bridge and caught her by her wrist.

"AH!" The pain from his wound caused him to lose grip with one hand. "I've got you."

He could feel something tugging on the back of his pants, and he knew Bug was doing everything he could to keep them from falling over the side.

Finn gritted his teeth. "I think—Bug's helping too."

Kili looked up at Finn. "Let me go."

"No. We're all getting out of here."

Finn didn't have the strength to pull her up with one arm. There wasn't anything he could do. It was possible she could survive the fall, but he hadn't seen anyone who fell into the water resurface at all.

"It's okay, Finn. I promise I'll—"

Captain Palmer butt in and grabbed Kili's arm. "Enough of that, get up here." The captain and Finn pulled Kili back onto the bridge. "You kids are so dramatic."

Finn raised an eyebrow. "That coming from you?"

He was surprised when Kili hugged him. "Thank you."

"Guys?" Penny called. "We've got another problem over here!"

Mendez stepped in front of his crew. "WHAT ARE YEH WAITING FOR?! DER'S ONLY ONE LASS!"

He was frothing at the mouth. "KILL DEM! KILL DEM ALL, OR IT'LL BE YER HEADS!"

chapter 24:

A Hasty Goodbye

The yellow-eyed pyrates were frothing at the mouth, anticipating their next kills. All of them were shouting different things, but there were too many voices to make anything out.

Penny held her sword out to one side of the bridge and Captain Palmer's sword to the other. "Time to go!"

"What's the rule for dealing with these guys?" Finn asked.

"Do what you must if you can stomach it." Captain Palmer narrowed her eyes. "These monsters aren't human."

Finn sighed as he remembered the pyrate he tossed into the waters, "That would have been good to know *way* earlier."

Kili snatched Bug and they all headed across the bridge as the grotesque pyrates made their leaps. Penny caught one with a slash in mid-air as she tossed the captain's sword back to her. Captain Palmer spun around and caught another with a slash as he attempted another jump onto the bridge. The group rushed toward the opening, with Penny pulling up the rear.

With no one to hold the pyrates back, they swarmed the bridge and chased after the group. The sickening thumping and screams of the pyrates should have terrified Finn, but whether it was shock from his wound or adrenaline, Finn felt alive.

He was living his dream.

As they made it to the opening of the cave, they found a small staircase carved into the face of the cliff. It twirled down and dipped behind the edge of the cliff, but if it was some kind of victorious escape route, it was possible it would lead down to the beach.

Captain Palmer stopped and grabbed Kili. "You're first. Run ahead to the village as quick as you can. If it's safe enough, inform Trigger and Tobi we're leaving. We need to get our crew back to the ship. We'll meet you at the boats."

"Yes, Captain." She turned to Finn. "I'll take good care of Bug." In seconds, Kili had disappeared down the stairs.

The shouting of the pyrates was gaining on them in hurry, but Penny was ready to act. She pulled a pair of flintlock pistols from her belt and aimed them at the wave of pyrates.

- BANG! -

She managed to hit one of them, and all the others dove to the ground. Rather than jumping back to their feet, they all took their time, hoping to not become the next victim. It was a smart idea as Penny had tossed her first pistol and was now honed in for her next shot.

"What about us?" Finn asked.

"You two make a beeline for the boats," Captain Palmer said as she stepped forward. "I'll hold them back."

"No." Penny grabbed her hand, still with one pistol held toward the pyrates. "Let me make things right. You're my little sister. It's my job to protect you, not the other way around." She winked at her sister. "Besides, they wouldn't dare kill an official of the Royal Navy. It would place their ship on every bounty board across the seas. Go!" The captain hesitated a moment, but Penny wasn't having it. "Go, now!"

She might have been mad at her sister, but Captain Palmer didn't want to leave her behind. If the captain was the only person to ever survive an encounter with those brutes, the odds weren't in Penny's favour. Though if anyone had a chance to replicate Captain Palmer's feat, Penny probably had the best chance.

The pyrates broke back into a sprint.

- BANG! -

The second shot didn't stop them all again, but it did slow them as they tripped over their fallen comrade. Penny tossed her other pistol and pulled out her blade.

"We can all stay—" Finn began.

"Let's go," Captain Palmer said as she took one last look at her sister.

Finn knew it wasn't the time to argue, and he followed on Captain Palmer's heels as the clashing of steel sounded behind them.

For a moment, he could have sworn he heard Penny's voice. "Take care of her, Finn."

- BANG! -

"Is she going to be alright?" he asked through laboured breaths. "That third sho—"

"She better be." Captain Palmer's voice was filled with concern, but concern soon turned into annoyance. "Neither of us even got the blasted diadem."

"I meant the—"

"I know you meant the bloody gunshot," Captain Palmer snapped.

Usually, Finn would have taken her tone personally, but he couldn't blame her. Leaving her sister behind to battle an entire crew couldn't have been an easy thing to do.

"I'm sorry." she said.

Finn had a feeling that those words were quite rare for pyrates.

The stairs went on for what felt like forever. They were slick as if the ocean had sent a wave high enough to coat them all, making each step a difficult task. The sounds of fighting disappeared far sooner than Finn expected, but he had a feeling that didn't mean Penny had fallen.

When they finally stepped onto the beach, they spotted a curious sight. The only ships beside the Albatross were Poseidon's Deceit and Penny's ship.

Where was the Poisoned Rose?

"So, they knew better than to dive into a fight with three full crews." Captain Palmer scoffed. "The rest of the Poisoned Rose may be nearby, be on guard."

They made their way across the beach to where the rowboats were and looked over to the islander village. Bodies littered the ground, some islanders, some of Captain Palmer's crew, a few navy sailors, and some of the crew from the Poisoned Rose.

Finn was relieved to see some of the islanders from the previous night standing by the edge of their village.

Something even more relieving was seeing Trigger, Tobi, Smiley, Kili, and Bug as they all came running toward the boats.

Ximena wasn't anywhere to be seen, so he hoped she had retreated inland to where the islanders said they had more people.

"Those psychos did it," Captain Palmer said with a proud smile.

"What the hell is going on, Captain?" Trigger asked as they made it to the boats. "It was a small-scale war out here."

"Where's the treasure?" Tobi asked.

"Everything's gone to hell," Captain Palmer said as they pushed the boat into the water. "And Jonas sunk with the treasure."

"You sure he sunk?" Tobi asked. "We saw a boat row over to the Deceit as we were finishing with the last of the Rose."

"That son of a—" She rubbed her temples. "No time to thank the islanders. Row. Now!"

Whatever the guys had been through, all three of them were covered in dirt and blood. They were all too much of a mess to tell if the blood was their own or their enemy's.

Everyone was tired, but they gave it everything they had to get back to the ship. The entire time, Captain Palmer's eyes were trained on the section of the beach that the rocky staircase led down to, but not one Poisoned Rose member had made it through.

chapter 25:

The Calm Before The Board

"I want everyone ready for an all-out war!" Captain Palmer commanded.

Before they had made it to the ship, Captain Palmer was already barking orders at everyone. Once they all made it up to the deck of the Albatross, Finn and Kili watched as Poseidon's Deceit started back out onto the seas.

"They'll head under to try to escape. Walker, you're on the wheel. Take us under, get us next to them—ram them if that's what you have to do," she scowled at the retreating ship. "We're getting that diadem back."

Finn followed her around in awe. It was always great seeing her in commander mode, but she was on a different level. She was ready to toss Jonas into the ocean and leave him for dead.

"You need to get Stitch to look at your arm." Kili put a delicate hand on his wrist. "It's bleeding pretty bad."

Finn put a hand over his wound, he'd taken a moment on the rowboat to tear a sleeve off and wrap it. What effort he had put in was in vain considering he was bleeding through it.

"Captain Palmer needs me up here," Finn said.

I'll get her. Be right back." She gave him a concerned look before hopping into the hatch to the lower decks.

Captain Palmer stormed over. "That's pretty bad, you going to be okay to fight?"

Finn hid a pained wince with a smile. "I wouldn't miss a chance to smack that guy's smug face."

"Good." Captain Palmer looked toward the hatch to the lower decks. "Have you—"

"Kili just went to get Stitch."

"Excellent."

For a moment, just a quick instant, Captain Palmer looked like she was proud. Rather than bring her wrath on himself by teasing her, Finn looked toward the rival ship as it started sinking into the water.

"You did an excellent job back there." Captain Palmer placed a hand on his good shoulder. "You had no other options, and you even managed to make him look like a fool."

Finn looked up at his captain. "Let's get your treasure."

She smiled. "Let's."

The energy pulse launched around the ship and the shaking began again. Just as it had the first time Finn was on the ship, it started to sink into the depths of the ocean.

"Have a plan, or are we just going to wing it like always?"

"I thought I'd take a cue from you, my young stowaway, and come up with a plan. You and I will board the ship—I will locate the diadem—additional treasure optional—meanwhile, you and Kili are going to attack the heart of his ship."

He remembered her saying that if a heart was damaged, it wouldn't be good. If the hearts could explode, it would be the perfect plan for Captain Palmer to be rid of her two biggest nuisances. There was almost no way that's what would happen, but Captain Palmer's mischievous nature left about a one-percent chance for that to be the case.

"What exactly does that mean?" Finn asked. "What happens if we mess up the heart while they're underwater?"

"They'll know it happened, and they'll have enough time to make the preparations to resurface." Captain Palmer tilted her head to the sky as the deck levelled with the ocean waves. "We'll have to get back to the ship before that happens or we'll be left behind on their vessel."

Finn shuddered at the thought of being held prisoner by the pompous likes of Jonas.

The ship fully submerged into the ocean and Finn watched a school of fish swim by. "How will we know we did enough damage?"

"Just give it a good poke, you'll know. Same start to the plan as with Penny's ship, but we're going to have a lot more help this time."

"What if we don't get the diadem in time?"

"We will," Captain Palmer said as she walked off. "See you at the front of the ship."

"Aye, Captain Palmer."

The hatch leading below the deck swung open and Kili stared at her surroundings in awe. Finn wondered if that's how he looked the first time he saw the beautiful sight. She stumbled forward, nearly running into everything in her path before she made it back to Finn with Stitch.

"You really need to watch where you're going, that's a great way to trip over something. So, where's this injury you—" Finn untied the sleeve from around his wound. "FINN TOWNSEND!" Stitch's tone changed from one of anger to one of amusement as she pushed up her glasses. "What did I tell you the first time we met?"

"You're a pro at stitches?"

"They even managed to mess up your pretty face!" Stitch squealed with delight as she got to work on Finn's wound. "I'll have it fixed up, even better than new in no time." Her tone switched to one that was much more overdramatic. "I—will—not—let—you—die!"

It was the first time Finn had seen Stitch do any work on the ship, and she wasn't wasting any time. He only knew the basics of first aid, so he had to trust that Stitch really did know what she was doing. Time to see if the cooky tailor was a great doctor.

Kili sidled up beside Finn as he leaned against the ship's railing. "It's so incredible. How is this possible?"

"Long story, remind me to tell you later." Finn winced at whatever Stitch was doing with her sharp instruments. "You ready for anything?"

"Yeah, but… I wanted to say thank you—for not leaving me back there. You probably made your arm worse by catching me."

Stitch snapped toward her, "This is your fault?"

"Relax, glasses." Kili didn't surrender an inch. "He'd already been stabbed by the moron we're chasing. Finn saved my life."

"I'm not surprised." Stitch settled back into her work. "Finn's a good person the best. Pretty sure if I studied his blood you could even see it in the wet bits."

Finn stared at Stitch looking for anything to say, but his confusion was overwhelming. Few people had ever left him speechless, but Stitch managed to do it on a weekly basis.

He finally turned back to Kili. "Don't mention it. It's like I told you—we're a family. We stick together."

Kili looked at Finn's arm. "Does—does it hurt much?"

In truth, it was the worst pain he'd ever felt. Since the adrenaline had worn off, his wounds had become agonizing. That fact had to be written all over his face, but he wasn't interested in acknowledging it.

"It looks worse than it is. In a weird way, I feel a bit closer to my dad now."

"Your dad got stabbed in the arm?"

"Nah, his got blown off."

Kili blinked a few times. "I have not asked you nearly enough about your exciting life."

"No, you have not," they laughed, but it soon turned back into silence. "I'm worried about Penny."

"Fortune's sister?" She looked around the boat. "Oh, yeah. Where is she?"

"We had to——"

Stitch backed up. "Ta-da!" Finn's wound was freshly wrapped and there wasn't a hint of bleeding. "Just try to avoid getting stabbed again."

Stitch tossed everything she'd used into a small bag. A bottle filled with a glowing orange liquid was amongst the things she seemed to have used. It made him wish he'd watched because he had no idea what something like that would do.

"Unfortunately, I can't make any promises." Finn moved his arm a bit. "At least it's not my good arm." He glanced toward the ship they were gaining on. "You may want to head back under, Stitch."

"I'll be okay," Stitch said with a dismissive wave of her hand. "I'm always gonna be here to help!"

"You two, with me." Captain Palmer strutted by. "It's about time to board. Stitch, grab Bug, and head under."

Stitch picked up her medical bag. "Aye, Captain." She ran off low to the ground. "Here, Bug! Buzz, buzz!"

"That girl is so strange," Kili said.

"She's not so bad." Captain Palmer replied. They reached the front of the ship and Captain Palmer took four ropes from a crew member. She handed Finn and Kili each a rope but kept her gaze on Kili. "I'm still trying to figure out why exactly it is that Stitch doesn't trust you—be good."

It looked like that comment hurt Kili, but there wasn't any time to work through that minefield.

Walker swaggered over and took a rope from the captain. "All the preparations are made, Captain."

"Wait, who's steering the—" Finn's question was answered before he could ask it when he heard Tobi whistling a tune.

He looked even more carefree than he had when they were repairing the ship.

"I hate to disobey direct orders, but yer going to need some help in this fight," Walker said. "Tobi's just gotta keep us straight. Once we're linked, their ship isn't going anywhere without us."

"Thank you, Walker." Captain Palmer set her sights on Poseidon's Deceit. "Everyone ready yourselves, and follow my lead."

"Aye, Captain."

Everyone was focused on Jonas's ship as the two lined up. Finn could feel his heart beating in the wound on his shoulder as he tightened his grip on the rope. The back section of the boat came into range, and it was time to act.

"Now!"

Captain Palmer ran and launched herself over the railing. Everyone followed suit with a thunderous war cry as they swung through the air to battle.

chapter 26:

A Sword To The Heart

Captain Palmer hit the floor first and engaged a group of pyrates on the stairs to the main deck. Walker headed right for the pyrate manning the wheel, and Kili followed Finn down the stairs to the main deck. Two pyrates jumped in front of them with swords drawn, and Finn replied by pulling his own sword. They

He expected Kili to do the same, but she tapped his shoulder. "We have a problem."

"What?" Finn glanced back at Kili's waist and remembered she'd dropped her sword back on the island. "How did you not realize you don't have a sword?"

"It's been a busy day!"

The pyrates swiped toward them, and Finn managed to parry one before clashing with the other. The captain rushed into the fray and struck the pyrate in the face. The other pyrate rushed toward her and she nailed him with a heavy kick that sent him to the floor.

"You're welcome," Captain Palmer said.

"Glad you could make it, love," Jonas said as he and

Wade approached, twirling their swords in their hands. "Saved me the trouble of hunting you down later."

Finn waited to give Captain Palmer the first verbal jab, but it never came. She was more serious than he had ever seen her. There was a fire in her eyes, the kind of fire that burned away any sense of humour.

"How was that swim?" Finn asked.

Jonas glared at him. "I'll make sure you find out."

Finn started to step forward, but Captain Palmer raised a hand. "You two know what to do. I'll handle them."

"You can't take a whole ship of pyrates by yourself," Kili said.

At that moment, dozens of members of the crew of the Albatross swung onto the ship each with weapons in hand. The skirmish was on.

Captain Palmer turned and winked. "I think I'll be fine."

He didn't spot him as they dashed across the deck, but he figured Trigger had to be amongst the men. Something told Finn that neither ship could risk the use of their cannons while everyone was in such a precarious situation.

"What is it we're looking for?" Kili asked as they reached the hatch to the lower deck.

"Have you ever passed that door on the Albatross with the weird glow?" Finn asked as they each hopped down the stairs.

"The really big one?"

"That's the one."

"So basically a big glow."

"Something like that." They turned a corner to a set of stairs. "I've really only seen the one. Keep your eye out for where they might be keeping the diadem as well. I have a feeling Jonas is smart enough to keep it separate from the chest."

They threw open a few doors but only found empty crew quarters. It soon felt as if they'd run rampant throughout the entirety of the ship. They rounded another corner and came face to face with a large door with an unmistakable glow. The heart had to be through that door.

Kili held a hand to it. "That looks like a big glow."

"How could I have ever found it without you?"

"Ha—ha."

They pushed the heavy door and entered a room that was unlike any either of them had seen before. The chamber on the Albatross was a simplistic and cozy room, but this one felt rustic and unwelcoming.

The room had two floors, and the heart was down a flight of stairs from where they came in. Despite the distance, the heart still glowed brilliantly. The cold metallic surfaces made the ship feel so much different than the Albatross.

"It's strangely beautiful." Kili stared at the orange glow of the heart. "In a hypnotic—looks like it's going to explode if we touch it, kind of way."

Footsteps pounded from behind them, and Finn turned to face the door. It was one of the two people he wanted to see least. Wade. He came thumping down the hallway with his blade drawn, and it looked like he was ready to kill.

Finn cocked his head to Kili. "You ever shared a sword before?"

"Have you?"

"There's a first time for everything."

Wade tapped his sword along the wall outside the room. "I knew I'd catch up to you two."

There was no way Finn could beat Wade. It was possible that the extra hand from Kili could be enough to throw him off balance, but with two people fighting with one sword, one of them was always vulnerable. The best way they could get an edge on him was through a little psychological warfare.

"Remember that time my dog beat up your boss and I tossed him into a whirlpool?" Finn asked. "Good times."

Wade stepped through the doorway. "Yeah, and I'm about to restore his honour."

"You're not gonna get any honour with those untied boots," Finn said.

"What?" Wade looked down at his boots and Finn launched forward.

After striking Wade's sword out of the way, he tossed his own blade aside to Kili and nailed Wade in the face with a wicked punch. Kili caught the sword and with a spin, she slashed toward Wade. He managed to recover from the strike in time to parry the slash. After a small step back, Wade circled them.

The fact that the lie almost worked to perfection astonished Finn.

"You're doing better than you were in Bridger," Wade said as he shook a finger.

Kili raised an eyebrow. "You guys fought back in Bridger?"

"I smacked him with a stick a few times," Wade said.

"A stick is a hell of a lot different from a sword," Finn said. "How'd you even get down here anyway? I figured Walker would have cut you off before you had a chance to get down here."

"I gotta give Walker some credit." Wade twirled his sword. "He was smart enough to recognize that our crew had the same plan as yours."

"What?"

"A fight like this is only ever going to end in one way, and that's with a damaged heart." Wade pointed his sword down at the heart "Walker caught some of our heavier hitters heading for yours and he doubled back to hold them off. I wonder how he'll fare against five of our greatest swordsmen."

Knowing Walker was capable of holding his own against Captain Palmer, Finn liked his odds. If the rest of the crew was as pompous as Jonas and as dim as Wade, Walked would be able to take them all after a whole bottle of rum.

"Then I guess we'll just have to beat you now, so we can go help him out," Finn said as he pulled his grappling hook from his belt.

"A boy with a rope, and a little lady. I like my chances against a pair of wannabe pyrates."

Kili pushed the attack first. She spun in and clashed swords with Wade. Finn circled on the outside of the fight, twirling his hook, waiting for the right moment. Wade used his size to his advantage and brutalized Kili with swings until she fell to the ground.

Finn swung his grappling hook toward Wade. He managed to pull his head out of the way in time, but at least now his attention was turned back toward Finn.

Finn readied his rope again. "Bring it, ugly."

He swung his hook a few more times, but Wade had been studying him. A quick duck with a step back, and Wade cut the rope. Finn hooked what remained of his ruined rope back on his belt as Wade approached.

There wasn't anywhere for him to go, but if he kept Wade's attention a bit longer, Kili would have the advantage.

Unfortunately, Kili blew her advantage by advancing with a shout. "AAAAAHHH!"

She managed to graze the shoulder of the arm Wade was fighting with, but that was it. His sword fell to the floor, but he managed to bounce it back up with his foot and catch it with his other hand. A quick elbow strike sent Kili to the ground again.

Finn used the opportunity to get in close and land a

few strikes, but it didn't phase Wade's bigger frame. He took a step back and nailed Finn with a kick, sending him over the railing, and down to the floor below.

He was a hell of a lot closer to the heart, but he had no way to damage it without his sword.

"Finn!" Kili called from above before she was drowned out by the sounds of clashing steel.

He looked around for anything that could help. Kili was good, but it would only be a matter of time before she succumbed to Wade's strength and experience.

On the ground by the heart, Finn found a toolkit. He looked through it, pulled out the heaviest tool he could find, and tucked it into his belt.

By the time Finn looked back toward the fight, Kili was retreating over the railing. When she landed, Finn could see she had a fresh cut across her cheek, and it looked like Wade had grazed her midsection.

He rushed over and helped her up. "Why don't you let me handle the rest?"

"Someone better skewer that rat." Kili looked disappointed and irritated, but she handed him his sword. "My face and my body are half of my job."

"It suits you. You're a real pyrate entertainer now." She smiled as Finn pushed her behind him and readied his sword. He narrowed his eyes as Wade hopped down. "Don't worry, I'm going to make him regret what he did."

Wade laughed, "We already know you can't handle me on your own, lad. I'll tell you what, if the two of you head out of here right now, I won't spill your guts all over the floor."

"Tempting," Finn brought a finger to his chin. "But making you look like a jackass sounds way more fun. Savvy?"

"Yeah, screw you, asshole," Kili added.

Finn glanced back at her for her lame line, but all

she could do was shrug.

He sighed and rushed toward Wade again. From only a brief exchange it was clear that Wade was getting ready to finish things.

The only bright spot of the entire day was that Finn was happy to see how well his mother's sword held up under the stress test that was this adventure.

He swiped at Wade's legs, but Wade clamped his sword on top of Finn's with a cocky grin. Finn got some revenge for Kili, a quick elbow crashed into Wade's face —there was a wicked crack and blood trickled down his face.

Finn let a cocky grin of his own scrawl across his face. Wade knew he was going to beat them, and that was making him arrogant. That was Finn's key to victory.

"I'm gonna kill yeh, lad." Wade wiped some of his blood and looked at his fingers. "I'm gonna kill yeh."

"You seem to be having an awful lot of trouble with that." Finn sheathed his sword and held his arms out. "You have an estimate on when you might be getting to that? Pretty sure we've got a skirmish to win."

Wade growled and made another run at Finn, just like he hoped. Finn waited until he suspected Wade wouldn't be able to get out of the way in time before he finally made his move.

Wade raised his sword and Finn wrapped his hand around the tool he'd stuffed into his belt. He pulled it out and chucked it as hard as he could.

The tool whirled through the air and planted itself squarely in between Wade's legs with a deep thud. His speed sent him tumbling across the ground, landing in front of Finn.

He knew the fight was over from the noises Wade was making on the ground. Kili ran over and picked up his sword as Finn used what was left of his grappling hook rope to tie him up.

"Why—would you—do that?" Wade asked through high-pitched sobs.

Finn clicked his tongue. "You were right, Wade. We weren't going to beat you, so I had to get a little—"

"Pyratey." Kili chimed in.

"Exactly. Now if you'll excuse us, we have to sabotage your ship."

The duo approached the heart, not sure what to expect. Kili's slight limp had Finn worried, but her smile reassured him.

"You gonna be okay to run out of here?" Finn asked.

"Just try and stop me."

"I have no clue what's about to happen." Finn took a breath and stabbed his sword into the ship's heart.

The ship's orange glow flashed all around and everything started to shake.

"Here we go."

chapter 27:

Just Another Thursday

"Why does everything have to shake?" Kili asked as she brought a hand to her stomach.

Finn grabbed her hand and they headed back up to the main deck of the ship where the brawl was still going on. Bodies covered the floor of the deck, but it was hard to tell who was dead, and who was knocked out. Regardless of who was who, it was going to make getting off the ship a pain.

Jonas and Captain Palmer were still locked in combat. He looked like he had the upper hand, but she spun away from him and kicked a barrel his way.

The glow of the energy field around the ship had dimmed and water was dripping onto the deck from all sides. If they weren't underwater Finn would have sworn it was pouring rain.

"Good job you two." Captain Palmer turned toward Finn. "Get back to the ship and tell Tobi—Walker—whoever's at the wheel to prepare our getaway."

That barrel came back to haunt the captain in a big way when it slammed into her from behind, courtesy of Jonas.

"Sorry, babe. Love hurts." In seconds, he was over

top of her. "I really hate to do this, but—" Jonas stuck his sword into Captain Palmer's abdomen and twisted. "If I can't have yeh, then I guess no one can. *Savvy?*"

Finn nudged Kili. "Once I get him clear, check on Captain Palmer and then get back to the ship, I'll handle this."

Kili gave him a worried look. "Are you sure?"

One final look was all the convincing Kili needed.

Finn moved to protect his downed Captain. "What kind of man hits a woman from behind?"

Jonas backed off as Finn approached. "A pyrate."

"Right. I walked right into that one."

"And now you can walk into my sword." Jonas rushed forward and the two clashed blades.

Finn wasn't sure if he was getting used to fighting more skilled opponents or if his senses boosted when he saw Captain Palmer get hurt, but he had no issue blocking Jonas's strikes. He was moving as fast as the captain had all that time ago when Finn first saw her in Embar.

Jonas was focused, but he seemed angry, almost like he regretted what he'd just done to his captain.

"How could you do that to someone you say you love?" Finn asked.

Jonas swung wild. "Shut up!"

Finn ducked the swing and threw a heavy fist into Jonas's stomach. He replied with an elbow to the back of Finn's head and they stepped back from each other.

Jonas chuckled. "If it took two of you to deal with Wade, you have no chance against me alone, lad."

"But we did still deal with Wade." Finn twirled his blade. "Today I've avoided hungry crocodiles, beaten ancient warriors, and gone toe-to-toe with the most vicious pyrates on the open seas—then I beat your first mate and sabotaged your ship. I'm on a roll today, and I'm not planning on slowing down."

"You think that's some kind of accomplishment?" Jonas asked. "For me, that's just another Thursday."

He pushed the attack, forcing Finn on the back foot. Jonas forced him up the staircase toward the wheel, a wheel that had no one at the helm. They fought their way around it and Finn used it to get some distance.

Jonas missed a few stabs. "Hold still and let me skewer you."

"Gonna take a hard pass on that one." Finn dodged a stab Jonas had thrust through a gap in the wheel, and used it to his advantage.

He spun the wheel, sending Jonas's sword out of his hand. Both ships took a hard turn, causing them to stumble and slip. As Finn moved to a better position Jonas snatched his blade from the spinning wheel and brought it to a stop.

"You're really going to make this as irritating as possible, aren't you?" Jonas asked.

"Annoying you is a win in my books."

Jonas launched a flurry of strikes, causing Finn to take a dive over the railing back down to the main deck. His foe was right on his heels, dropping down in an attempt to impale Finn. The sword landed right between his legs and he thanked the heavens he hadn't been about a foot forward.

Finn raised his sword, but Jonas hit him with a stiff kick, sending him sprawling backward. He backed into the mast of the ship and his hand met a rope as he stood up. He needed to stop trying to formulate a plan and start trusting his gut.

His gut told him that rope was the right move.

As Jonas rushed toward him, Finn cut a tied-down rope, and the one he had in his hand sent him up to the sails of the ship. An ornate sail unfurled as he sailed to the top of the ship. He landed on the mast and struggled to catch his footing on the slippery surface.

"Alright. That should give me a second to catch—"

Before he could finish, Jonas was already beside him. "So you've chosen a fall from the top of my ship to be the way you die?"

"I was—" Finn lashed out with a sword slash and nearly slipped off. "About to ask you that."

He looked for a way out of the situation, but the only thing he could see was a sail that was a solid leap away. It looked a bit out of his range, but his gut was saying he could make it.

"We both know you aren't allowed to kill me. What would Fortune do without me in the world?"

Finn couldn't hide how worn out he was. "I'm gonna veto Captain Palmer—and say that I think she'd probably be better off."

Jonas attempted a stab again, Finn barely managed to shift his body out of the way in time. Silver-Tongue grinned as he shifted the blade and sliced it across Finn's side as he pulled it back.

"AH!"

Finn wasn't going to look down at the wound, but he knew it wasn't good. It was never a good sign when you could feel blood leaving a wound, and a lot of blood was leaving his body. As long as his guts were still inside, he could keep fighting.

Jonas readied another strike, but Finn was ready to take his chances with fate. He leaped toward the sail and stuck his blade through it. It slowed his fall just enough for the last few feet to the floor to only be mildly painful.

"Ah—" His fresh wound stung and he brought his hand to it in order to check the bleeding. "At some point, Jonas is going to stop pissing me off."

His shaky hand was drenched in blood.

Jonas dropped down in front of Finn, far more gracefully than he ever could have. "Are you done with this foolishness, lad? Just put your sword down, and take your stabbing like a man."

"Come on then," Finn sheathed his sword and held up his fists. "Or are you too afraid I'll bust up that pretty face of yours?"

"Someone as pitiful as you could never ruin a face like mine." Jonas sheathed his own sword. "An honest challenge is something I'll never back down from."

He rushed forward and threw a few strikes. Finn wasn't able to do anything except absorb them. When an opening came, he used a spin to mask redrawing his sword, but Jonas met it with a sword of his own.

Jonas waggled a finger. "That's not honest fighting."

"No." Finn winced. "It's fighting like a pyrate."

"Pyrate or not. This is where you die." Jonas went for a final stab.

Finn was in a bad position. His only option was trying a move he'd seen Captain Palmer do a dozen times. She'd never actually taught him to do it, but he had to try.

In one motion Finn ran his blade along Jonas' and whirled it until it was at a bad angle. With a hard flick, Jonas lost his blade entirely.

There was a brief moment of joy. A moment when Finn knew he'd won, but that joy dissipated when he was grabbed from behind.

"Told you I was gonna kill you," A familiar voice said. Finn cranked his neck to see that Wade had grabbed a hold of him. "How do you wanna kill this little twerp?"

Things weren't going well before, but now, things were much, much worse.

Chapter 28:

The Devil's Charm

"How'd you even get free?" Finn asked.

"Yelled loud enough for the ship doctor to come running," Wade said. "Did you think the crew would just leave me there?"

Jonas paced back and forth. For the first time, Finn spotted that Jonas was keeping the diadem tucked just inside of his vest.

"We don't have much time, but I have an idea." Jonas looked toward the waning energy field around the ship.

Wade pulled Finn over the ship's rail and grabbed him by the hair. "Any last words?"

As he went to make a sarcastic remark, Wade shoved Finn's head out of the energy field into the depths of cool, dark ocean water. The salty ocean filled his mouth, but the drowning wasn't what was hurting Finn the most —at that point.

The speed the ship was moving through the water, and the resistance of his head leaning out of the energy field put so much pressure on his head and neck, it was unbearable.

Finn thrashed his arms backward, hoping to get

lucky and hit Wade in some vital spot. He must have hit something because he managed to get back through the field for a quick breath of air.

Quicker than he had come out, he was shoved back in, this time by two sets of hands.

Finn kept fighting, thrashing, lashing out. Nothing worked. He could just try to toss himself into the water, but there was no guarantee he could swim to the surface without drowning. Even if he could make it, if he was stranded in the middle of the ocean, he'd be good as dead regardless.

Finn knew he was going to die.

He'd never get to say goodbye to his pop, Bug, or Diego.

He'd never get to say goodbye to Kili, Captain Palmer, and the rest of the crew.

He'd never get to find out what happened to his mother.

His lungs were sore and his vision was getting hazy. His body felt heavy, and he didn't have the strength to fight anymore.

He was dying, he just had no idea it would be so painful.

One of the sets of hands let go, and then a moment later, the other set. A hand grabbed his shoulder and yanked him back onto the deck.

He gasped for air and coughed all the salt water out of his system. Captain Palmer was standing over him with her sword pointed toward Jonas and Wade, each on the ground. Finn had no idea what had happened, but blood was dripping from the tip of his captain's sword, and Wade wasn't moving at all.

"What did you do?" Jonas growled.

Captain Palmer's breathing was shaky and her skin was pale, but she still managed to choke out a few words, "You're really going to try to be—morally superior while the two of you grown men were trying to—drown a child—after attacking a woman from behind?"

Finn tapped her leg as he caught his breath, and she moved so he could stand. "Captain, he's got the diadem."

"I know."

Jonas stared at her. "I thought you never kill."

Captain Palmer spat toward him. "You went after the diadem without a contract. You made a deal with the Blues. That makes you and your crew renegades— suitable to kill." She gripped her blade tighter. "You try to kill me—you try to kill my boy—your life is forfeit."

Finn looked at Captain Palmer, utterly bewildered.

Her boy?

She had to be woozy from the wound.

"Wade." Jonas stared down at his first mate. "Wade, open your bloody eyes!"

Captain Palmer turned to Finn as the let out a violent shake. "We need to leave, now."

Finn stepped in front of his captain and readied his blade. She hadn't noticed Jonas sprinting toward her with his sword ready to strike. With a quick flick of his wrist, Finn slashed Jonas's hand sending his sword right over the rail of the ship. Captain Palmer followed up with a running knee to Jonas's face.

Finn ran over toward Wade and held two fingers to his neck, but he couldn't find a pulse. It was possible he was dead, but it was also possible Finn had lost so much blood that he couldn't feel his hands anymore.

He turned back toward Captain Palmer as she dropped Jonas's unconscious body by his vest. She limped over and threw Finn's good arm over her shoulder. As they reached the gangplank the ships were coming apart, causing the plank to fall into the water below.

They had no way to get back across.

Finn looked around for any options, and spotted Kili jumping and waving her arms from the Albatross. She had a hold of two ropes that were tied to the mast of the ship. They were only going to have one shot.

Kili ran and jumped across the gap, holding both ropes, and as she approached tossed one rope to Finn. He barely managed to get his fingers wrapped around it before it swung back out of reach. Kili swung back toward the Albatross and watched on.

Captain Palmer smiled at Finn. "Let's get off this wreck."

Finn smiled back. "Let's."

In unison, they stepped up onto the rail with the rope in hand. "One, two, three!"

Finn and Captain Palmer managed to clear the gap by a hair. They poured over the rail in a mangled and bloody heap. The crew of the ship crowded around their injured Captain, but Trigger pushed them all back.

Kili rushed over with Bug and helped them to their feet. It was good to see Bug again, but the last thing Finn needed was dog saliva in his wounds.

"Someone send for—Stitch." Captain Palmer winced. "She'll be excited and—horrified." She threw a finger toward the wheel of the ship. "Tobi! Take us to the capital."

Finn watched Poseidon's Deceit as it stalled in the water behind them, and then shot up to the surface. "Whoa."

Walker raised an eyebrow. "Yeh managed to find the diadem?"

"No." Finn hung his head. "We couldn't get it from Jonas before we—"

"Speak for yourself." Captain Palmer pulled the silver diadem from her coat. "The Devil's Charm—" she moaned in pain. "Captain Fortune Palmer never—and I mean never—loses."

The entire crew erupted in cheers. Finn couldn't help it, and despite his wounds, he joined in. Going from a feeling of failure and waste to one of relief and victory felt so good. Having that diadem made the sacrifice of the crew members they lost worth it.

"I don't care what anyone says." Captain Palmer climbed onto the railing of the ship. "Not Sig, not the Blues, and certainly not Jonas. There is not a single ship on the seas that can match us in strength, speed, and heart." Whether she'd admit it or not, her admiration for her crew was apparent. "We lost good men today, but our victory is the start of a new era for the Albatross. You don't know it yet, but I've got big plans—plans that'll make all of us rich beyond your wildest dreams."

The entire crew started to murmur and look amongst each other. There was nothing more enticing to a pyrate than the promise of treasure.

Captain Palmer cleared her throat and continued. "The bad news is, we're missing out on the payday of a chest full of gold. The good news is, Sig owes me a whole lot more than two crates of cells. We'll have a fresh contract in no time at all. Today, a bloody diadem— tomorrow, Red Beard's lost treasure."

Chapter 29:

The Woman Named Fortune

After what felt like spending forever under the seas, the ship had surfaced into the dark night. The only light came from the few torches strewn about the deck, and the bright stars shining down. Everyone had gone to get some shut-eye after the hectic day's events, but Finn was restless.

He tip-toed his way out of the crew's quarters, and as he neared the hatch leading back out to the deck, he spotted Captain Palmer.

It was strange to see her up and below the deck considering she had demanded much of the crew who'd spent some time fighting to get their much-needed rest. Knowing her, she was probably checking in on the injured members of the crew before getting some rest herself.

He crept through the ship and headed out into the dark night. It was haunting and almost eerie, yet calming. Finn admired the stars overhead as he looked around for Captain Palmer. He spotted her limping toward the front of the ship, and Finn followed.

The flames of a nearby torch licked the captain's face as she looked up to the stars. She looked sad, despite the day's victory.

Wade's lifeless body flashed in Finn's head and he wondered just how many people Captain Palmer had killed. It was clear she didn't like taking such drastic action and he wondered what it was that led her to implement a strange no-killing rule.

"Captain Palmer? Everything alright?" Finn asked as he approached.

"Everything's fine." She didn't take her eyes off the stars. "It was a long day, you should be asleep."

"I could say the same for you. I feel like I was made into a human pin cushion today. Thought some fresh air could help."

"Mmm." She brought a hand to her wound. "Yes, I'm in a similar situation."

"I wanted to thank you for saving my life." Finn took a moment to look up to the stars the captain was admiring. "Even though—"

"Don't mention it, kid." Finn could feel a sense of apprehension in the air. "How's the arm—and the midsection?"

They were both still burning every time he moved his body. As Captain Palmer had predicted, Stitch was horrified and excited to work on him again. Once again, whatever she'd done had worked wonders.

"First official stabbing, not so bad." Finn rubbed his wounds. "I'd like to avoid it in the future, but it could have been worse. How's yours?"

Captain Palmer let out a half-hearted laugh. "Not the first time. Likely won't be the last. I've been worse off, though. Nothing I can't bounce back from."

"It's kind of cool."

"Oh?"

"On my first adventure with you, we both got stabbed. It's like a neat little thing that'll connect us."

She stifled a laugh. "I'm glad you're looking at things

in a positive light, even if it's a bit twisted."

She looked as if she were longing for something.

He wanted to ask about Penny, but he wasn't sure what he could say.

There wasn't anything he could say that would comfort Captain Palmer. She would have known her own sister better than anyone, and she seemed to know more about the Poisoned Rose than she let on. The captain would likely know exactly whether or not Penny would have been able to survive on her own.

"Have you—ever killed someone before? Before Wade, I mean. Is that why you have that rule, or—" Captain Palmer's attention snapped to Finn, but not in an angry way. The look she gave him reminded Finn of the look his father would give him when he was trying to protect him from the world. "I shouldn't have—"

"I have."

Finn stared up at his hero. All the years he'd heard stories of Captain Palmer, he'd never heard one that involved her taking someone's life. That's one of the things Finn admired the most about her. He wasn't sure exactly why, or what it was, but Finn was looking at his captain in a new way.

"I put the rule in place because I love being a pyrate, but I don't love what being a pyrate can do to people. I've seen perfectly wonderful people dragged down into becoming the worst humanity has to offer because of piracy." She took a shaky breath. "Killing people—slaughtering innocents—it changes people."

"Has it changed you?"

"It has."

"You could have just let them take me out." Finn looked out across the star-dotted ocean. "It's my fault I ended up in the position I was in."

To his surprise, Finn could feel himself getting emotional. It wasn't due to his shortcomings, but instead due to his near-death experience. The feeling of drowning was scarier than any of the yellow-eyed pyrate brutes he battled.

Captain Palmer shook her head. "I was pulling my strikes against Jonas. I should have beaten that fool long before you returned from the heart of the ship. Long before today if I'm really being honest. It is my duty to ensure the health and safety of my crew."

"Yeah, but—"

"We wouldn't have even made it to the treasure in the first place if it weren't for you and Bug. You may have been an annoying little brat only a short while ago, but you've already become a wonderful pyrate." Finn must have been smiling because she switched her tone. "Don't get me wrong, you're still an annoying brat, but now you're a *useful* annoying brat. You'll become the kind of pyrate anyone could be proud to tell the tales of."

He couldn't help smiling. It was really nice for Finn to hear a rare compliment leave the lips of Captain Palmer. It was probably the only one he'd be getting for a long time, so he felt the need to relish in it for the moment.

"If I may, how many people have you killed?" he asked.

She sighed, "As of today—three people."

Finn cocked his head. With the way Captain Palmer had been acting, he expected a much higher number. She had been a pyrate since Finn was a boy after all. Finn couldn't imagine how difficult it would be to take one life, but tales of pyrates often came with mentions of bloodshed.

"Three people?"

She nodded. "The first was about a year into the first crew I joined. I had no choice. The man in charge of that particular crew was a loud-mouthed drunk—a real fool of a man. He got himself on just about everyone's bad side, which led to bounties. A group of pyrate hunters tracked the crew down one night and launched a surprise attack while we slept." Captain Palmer's hands balled. "By the time I managed to get to the Captain he was already dead. The hunters attacked me, and I had no choice. It was either them or me, and I chose me."

At that moment, Captain Palmer reminded Finn of Vi, the old woman who originally told him the stories of the legendary pyrate. Hearing about her life from Vi was one thing. Hearing about it from Walker was another. Being told a story by Captain Palmer herself was a dream come true.

Finn leaned over the railing. "It's weird to think about you as just another pyrate on someone else's crew."

She let out an amused chuckle. "It is, isn't it?"

"Is that group of hunters still active?" he asked.

"The group? No. The brother of the man I killed that night? Yes. I doubt he'll ever stop, but I can't blame him. I'd do the same if anything happened—" Captain Palmer's thoughts clearly flipped to Penny, and Finn could see the emotion getting the better of her.

"The other person?"

Captain Palmer looked surprised when she turned her attention to Finn. It was like she was unsure of what to say next or how to even say anything at all. Her mouth opened like she was going to speak, but she thought against it a few times.

She set her sights on Finn again, this time more serious. "It was necessary, but it was a mistake."

He raised an eyebrow. "I'm going to need some elaboration on that one."

"It was the second time I was in a clash with the Poisoned Rose."

As soon as those words left her lips, she had all of Finn's attention. He'd always felt that Captain Palmer knew a bit more than she was letting on about the band of brutes. Maybe he'd finally get to learn a bit more about the crew that took his mother.

"So it is true, but—you're the only person known to survive a battle, and you've done it *multiple* times?"

She nodded. "A one-on-one skirmish, yes. It was horrific. Those monsters killed so many of my friends. They almost killed me—they probably should have."

"What happened?"

"They like to play with their food. They had me dead to rights. I was surrounded and on my own. The ruins of a ship doomed to sink around me. The twisted cap thought he'd make an example of me for his crew."

Of all the stories Finn had heard, and he'd heard a lot, he'd never heard one where Captain Palmer was in a losing situation. Things didn't always go her way, but by the end of the tale, she managed to set things right.

Finn needed more details. "And?"

"We duelled. I don't know if it was because he was toying with me, or if he secretly wanted to die. Maybe he was craving freedom from the life he'd led for so long. He left me a huge opening. I took it, and the crew went into a frenzy. Before any of them turned their attention back toward me, I had already hopped overboard to take my chances with the sea. I found a couple pieces of wood to float on, and after—who knows how long—I landed on an island."

"So what was the mistake?"

"The mistake was the act. The new Captain of the Poisoned Rose has been even sicker than the last. I inadvertently added to the strife of the seas by killing that man."

Finn wondered if that man had been the same as the one that had taken his mother. The man that likely killed his mother. He felt a strange sense of justice that if he couldn't be the one to avenge his mom, at least Captain Palmer had, whether she knew it or not.

"Do you think—"

"Don't," Captain Palmer warned.

"I need to know." It was Finn's turn to ball his fists. "Was there a woman? On the crew, maybe as a pri—"

"There are no men or women aboard the Poisoned Rose." Captain Palmer put a hand on Finn's shoulder. "Those people are all monsters. Whether mother, father, son, or daughter—the instant you join that crew, you become something different. Something terrible."

"Something terrible?"

"Aye. You lose your soul—your regard for human life —your will to seek happiness. Once you see those gaunt yellow eyes, you know there's no turning back."

What she was saying made sense. None of the monsters they faced in the cave looked like they had any regard for human life. Their yellow eyes were more animalistic than they were human.

Finn looked Captain Palmer in the eyes. "Did you see a woman that night?"

She nodded. "There were three, all too far gone."

"Would they have taken a normal woman into their crew? Someone with no experience, or—"

"No, Finn. Your mother is gone. Even if a woman with no experience became a member of the crew, the average member of that crew lasts less than a year. You aren't a person to their twisted leader, you're just meat puppets, there to do as you're told."

His whole life he'd been told that his mother was dead, but he always held onto a tiny piece of hope. Hearing Captain Palmer speak about her run-in with the crew diminished that tiny piece of hope. He knew he needed to drop it, but if they ever ran into the Poisoned Rose again, he'd do whatever it took to get the answers he needed.

Captain Palmer's words were one thing. Finn needed to see the crew himself, look them all in the eyes, and demand an answer. He knew it was stupid, but he wasn't about to give up on his mother, even if the chances of her survival were next to nothing.

"Come here," Captain Palmer said.

Finn almost jumped in fright when she wrapped her arms around him. He was so in his own head he hadn't been aware of her approach. For someone who lived a life at sea, she didn't smell like other pyrates. Her jacket smelled of freshly picked fruit, and Finn found comfort in her arms. He was upset, but the gentle beating of Captain Palmer's heart calmed him down.

"Time for both of us to go get some rest, savvy? Who's going to annoy the crew if each of us is sleeping all day?" she asked.

"I have a feeling Kili could fill that void for us."

"I'd imagine you're right. Go on. I'd like to be out here on my own a bit longer."

Finn nodded and headed back toward the lower deck. As he reached the door, he looked back at his captain. She'd removed her hat, and it looked almost like she was paying respects to the man she'd killed.

chapter 30:

A Promise To Be Wed

Walking into Sigourney's chambers for a second time felt far less daunting to Finn. Perhaps it was how the entire adventure had changed him, or perhaps it was due to the confidence the crew's victory had instilled in him. Whatever the reason, Finn had no fear of coming face-to-face with the Pyrate King.

Captain Palmer had given Finn the diadem to hand over to Sig, but he wasn't sure why. It seemed like a given that a pyrate would want the credit for their actions. The captain was the one who got the diadem from Jonas. He wondered if it was a kind of honour system.

Finn *was* the one to claim the treasure back on the island, so maybe Captain Palmer felt it was only right.

He wasn't going to ask too many questions.

"Best behaviour this time, savvy?" Captain Palmer said.

"Aye, Captain," Finn said.

The large doors swung open and Finn's sight set right on Sig, relaxing on his throne. Beside him, a large wooden table was filled with foods Finn had never seen before. Sig had just taken a bite of a chicken leg when they walked in.

Sig tossed the piece of chicken. "The scourge of the seas returns. With my daughter's diadem, I hope?" Finn flashed the diadem. "Excellent." Sig reared back in his seat. "DAUGHTER! GET IN HERE! NOW!"

The large hall filled with smashing, thumping, and unintelligible shouts as Sig's daughter made her way into the hall. A small door behind the throne flung open and she stepped into the room.

"What do you want now, father? I'm trying to work on my paints."

Sig rolled his eyes and looked at the crew. "It's her latest life pursuit." He turned back to his daughter. "AN INCREASINGLY EXPENSIVE, POINTLESS ONE!"

She stomped her foot. "YOU NEVER LET ME DO WHAT I WANT TO DO!"

"YOU ALWAYS GET EXACTLY WHAT YOU WANT YOU LITTLE BRAT!"

Finn stepped forward and held out the diadem. "This—uh—this is for you, ma'am."

The princess's attention snapped to Finn as she slowly waddled toward him. He started to sweat as she studied every inch of him. Instead of going for the diadem right away, she circled him, looking up and down. Captain Palmer gave him an amused grin when he looked over for some assistance.

Kili looked far less amused.

The princess stopped in front of him and put a hand on the diadem. "Where were you last time Palmer was here?"

Finn's face scrunched. "I was right beside her."

Captain Palmer chuckled. "I believe your exact words to him were, *quiet you dirty little twerp.*

The princess narrowed her eyes at the captain. "Shut up, tall person. That doesn't sound like me at all." She snatched the diadem. "Daddy, I'd like to marry this man."

Finn's mouth hung open, but Kili was the first to speak. "Excuse me? Finn is his own person." The room went quiet and both Sig and the princess stared at her. "Your highness."

He was glad that someone was willing to help him out. Despite their little heart-to-heart, Captain Palmer was still more interested in watching him squirm, so long as the situation wasn't dire.

Sig ran a finger along his brow. "I can't just *make* the boy marry you."

"Well, why not?" the princess asked. "You're in charge! Everyone has to listen to you!"

Finn's confidence was fading fast as the shrill woman continued bargaining for his hand in marriage. She wasn't unattractive, but her personality certainly was.

"Palmer, how old is the lad?" Sig said.

Captain Palmer looked down at Finn. "He's of age, but nowhere near mature enough to make a suitable suitor for a princess."

Finn mouthed the words, '*thank you*' and Captain Palmer gestured toward Sig.

The princess stomped her foot. "I don't care if he's not mature. He's a handsome pyrate and he'll give me the most beautiful babies and they can rule, and—"

Finn tuned her out and thought of how horrific a life that would be. "Do I get any say in this?" It was like the words fell out of Finn's mouth and he regretted it immediately.

Sig raised an eyebrow. "No. Thank you, Captain Palmer, for fulfilling the contract. As promised, your punishment will be forgotten about. You and your crew may return to port for a week as a reward. When you return you will have your pick of any new contracts. The boy will be wed to my daughter after two years' time—if she is still interested in the lad."

Finn gulped.

He didn't think he'd ever get married once he got out on the ocean. Love and marriage never seemed to be in the cards for pyrates.

"Is that fair for everyone?" Sig asked when no one spoke up.

The princess sauntered over to Finn. "I don't like waiting, but it is kind of romantic." She kissed Finn on the cheek. "I pray you have safe adventures, my lord."

Finn's eyes darted around. "Uh—thanks. You too?"

His eyes landed on Kili, and it looked like she was ready to put an end to all pyrate royalty.

The princess skipped back from where she had come, slamming the door as she went.

Sig raised his voice. "I ask yet again, is that fair?"

"Aye. Thank you, Sig," Captain Palmer said.

"One of these days you'll address me properly," Sig said as he waved his hand. "All of you, out."

The entire trip back to the ship, everyone made fun of Finn and his bride-to-be—everyone except for Kili. It was funny, but Finn was genuinely distressed that he suddenly had an arranged marriage to a pyrate princess. He'd met her a total of two times, one of which she'd insulted him.

That sounded like a horrific marriage to Finn.

At Finn's behest, they set sail rather quickly. He wasn't the only one who didn't want to spend more time than needed at the capitol. It was a strange and interesting place, but it felt like everyone needed to walk on eggshells constantly.

Luckily, everyone was already focused on what adventures the future held.

Chapter 31:

The Iron Heart

As Finn looked out across the open seas, he wondered what the future would hold. Being able to return to port for a few days would be nice. As marvellous as being out on the water could be, a part of Finn always missed being on dry land.

Off in the distance sat a small island, and Finn thought about his family as they approached it. He wondered how his pop was doing with the shop, and whether or not Diego would ever be able to forgive him if he ever returned.

His thoughts were interrupted by the grunts of someone climbing up to the crow's nest.

Finn leaned over the side and watched Kili struggle to make her way to the top. "I'd say the view is nice, but that is quite the face you're making."

Kili blew out a puff of air. "Oh, shut up. How are your injuries?"

"Good enough to climb up here."

"You sign your contract yet?" Kili said through shallow breaths. "I think you're the last one."

Finn shook his head. "It feels like I'll just forever be a stowaway."

He wasn't sure if that was all that unfortunate. Leading the life of a pyrate, but forever technically being a stowaway could lead to a unique moniker, something he still didn't have. Plus, if he never signed a contract, he'd never technically be an outlaw.

"At least you're getting what you want. We went on that whole adventure and I didn't get *any* gold."

"There'll be other chances."

She climbed into the nest next to Finn. "You've been up here alone all morning. Everything okay?"

The wind blew a few strands of Finn's long curly hair into his face. "Yeah. I told Captain Palmer I'd keep an eye out for any approaching ships."

"But you're not looking for the Poisoned Rose, are you?"

"No. I finally got to see those monsters in person. The man I remember from when I was a boy wasn't there, but—the life of a pyrate, right?" Finn looked across the water once more. "My pop was right. My mother was probably dead the night she went missing."

"You know, they've got to be so proud of you."

That was a strange thought. Finn's pop being excited about him adventuring around the world. Archibald probably would have screamed at him for nearly getting killed by someone like Jonas.

"One of the last things my pop said to me before I joined the crew was how evil all pyrates were," Finn said.

Kili gave him a dull look. "I know I'm not one to talk about parents, but even if your father doesn't approve—I know your mother is smiling down on you with pride. You're a hero."

They each looked out to the horizon in silence. Finn had no idea how much time had passed, but it didn't matter to him. Just having Kili's company at that moment felt right. It was nice to feel close to someone for the first time in a long time. Kili slipped her hand into

Finn's without looking away from the sea. They just stood there together, enjoying the moment.

Finn's body tensed. "I'm worried about Penny—"

"Where, oh where are the wonderfully pure young ones?" Captain Palmer's mocking voice carried from the deck. "One of them has a dog that has not only pooped on my sparkling deck, but that very dog is now napping ON MY BED!"

If he had any doubts before, it was clear their late-night conversation hadn't changed much between the two of them.

"Oh, look," she continued. "The little love birds are up in the nest. I don't want to know what you two are doing up there, but I can imagine that is not what it's meant to be used for. We need to keep that purity intact in case we have more ridiculous temples to plunder." Captain Palmer's mischievous grin was clear, even from the crow's nest. "Kid, get down here. I've got something special for you."

They each took their hands away, a bit red in the face. Every time he got to hold her hand was nicer than the last, and if he was honest, he didn't want to stop. Kili had quickly gone from his least favourite person on the ship to his favourite.

Kili sighed, "I'll stay up here and keep watch. Looks like it's finally contract time." Finn nodded and started his climb down. "Finn—"

He stopped and leaned back up to the nest, Kili had leaned over and their faces were hovering just inches from each other. The sweet scent of exotic flowers overpowered the salty smell of the open sea. Kili opened her mouth to speak, but no words came.

Finn simply smiled at her and climbed down.

When he reached the deck, he was met with Trigger, Tobi, and Smiley as they worked on repairing some breaks in the deck. "How're the repairs, fellas?"

Tobi flashed a thumb. "Things go much quicker when I've got the extra hands to help me. One of you, remind me to find Finn later so I can dangle him over the side of the ship again."

Finn flashed him a thumb right back. "That's the last possible thing I want to do."

"Get out of here and sign your contract, lad," Trigger said. "We need to be able to welcome yeh aboard the crew properly."

Exactly what a proper welcome entailed was a good question. He had a feeling that if he asked, Trigger would go into far too much detail.

He started toward Captain Palmer but stopped. "I was meaning to ask, how'd you guys manage on the beach—while we were in the temple, I mean."

These two fight like savages." Smiley cracked the first smile Finn had seen from him as he continued. "As soon as the fighting started I knew we were going to be fine. With the help of the islanders, everyone against those barbarians wasn't much of a problem at all."

"He's being too modest." Trigger slapped a hand on Smiley's back. "This fella must have taken out at least twenty men all on his own. He may favour a mop and a frying pan, but I'll fight alongside him any day."

"Remind me to never complain about the cooking," Finn said before heading off to find Captain Palmer.

When he reached her, he gave her a little salute.

Her head jerked back. "We don't do that here. Pyrates never salute."

"Just thought I'd try something new," Finn said.

"Let's leave the new ideas to me."

"The pyrate who rushes headfirst into everything said to the idea man."

"*Captain,*" she corrected as she rolled out a piece of parchment. "Do you want to join my crew or not?"

Finn's eyes poured over the piece of parchment.

There were lines of text, but what any of it said didn't matter to him. All he was focused on was a small line at the bottom awaiting his signature.

"Well?" Captain Palmer held out a quill. "I'd be honoured if you'd officially join the Curse of the Albatross."

Hearing those words felt far better than he ever could have imagined. He was about to officially join the crew he'd dreamed about his entire life. The quill was right at home in his hand as he signed his name.

She rolled the piece of parchment up with a smile. "Welcome aboard, Finn." She took the quill from him and headed up toward the wheel.

Finn stared at her as she went. That was the first time she'd ever called him by his name without immediately making fun of him afterward.

Walker's laugh pulled his attention from Captain Palmer. "Looks like yeh graduated from kid. Happy to have ya, Finn."

Finn rushed up the stairs. "What exactly am I supposed to do?"

Captain Palmer placed a hand on the wheel, and Walker headed down the stairs. "I have a very special job in mind for you." She stepped to the side. "Here, take the wheel."

Finn stared at her. "I don't know how to steer a ship."

"It's easy. I'll teach you," Captain Palmer said as Finn grabbed the wheel. "Our recent adventure—and my close calls made me realize that my time on the seas could end at any moment. Someone will need to step up as captain if anything were to happen to me."

She was getting at something, but Finn couldn't believe she was going where he thought she was going. If he didn't know any better, she was getting ready to ask him something big.

"Wouldn't taking over be Walker's responsibility?"

"He's a wonderful second, but he's no captain." Captain Palmer's kind tone morphed to one that was more matter of fact. "He knows that—drinks too much, hates all the responsibility. You on the other hand— you're young, ambitious, and you've got some semblance of wits about you. I'd like you to be an apprentice of sorts."

Finn looked up at Captain Palmer. "You want me to be your apprentice?"

She nodded.

"To one day Captain the ship?"

She nodded again.

Finn's jaw hung open. "I don't know what to say."

"You will say nothing." Captain Palmer looked out to the sea. "This conversation is between the two of us. If anyone finds out about this, you could be in grave danger."

"Grave danger? Why?"

"If word were to get out about my training someone to take over as captain, you would become the biggest target on the seas." She looked out across the sea. "Pyrates, Blues, and likely all manner of strange ancient dust warriors would be coming for you."

He couldn't believe what he was hearing. His hero wanted to take him under her wing. One day, Finn would take the lead on the Curse of the Albatross. Hopefully, that time wouldn't come anytime soon.

"Thank you, Captain Palmer."

"You as my apprentice—it comes with perks. You are not my equal, but when none of the crew is around you may call me Fortune and you may visit my private quarters." She stuck a finger in his face. "You will *always* knock, or that privilege shall be revoked *immediately*. You've proven your loyalty to me in impressive fashion."

The captain's words were a lot for Finn to take in. It

felt as if each word were leaving her lips in slow motion. He'd finally get to see all the exotic treasures she kept as mementos.

"Now then," she continued. "Every self-respecting pyrate needs a moniker, and I've got the perfect one for you—The Iron Heart, Finn Townsend."

"Th—thank you, Fortune."

"Captain, we have a problem." Stitch's voice came from below.

"What now, Stitch?" Captain Palmer asked.

"Well, it's not so much a problem, because more friends is never a problem, but—" Stitch said as she headed up the stairs with Ximena. "Ta-da!"

She liked just like she had on the island, but it had been days since then. She'd have had to have stowed away on the ship without anyone ever noticing.

Fortune's eyes snapped open as wide as they could. "What are you doing here? How did you even get here?"

Ximena rubbed her arm as she looked around. "While everything was happening with the fighting, I swam to your ship and climbed up the line that ran into the ocean. Then I used my knives to climb to the top. When I had the chance, I ran to the door and found a place to hide."

"Is that Ximena?" Kili called from the crow's nest. What's she doing here?"

Ximena's eyes darted around. "Please don't make me go back there. What you saw with the men and their spears—that happens once every moon. They hate me, and I fear they would kill me if I stayed."

It didn't seem like she was putting on an act. Ximena seemed genuinely terrified to return to her island. Whatever those people had done to her, it wasn't right. She'd helped them without asking for a thing in return, something Finn could admire.

"Hey, it's okay. You're safe here." Fortune walked

toward her. "You're welcome to stay, but you need to go with Stitch so she can make sure you're healthy and not injured, savvy?"

"Savvy—do I understand?" Ximena asked.

"That's right."

Kili made her way up the stairs and surprised Ximena with a tight hug. "Oh thank the Gods. More girls on the ship."

She hugged her back. "Kili, it is so good to see you again. I have a—a surprise—for you."

"I love surprises, so long as it's not a crocodile."

Ximena chuckled as she reached into a small cloth bag she had on her waist. She pulled out some clothes that matched her garb.

"You said you wanted clothes like mine, so I brought extra for you."

Kili took them. "Are you sure?"

"My people value sharing our culture with our new friends." Ximena nodded toward Finn. "If I had the time, I would have brought enough for everyone."

Kili laughed, "I don't think Finn could pull it off, but thank you. I can't wait to match you—OOH! We can do a performance together for the crew." She turned her attention to Fortune. "She can stay, right?"

Fortune nodded. "It's already been decided. Now then, Stitch."

Stitch linked arms with her. "I like this one." She led Ximena down into the ship with Kili.

Captain Palmer smiled at them as they walked off. "I think I do too."

Finn turned his attention back to the wheel—to learning everything he could about the ship. Captain Palmer placed a hand on his shoulder and looked out to the sea. Their adventures could take them absolutely anywhere, but Finn knew that wherever they were—or whatever they were doing, everything was going to be alright.

His mind wandered again to his mother. He couldn't help wondering what really happened that night she went missing. Was she scared? Did she suffer? Did those monsters laugh as they did what they did? Finn achieved one dream, which gave him an inner fire to achieve his new one.

Finn was going to destroy the Poisoned Rose—for the uncle he barely knew, for the father that raised him on his own, and especially for the mother that could never be replaced.

Epilogue:

The Black Heart

Mendez stepped onto the deck of the ship with what was left of the men in his command. From the first heavy step, everyone stopped what they were doing. He and his men were all covered in blood, but whose blood it was didn't really matter.

Every crew member in sight averted their eyes as he stalked his way across the deck. As he reached the stairs to the wheel, he looked back to ensure their prisoner was keeping pace.

Mendez relished the disgust and fear he managed to instil in those around him. It was the one thing he had to bring him joy as he knew Locke wasn't going to be happy. As he reached the top of the stairs he locked eyes with his Captain. There was one person's wrath he feared, and that was hers.

"Well?" Locke asked.

Mendez pushed a bloody and beaten Penny onto the ground. "All teh inhabitants on teh shore of teh island are dead. We didn't bother chasing teh few dat managed teh escape inland. A few women and children weren't wor' teh hassle. We saw teh slaughter and destruction of teh remaining Blues. Deir ship included." He pushed his prisoner forward. "Dis is teh head of teh Blues. She's teh reason teh others escaped."

"Do you think I care about a bunch of tribal freaks and pathetic turncoats?" Locke snarled. "Where is the diadem? That's the only reason we even came to this bloody rock."

"It was tossed off a cliff, along with some of our men. None of teh men ever resurfaced. Der's no way teh retrieve it."

The way Locke stared through him with those piercing yellow eyes unnerved even him. "You're certain?"

"I don't know how someone could have survived teh fall." Mendez's eyes fell on the deck.

"Then the diadem is lost. That is disappointing."

"Well…"

Locke's eyes snapped onto Mendez. "Well? Well, what?"

Locke was already growing annoyed with Mendez. The brute was as stupid as they came, but he was able to fool the rest of the crew into fearing him. In reality, Mendez was as soft as all the others, he simply had the gall to put himself in a higher position than them.

Mendez tried to remain composed. "Der is teh possibility Silver-Tongue managed teh survive teh fall and make it back out teh his ship."

"A ship which is no longer anchored off the island?" Locke asked.

"Aye."

"You do understand that we can't get through that bloody door without that stupid little diadem?"

"Aye, Captain." Mendez confirmed.

"And if Silver-Tongue managed to escape, Palmer no

doubt gave chase," Locke growled.

"You tink she'd win dat skirmish?" Mendez asked.

"Of course she would. Which only complicates things further." Penny started laughing, and the Captain's eyes snapped to her. "You seem to not realize the gravity of the situation you are in, my dear."

"I don't care what happens to me." Penny spat a glob of blood onto the deck. "All that matters is that you monsters didn't get your hands on your prize."

Mendez kicked Penny hard in the stomach before he got down on his knees and hung his head. He knew what the punishment was for failure. No one was allowed to fail aboard that vessel.

"Do what you must Captain. I understand." Mendez closed his eyes as he heard Locke's sword slide out of its sheathe. The cool steel of the blade pressed against his neck, and he waited for it all to end.

The Captain pressed the flat end of the blade to his chin and lifted his head. "This is disappointing, but I'm feeling charitable. Are you aware of exactly who it is you've brought me?"

Mendez shook his head. "No, Captain."

The Captain grabbed a fistful of Penny's hair and looked down at her. "This is the older sister of The Devil's Charm."

Mendez's eyes went wide. "What?"

Locke smiled. "You know what that means?"

"A woman scorned—"

"Set a course for the stronghold. It's only a matter of time before we clash steel with the greatest captain this side of the seas," Locke said in a mocking tone.

"Aye, Captain Locke," Mendez said as he took the wheel. "What about her?"

Locke turned her attention from Penny toward Mendez. "Mind yourself."

Without a word, Mendez turned his gaze to the

horizon, keeping Locke and Penny on the edge of his vision.

Locke brought a finger to her chin as she circled Penny. Mendez couldn't tell if she was thinking of ways to interrogate information from her, or simply how she wanted to kill her.

Penny stared up at her. "What? You think you can use me as bait to draw my sister into a fight? She's no fool. She'd have something planned to save me and kill each and every one of—" Locke drove her sword through Penny's hand, causing her to let out a blood-curdling scream. "You bitch."

"Tell me," Locke practically hissed. "How does a girl from a Royal Navy family end up as one of the most notorious pyrates alive?"

Penny held her wounded hand. "How do you know that we're a navy family?"

"I know far more than you could ever imagine." Locke crouched down, grabbing a handful of Penny's hair again in the process. "Now then, tell me—"

"She wasn't big on the uniform."

Locke drove her sword into the captive's knee, and as she twisted the blade, Penny replied with another scream.

"I'm glad that classic wit extends to the entirety of the family," Locke said with a sickening grin. "Let's try another question, where might one head in order to find your sister when she's got her guard down?"

Penny's breaths had become shaky and shallow. "Where do you find any pyrate? Lost at sea with a bottle on her lips."

The scent of blood was rich in the air. Penny had been pretty banged up in the schedule already, and Locke was only making things dangerously worse.

A menacing smile scrawled across Locke's face. "This disrespect in the face of imminent death really is getting tired." Locke drove the sword into Penny's shoulder. "There are so many places for me to stick my blade. I'm trying to decide—I could kill you now and be done with your insufferable attempts at defiance, or I could keep you alive and torture you every few days when I get bored."

"You talk big for someone who sent a man to face my sister." Penny looked up at Locke. "If you ever find her, she'll kill you—and your crew without breaking a sweat."

Locke sheathed the blade and stared into her eyes. "I did not come here to kill your sister. I came here for a treasure that was clearly of great interest to many parties." She crouched down again, but this time ran her hand along Penny's bloodied face. "However, the next time I come across the Devil's Charm, I will watch her bleed to death at the end of my blade."

Penny had been so focused on Locke, that she hadn't noticed when Locke readied a knife. "Don't—"

"Are you afraid?" Locke ran the knife along Penny's face. "Does it scare you that at any moment, all it would take is a little bit of force—" Locke dug the blade into Penny's cheek. "To end your pitiful existence?"

Light torture was a favoured pastime for Locke. Sailing the seas had grown old after more than a decade, so finding new ways to keep things fresh was a must.

"You kill me, and the entirety of the navy will be after your ship." Penny winced. "You'll be sentencing yourself to death."

"Oh, sweetheart." Locke started to drag the knife across Penny's face creating shallow cuts. "I've been awaiting my sentence for years now."

Locke licked the blood from the knife. Without missing a beat, the twisted pyrate sauntered toward a box. After pulling out a bottle of alcohol, Locke gave the bottle a whiff and took a swig.

It was good enough to share.

Locke splashed the booze onto Penny's cuts. "Good, isn't it?"

Penny's body had started having involuntary convulsions. She knew she was going into some kind of shock, and that death wasn't far off.

Locke threw the bottle at the ground beside Penny, causing it to shatter all over the deck. Penny's face shot toward the glass thanks to a heavy push from the pyrate. She fought against Locke, but it was no use.

Locke took a finger and dug it into the stab wound in Penny's knee.

"AAAARRRRGHH!"

The horrid captain smiled and leaned into Penny's face. Penny could feel stinking, hot breath beating against her skin. "Now you're going to tell me exactly how to hit your sister where it hurts, or—"

Penny spat a glob of blood into Locke's face.

Locke didn't blink.

Locke didn't even move.

Instead, the pyrate took a deep breath, before letting go of Penny, and standing back up. Penny looked down at her hands which were both full of jagged glass.

Locke looked out across the sea as if Penny had blinked out of existence. It was as if something inside had pulled Locke's attention elsewhere.

Mendez couldn't help himself. "Captain?"

All he saw next were a flash of Locke's wild yellow eyes and the glint of steel. Locke whirled around and sliced Penny's head off with one clean swing.

It happened faster than Mendez was even able to register in his brain. Penny's corpse dropped onto the broken glass as her head rolled toward the pyrate.

Locke picked Penny's head up by the hair and stared down at it. Without a word, she moved toward the body and removed a silver watch. She smiled and pocketed it before once again returning her attention to Penny's head.

It was as if she were admiring her work. Even Mendez became unsettled when Locke started to sing a sea shanty as she moved toward the railing.

Captain Locke tossed Penny's head into the ocean and climbed to the crow's nest. She knew much of the crew felt safer while she was up there because even if someone managed to piss her off, they had a chance to hide.

As she reached the top she removed her hat and allowed her long curly hair to flow in the wind. As she leaned back, she blew a strand of her fiery red hair out of her face.

Her eyes locked on the horizon and she pictured Palmer and her crew of misfits rowing back to their ship to flee.

One day soon, there wouldn't be anywhere for The Devil's Charm to run.

The Black Heart, Sophia Locke, knew she would be the one to kill Captain Palmer and the rest of the pathetic dregs aboard the Albatross.

The End.

Enjoy more novels from Cameron Stewart Miller:

(Available in paperback and EBOOK on Amazon)